THE ULTIMATE MOTOR

John Parker

Order this book online at www.trafford.com
or email orders@trafford.com

Most Trafford titles are also available at major online book retailers.

Printed in the United States of America.

ISBN: 978-1-4269-7315-4 (sc)
ISBN: 978-1-4269-7314-7 (e)

Trafford rev. 08/10/2011

North America & international
toll-free: 1 888 232 4444 (USA & Canada)
phone: 250 383 6864 • fax: 812 355 4082

This book is dedicated to all the inventors including my uncle and nephew that have struggled with getting their inventions to market, no matter what the reasons.

Chapter One

Spring in the fabulous Green Country of East Oklahoma was warming the days into the beginnings of summer while the evenings and night struggled with letting go of winter. When we arrived at the racetrack it was about three in the afternoon, and we were very early to register for the race but since this would be the first time that I had driven this car, I did not care. I hoped to spend some time on the track with it to get acquainted with it. There were a lot of variables in running on an asphalt track that I had heard about but had not actually experienced even though I had plenty of experience on dirt tracks. When I asked my new boss about taking the car on a few practice laps, he just laughed when he declined saying, "This car is so fast, you can't lose unless you drive in reverse." I found my new boss to be somewhat different or maybe a little odd when compared to the rest of the car owners that I had known. Sidney Cain was definitely a strange man. He looked as if he were a fireplug, short, stocky, and appeared very strong. His arms were massive and his chest was big and round, but age and an obvious love for food had left him looking as if he were the same size from his shoulders to his feet. He had a fat round face that appeared reddened and topped with neatly trimmed graying hair. His horn rimmed glasses overlooked his ever present smile that he had on his reddened face that made him look like he had permanent high blood pressure.

When had lined up on pit row to park the truck, he made sure that he would get the spot that he wanted because there was no one else there except for a couple of the track crew who looked a little surprised to see us this early.

"We run in the late model modified class, so we have a lot of time to kill," he was stated the obvious but I really did not care. He was paying me good money to drive his car. Something that I would have done for free, because I could think of no one that would outfit a modified racecar and tell me to drive it. He pulled the race car with a big Kenworth tractor and in big drop deck trailer equipped with all the tools, equipment and spare parts of all kinds neatly arranged in bins mounted onto the walls of the trailer.

I was setting in the cab of the truck wondering what we were going to do for the next three or four hours. When he jumped out of the truck, "Well come on, let's give this thing a spin around the track." I could not believe my ears as my excitement level shot into the stratosphere. I quickly followed him to the back of the truck. He opened the big double doors and hit a lever to operate the hydraulic ramps. "Jump in there," he motioned for me to get into the car over the roar of the hydraulic ramps, "let's give it a spin or two before everybody else gets here." I could sense the excitement in his voice like he was showing off his baby to someone. I had my race suit in my hand and started to take my shirt off to put it on but he motioned for me to stop. "Don't put that on now," he said, "we won't be out that long." I laid my suit on the toolbox and climbed in the car, excited to be in this car. I was just checking out the car when he suddenly appeared, tapping me on the shoulder to get my attention. "Now just take it out there and get acquainted with it and," he stopped and retrieved a helmet from one of the cabinets. "here," I could see that he got a thrill from my excitement as he handed it to me, "put this on. It has a headset built into it. To transmit push that button on the dash." I flipped the switch on the dash and the motor roared to life and I backed out of the trailer.

I was gunning the motor expecting that I would burn the tires a little but it did not and the front end jumped and felt like it was going to leave the ground. "Okay, now just take it out on the track and go around a couple of times." His voice bellowed over the headset as I pulled out of pit row and onto the track.

I pushed the motor up a little knowing that it was still cold and I needed to warm it up for a lap or two before I really let it out. I pushed it up to about eighty and held it there as I pushed through the first turn. I accelerated through the turn and it quickly picked up to ninety. Liking the way the car handled I pushed it to one hundred down the straightaway. I could see the boss smile as he watched as I passed him by. I knew that I had to check out how it handled on the high groove and in the low groove and how it maneuvered in and out of the curves because most of the times in the curves are where the passing occurred. In the next curve I would start out in the high groove and drift into the low groove and then reverse the process. I had pushed it up to about one hundred ten miles an hour and was attempting to test my maneuvering skills out skidding through the curve and powering down the straightaway. "Okay, bring it in." His voice demanded in my headset. I was trying to remember how many laps I had made it around the track and could not remember whether it had been three or four laps, but I guessed that it did not matter, because I was headed into the pits.

I rounded the curve onto pit road and the boss again spoke, "Go ahead and put in the trailer." He was motioning to me to pull between the screens and onto the trailer. I had seen the screens in the front of the trailer but I had no idea of how he was going to use them. When I shut the motor off in the trailer I heard the ramps come up and was confused as to why he would be closing the doors or for that matter why would he want the car back in the trailer, but he was the boss.

"How did it do?" he asked as I was climbing out of the car and taking my helmet off.

"It goes really good and handles even better." I could not help thinking that I would have no problem winning every race. I was developing a base of knowledge about how the car handled and that would definitely help me in the race.

"Come on we've got about three hours before the heat race," he said closing one of the trailer doors and stood holding the other waiting for me to get out of the trailer. "Let's go get something to eat." He added as he closed and locked the trailer. The only things that he left out of the trailer were the screens that he had lined up to mark out place on pit row.

We had walked over to a little restaurant that Sidney acted like he had been before. Sidney had always been very gregarious but as we sat in the restaurant he avoided talking much about the car except to give me pointers on how to drive the car from time to time. He made strange comments about not wanting the other "gear heads" to get a look at the inner workings of his car. I got the feeling that he could care less about racing and more about keeping his secret about what was in the car. With all of his precautions I was getting curious about the car myself and I was the driver.

When we got back to the race track we had about an hour to go before the start of the race and other cars were on the track making their hot laps and making their final adjustments and I fully expected to get the car out of the trailer and maybe take a lap or two. But he looked at me like I had lost my mind and drew up a lawn chair at the end of the trailer. "Pull up a chair and let's watch a couple of races." He pointed at the chair that he had set out for me.

"Well Ricky, tell me about yourself," he said over the noise of the other cars on the track. "Are you married? Have a family?" He asked as if he had not read my resume or had a hiring interview with me. Of course, about all we talked about during the interview was racing.

"I was married," I began, "but it didn't work out and we split about six months ago." I waited to let the cars pass on the track to see if he had anymore questions.

"Kids, did you have kids?" he asked excitedly and intently waited on my answer. I was afraid to say no, but of course that was the truth I did not have any kids that I knew of, of course.

"No, no we didn't have any kids," I was almost happy to have another screaming race car come by to prevent further expounding on my childless ex-relationship. The car passed and I needed no further reminders of my ex-wife. "Don't you think that we ought to get the car out of the trailer?" I asked attempting to change the subject.

He looked surprised when he answered. "No, no, we need to keep the car in the trailer until the last second before we line up for our heat race." He stated flatly and sat back in his chair. "I don't know why I like racing so much," he said swallowing hard and turning to look me square in the eye, "but I want you to know that everything about my car is experimental and I don't want a lot of questions about what makes it tick." He swallowed hard, his eyes boring wholes through me, "do we understand each other."

"I, I," I began and my thoughts quickly ran to all that I had riding on this job and the hope that I could get out of the little trailer that I was living in and let alone buy me a better truck.

"Sure thing," I said sounding a little more contrite that I wanted to.

"Anything, that you say." A racecar sped by drowning out my words but I knew that he understood what I had said because I gave him a little two fingered salute to let him know that he was the boss.

"Look," he began apparently sensing my displeasure with his statements, "I know that everyone thinks that I'm a little paranoid over this car, but it has been my life's work to develop it. I cannot tell you all about it just yet, but I will tell you this. This car is faster than any car that has ever run on this track. You will not want for power. And I've tried to build the best car possible." I could see and hear the pride that he had in the car as he talked about it.

"I will do whatever you think," I began, "I need this job and I really would like to come in second place tonight." I stood up as I was handed a copy of the heat race positions by one of the track officials that rode through the pit area on a golf cart.

"You'll be lining up for the first heat race," he flatly stated handing me the paper. He was an older man, with graying hair protruding from under his ball cap and looked like he was a little pudgy around the middle. "You better get unloaded, if you want to take it a couple of laps." He waved and moved off down the line. I heard the car next to us fire up and could not help but to stare in their direction. I had seen people walking up and down pit road for a while and they looked as if they were giving each car a close up inspection and I could see why Sidney felt the way that he did about prying eyes of the public and other race drivers. Sidney was very quiet and secretive about me wanting to do anything with the car. I had run on dirt tracks all over eastern Oklahoma, Kansas, Missouri and Texas for several years, and when I happened to see an add in the city newspaper for a race car driver and a part-time installer for security equipment. I loved the car, it seemed to have all the power in the world and hugged the racetrack because of the little extra weight that he had in the rear end. He had said some new kind of differential in the car that acted as transmission and a differential. That was all right with me but he had the back floorboard arranged so that you could not even see the rear end. It was strange. And another thing strange was he did not want me working on the car.

"You think that we could take it out now?" I asked letting my anxiety show a little too much.

"Just calm down," he said slowly sort of laughing at me, "we can't do anything until the stock cars get off the track. Besides they have already got your place set." He eased back in his seat with a big grin on his face. He was right, of course, they were not going to start our race until the other race finished. I had not even been paying much attention since we got back from the restaurant and had changed into my racing suit.

"I think that they have got two laps left," he said calmly and suddenly seemed interested in the race. "Look at that thirty three is going to take it." He slapped and his hands together and jumped straight out of his chair. "Let's get this thing out of the trailer," he nearly yelled as he moved the few feet to the trailer and opened the big double door. I started to open the other door but he motioned for me to get in the car.

Adrenaline flowed through my veins as I started the car and pulled it into reverse to back off the trailer. Sidney motioned for me to stop for a second, "Look, it is against the rules for me to transmit to you during the race, but if you need to know something I will tell you." He smiled at his revelation that he was willingness to be an outlaw racer.

"Just don't try to transmit to me, transmitting from the car is easier to detect." He motioned for me to move into position.

I was glad that I was not the only one that was late getting to the line up. We had to line up and shut our motors off. Then they race officials would give the famous, "Gentleman, start your engines," then we will pull onto the track and wait for the pace car to take us around the track to get the green flag. Sitting out the outside pole I had to be sure to stay back from the pace car long enough to let him get down pit road before the green flag started the race. Most tracks made a big deal out of the starting ceremony but I always thought it was more for show than anything else, and some tracks would have you park your car on the track and have you run to it when the announcement was heard over the loud speaker.

"Gentlemen start your engines." The call came over the loud speakers followed by a deafening roar of motors coming to life. This heat race with about twenty cars was only ten laps and I knew that I had to stay in the first five to win a spot in the feature which was the money race.

The pace car stared rolling slowly and I could not wait to finally get moving and I checked the car on the inside pole and he moved ahead of me a little and I quickly followed. We moved around the track and pushed our speed up to about fifty miles an hour. I could feel the excitement boiling within me and I could feel it building in the crowd as well. I noticed the pace car pull onto pit road and I picked up the pace as just to stay even the fifty one car on my left. He was acting like the race had begun and was really pushing it faster and faster, but we had about a half a lap to go on the quarter mile oval to the flag stand to get the green flag. Going to fast at this point in the race would get you a fine and it could get you kicked out of the race.

We were doing about eighty when we got the green flag. The fifty one car definitely had a good motor because he shot out ahead of me and the rest of the pack about two car lengths upon getting the green flag. I decided that I would push him to the limit. By the first turn I was pressing close to his rear bumper. I could see him react when he saw me in his rear view mirror. He clearly jumped and sprinted down the straightaway. By the time we were halfway down the backstretch we were neck and neck and I knew that he would have to start slowing down for the turn ahead, then I would have my chance to pass him. He started to slow a bit and hugged the inside bottom of the curve. I knew that I could take him by splitting the low and high grooves and forcing him to stay on the apron. I thought that I could take him easily if I could force him into giving me a clear path by the time we hit the straightaway. He took the bait and when I accelerated to power out of the curve. I was surprised when I hit the gas that the front jumped up and the car just exploded down the track. When I calmed down enough to look back I was about two car lengths ahead of the fifty one car and no one else near me.

"Hold up a little," Sidney surprised me talking to me in the headset, "you don't want to lap the field." He was laughing as he faded into the background. I watched the rear view and allowed no one else to get close. In heat races it was common for one car to take the lead early and hold onto it to the finish and I was hoping that I could hold on.

I decided to test the car out a little more than I had the chance to do before the race started. I headed into the south curve and took it from the low groove to the high groove and the car came through alright but it something was wrong and it didn't feel just right. I checked the rearview mirror and discovered that the five car was closing the distance between us quickly. I couldn't even see the fifty one car anymore. The five car pressed close to me on the straightaway and I started to go into a little defensive blocking move but the curve was coming up and I knew that I had to power out of it a little to get around the curve cleanly to have hopes of running off and leaving him on the straightaway.

He bumped me a little going into the curve just to let me know that he was there I guessed. I smiled to myself as I touched the brakes, knowing that in a couple of seconds I would be able to apply the power down the straight. Now. I punched the gas and the car lunged forward. In the rearview I could see the distance growing between me and the five car, much like I did with the fifty one car.

I was having so much fun driving this car. This is the first time that I ever had a car that had the power to do anything but get on the track and run last or next to last. I had dreamed of being able to spend the money necessary to win and to run with the "big boys" as we called the guys that were able to spend money on their cars.

I was zooming down the front straightaway when I saw the flagman holding the white flag. This race had gone quick, I thought as I took the white flag. "Okay," Sidney said excitedly, "bring it on home." I could tell that he was thrilled about the race and the potential victory.

I rounded the curve to the backstretch and ninety car tried to cut me off diving low into the corner. I didn't even try to block him instead I just slid a little high at the apex of the curve and smashed the accelerator to power down the backstretch. I could see in the rearview mirror that he was going to try to cut me off in the low curve coming around to take the checkered flag. I knew that I would have to be ahead of him going into the curve or force him to the outside into the high groove. I knew that the car had the motor to pass him flat out on the straightaway but if I didn't watch it I would be going so fast that I couldn't make the curve without ending up in the wall.

I knew that he had a lighter car than I did so his apex point in the curve would come quicker in the curve than mine would and I could slide through the curve going from the low groove to the high groove and be prepared to accelerate down the front stretch and take the checkered flag.

It worked out just as I had planned and I pulled ahead out of the curve by at least a car length and took the checkered flag by at least a car length. It was customary to take a victory lap around the track and I started past pit road and I could see Sidney standing on top of the trailer waving at me. I was thrilled at the way my plan had worked and I zoomed down the straightaway to take the checkered flag.

"Good job," Sidney said in my headset, "take it around the track and I'll have the trailer ready for you to pull in." I could tell that he was pleased with the race, but I knew that we had the fifty-lap feature following the rest of the heat races.

I had worked on every car that I had ever driven in a race, but Sidney wasn't talkative when I climbed out of the car after pulling into the trailer. "You can wait on top of the trailer or in the stands over there," Sidney said as I started to pull the pins to raise the hood. "I'll take care of the motor." He continued casting me a look that looked as if I were trying to steal something. "Is it holding the track all right?" He asked surprising me as I was recoiling from his tone and suspicious nature.

"Sure," I said slowly coming to my senses enough to answer. "Sure, I think that it's all right," I stroked my chin as I was looking the car over and taking stock of what might be problems in the feature race. "We might want to change the tires on the right side." I said putting my helmet on the top of the car.

"Okay," he said way too quickly, "you get the front one and I'll get the back." I grabbed the jack and started for the front tire. He had a trailer and equipment that would make some of the NASCAR crew chiefs envious. It had a compressor mounted inside the trailer and the airlines were on reels that extended out to the pit area. One whole side of the trailer was compartments and drawers that I assumed were filled with parts and extra components. Up front he had three rows of tires.

I questioned his secrecy, but obediently climbed up on top of the trailer to watch the rest of the heat races. I could see why Sidney wanted to get here early, this was a great spot to watch the race let alone having the first place on pit road.

It was such an exciting car to drive that in my heat race that I quickly out paced the rest of the other cars. It was so technologically advanced that I had never experienced a car like it before. It was balanced. As heavy on the front end as on the rear end. Strange, I thought but I didn't question it, even though I noticed that the weight tag read about three hundred pounds more than the limit and I was glad it was in the rear of the car.

Finally, we got the call to line up for the feature. I was excited a nearly jumped through the window and into the drivers seat. The car had a detachable steering wheel that made it easier to get in and out of the car and I was buckling myself in and locking the steering wheel in place when Sidney suddenly appeared taping me on the shoulder.

"Remember Ricky, we just want to come in second." He was very deliberate and calm and I motioned to him that I understood and started the car and he moved away.

I lined up in my position for the start of the race there were about twelve cars in the feature race and I always got very excited every time I lined up for the big race.

"I want you to know that you are sitting in the finest car out here," Sidney chuckled over my headset as if he was taking pleasure in his car and he certainly deserved it. "Just try to have fun."

I started to say something back to him but I would have had to press the button on the dash to talk to him and I did not want to take my hands off the wheel gearshift that long and he had warned me not to because it was easy to detect. The green flag was dropped and the race was on.

The first few laps I was content with just trying to hold my place and get accustomed to the track and the other drivers. A couple of times I was bumped from the side or the back but tried to hold my position and not allow too many cars to get ahead of me.

I pushed the car a little thinking it was about time to make my move. We had twelve laps to go and I was still in fifth place. I really wanted to finish at least second place and I had a least three places to make up. The number ten car was directly in front of me and for the last couple of laps he slowed down on the corners and took a deep low groove and I decided that I would take the medium groove and force him not to block me while he was in the curve. I gunned the motor and it responded quickly and I was confident that I could easily get past him on the upcoming curve.

The ten car did exactly as I thought he would and I pushed the car into the middle groove and quickly slipped around him. He bumped me a little as I cleared him but it was too late I was completely around him and in third place. A couple of times cars behind me tried to get past me but with the ten car next to me we were pretty much blocking the rest of the pack from advancing on the front runners.

Boom, the ten car bumped me in the rear, but I knew that it was too late for him and I knew that he was letting me know about his displeasure in my passing him. The five car was making a move on the ten as well and when he attempted to pass the ten he attempted to put him into the wall. I was so engrossed in the rearview mirror that I nearly hit the car in front of me. I was running out of time. I needed to figure out how to pass the twelve car in very little time. The only thing that I could think of to do was to take him in the high groove when he rounded the next curve when he went low I had to go high and hope that I could hold traction and not cause the biggest pile up that the track had ever seen.

He was blocking me pretty good until we started into the curve and when he dipped low, I took the high groove and smashed on the gas cautiously not wanting to loose control in the curve. I slid around him with surprising ease. And I was feeling so good about getting around the twelve car that I quickly closed the distance between me and the car ahead of me.

I slid into second place gunning my motor for all that I thought it was worth. The number five car bumped me from behind and when I accelerated and the car lurched forward. My God, I thought, what kind of motor does this guy have in this car. He told me that it was a little heavier in the rear than most cars that I had driven on the racetracks around here. Night had overcome the field and the lights burned brightly but there were areas that were shaded especially on the far side of the track opposite the stands and where pit row was.

"Ease up a bit," I heard the voice of the owner of the car in my ear, "we don't want to run off and leave them in the dust." He chuckled to himself over the radio. What in the world does he mean by that, I thought as I pushed on the gas pedal a little more and the car responded by jumping forward. "One twenty," he shouted over the radio. "Slow down a bit, remember we just want to come in second." I could not understand his absolute demand that we not win the race, but since this was my first race with him I agreed to his terms. I never understood what he was so secretive about. Yes, we were running in the modified class and that meant that we pretty much had to run a four-barrel carburetor and that was about it.

Boom, the number five car bumped me in the back again and I decided that I would let him pass and slid a little high in the curve and he took the hint and went low. My thoughts returned to my thoughts about my boss and owner and why he was so careful not to let anyone know much about his car. But I was learning more and more about this car the more I drove it.

"Five laps to go," he shouted into my headset. "Just try to hold your position at number two. When you hit the pits, we'll have the screens set up just drive into the trailer and we'll take care of the rest." He had told me about the screens and I thought it was peculiar but there were other outlaw teams that used screens.

I pressed on the gas and pushed to bump the number five car, just to let him know that I could give him a better race than he was getting from me. I backed off and let him take the lead through the last five laps. I began playing with my new ride in an attempt to learn more about the car. I had noticed that when I pressed on the gas there was a little gap in time before I could feel the car respond. And it did not sound to me like the motor was under any kind of a strain at all and the motor did not retard the engine. He told me he used an automatic transmission and I didn't think much about it, because I knew that I would have to use the brakes more going into the curves. It would run up and sound like a motor should but it gained revolutions per minute to fast. I decided that I would bump old number five a little bit again, just to make the race look good. I pushed the gas to the floor and I thought I felt the tires spin a little bit, then the caught hold of the slick pavement and the car almost lunged onto the trunk of the number five car. His car shuddered under the impact and he swerved from side to side as if he were fighting to regain control. He finally managed to get his car under control but both he and I had slowed so much that the number ninety car took the low groove and slipped by both of us.

I could not help but laugh about the situation and possibly how ticked the number five car was going to be.

"Now you done it," the boss's voice boomed into my headset, "you probably cost us a fine or something." I started to say something back to him but thought I had better block the car behind me or I would end up in fifth or sixth place. I did want to end up in the money and second would be better than third or fourth any day. The number five car was back underway and challenging the number ninety car for first place even though he had a pretty severe dent in his rear. I noticed that he was going to take the inside groove to pass the ninety car and I decided that I would hug his bumper and when we both passed him, he would be forced to stay in the high groove. I had no doubt that I had the motor to get the job done.

"We've got two laps left and I'm starting to run a little hot." I said as the heat gauge starting climbing. "I think that I can finish the race though."

"My God, did you puncture the radiator with that stupid move that you made?" he asked sounding upset with me. "Just bring the damn thing in."

"No," I cut in to protest as we cleared the ninety car and I took the high groove to allow my motor to get all the fresh air that I could give it but I was afraid that the ninety car would try to pass me on the inside on the next curve. "I can finish the race, but the motor is going to run a little hot." I was taking a lot for granted with the boss. He had just hired me last week not to drive the car but to work in his security business as an installer and offered me a deal to drive on Saturday nights as a bonus. Our deal was that I get fifty percent of the winnings or two hundred dollars whichever is more. I knew that second place would pay me a thousand or two and I could really use the money.

"All right," the boss shouted into my headset, "but you had better not blow up my motor." The ninety car gave me a bump on the side like he was trying to spin me out or something but the car held traction beautifully due to the added weight that the car had on the rear axle. I pushed ahead of him by about a half a link and started to turn into him and push him off the track but thought better of it.

"Okay, this is the white flag lap," the boss sounded calmer now, "we've got one lap to go." Boom, somebody bumped me from behind, I checked the rearview but could not make out what car it was. Evidently my scrap with the ninety car allowed the five car to move out three or more lengths. Boom he hit me again, as we took the white flag. Second was my place and I was not going to allow anyone to get by me, if I could help it. "Watch him," the boss shouted at me. I looked in the rearview and saw him getting ready to ram me again.

"Who's this jerk hitting me in the rear?" I was tempted to ask over the radio but decided that I had better not. I had to just get out of the way. I pushed the gas pedal down and the car moved past the ninety car on my left and I moved within a car length of the five car.

"Watch the twenty one car," the boss shouted into my headset almost like he could have read my mind. "He must still be pissed from when you passed him early on in the race." I could see the number on his hood now that I had moved away from him a little as we headed into the first curve of the last lap. I knew that I could hold my position on the high groove because of the way that the car was handling but I was not going to let the ninety car have second place.

I sprinted down the straightaway almost running into the number five car to separate myself from the ninety and the twenty one. Surprisingly the twenty one slid by the ninety following me as we headed into the second curve getting ready for the checkered flag dash. I could see the flagman holding the flag limply in his hand. The twenty one car clipped me from behind as he attempted to pass the ninety car who had held position a little behind me in the low groove of the track.

"You got smoke," the boss shouted as the heat gauge glared at me with the needle pegged in the red zone. I checked the gauge and knew that I would have to shut it off soon as I watched the flagman wave the five car past the finish line. That would mean that I was second. "Turn the motor off." The boss shouted at me over the radio. "Turn the motor off," he began again coast around to the pits.

I switched the motor off and coasted around to the pit road and the car slowed so much that I knew that I was not going to be able to get to our section of the pits let alone pull into the trailer. I saw the boss coming towards me on pit row and started thinking that he was going to push me onto the trailer. He stopped about twenty feet from where the car had come to a stop and after he dodged a couple of other cars coming into pit road.

"Okay, just hit the gas easily and get it into the trailer," he said as he pointed what looked like a remote control of some sort at me and I noticed a green light click on in the dash panel. I figured that he meant for me to restart the car and drive it onto the trailer but the second he heard that I was trying to start the motor he yelled at me over the headset.

"No, no just hit the gas it will go." He was confusing me but I did what he said and jammed the gas pedal down about and the car spun tires and laid a strip of rubber on the pavement. I quickly traveled the hundred or so yards to our pit area and slammed on the breaks and slid into position to go in between the screens and onto the trailer.

I was taking my helmet off, perplexed about what had just happened. The car seemed to run better without the motor running. That is odd. I heard someone rolling the screens onto the trailer.

"Get your ass out of there and let's go." The boss shouted at me setting the first screen into place. I crawled out of the car and ran out of the trailer passing him as he was pushing the second screen into place. He looked at me like he thought it was about time that I showed up to help.

We quickly got the screens onto the trailer, the ramps up and doors closed. "Get in the truck," the boss said as we saw a group of men coming towards us and I assumed that they were from the five car. "I'll handle this," he said pushing me in the direction of the front of the truck.

"Hey you," I heard one of them say as the boss motioned for me to go on. He moved to meet them and I wondered what was going to happen to him.

In a few minutes he opened the door of the truck and shifted it into gear all in one smooth motion. "That was one hell of a race." He sounded like he was happy with my performance and I surely enjoyed driving his car.

"That was one hell of a race," he said with a little grin on his face as he pulled turned the truck onto the highway and shifted through the gears going a little faster with each shift. I took a long drink from my bottle of water, thankful that it was still a cool night.

"That is one beautiful car that you have there," I said curiously hoping that he would divulge some more information about it. He shot me a grin and turned his attention back to the road ahead.

"How did you do that thing with the remote control?" I asked hoping that he would give me some straight answers.

"I'll tell you this," he began and I was getting more anxious the longer that he paused. "You know your stuff about driving a race car." I know that my disappointment showed even though he paid me a compliment and he smiled at me a bit. "Well I can tell you this, you are driving a car with an experimental motor. And I cannot tell you much more than that. Do you still want to drive my car?" What kind of question was he asking, of course I wanted to drive his car. It was more fun driving it than any of the heaps that I had driven in the past.

"Oh, I want to drive your car more than anything," I responded excitedly to let him know that in spite all the mystery I wanted to drive his car.

"Believe me it is better for you not to know about the car." His mood turned cold as his facial expression turned somber. "Between the damn government and the oil companies a man doesn't know who to trust." He was confusing me. Government? Oil companies? What was he talking about? "It's just better that you don't know about the car." My head was full of questions but I knew that I did not need to press the situation so I just sat there quietly and watched as he took the exit to get off the highway near the warehouse.

"What did those guys want?" I asked as he pulled the truck into the warehouse parking lot.

They were the guys from the number five car," he began they had a crazy idea that you gave them the race because you dented their metal a little." He chuckled at their assumption. "Can you believe that?"

"One more question," I said somberly, "what is the deal with not winning the race?"

"If we win all those goof balls get to go over my car with a fine tooth comb." He slapped the steering wheel of the truck before continuing, "and I will not have those sons a bitches crawling all over my car." He sat quietly for a moment then added, "I guess I will see you Monday morning. I think I saw where you will have a lot of work to do."

Chapter Two

I saw Sidney for a brief few moments on Monday morning when he assigned me to an installation crew. "Joe," he said like he was a little nervous or something, "I've got a new guy for you, he's my new driver and I want you to take good care of him." Joe greeted the information by rolling his eyes, grimacing his square face before reluctantly extending his hand to me. I estimated Joe to be in his mid-thirties and stood over six feet tall and looked as if he rode his horse to work. He was dressed in boots, blue jeans, chambray western snap shirt that had the Alltech Security Company logo emblazoned on it. I could tell that Joe would have much preferred wearing his cowboy hat instead of the soiled curved bill ball cap that he nervously adjusted from time to time. Sidney quickly moved away from us.

"Let me tell you something right off," Joe began sounding more than a little perturbed, "if you're going to be on my crew, you're going to have to work." He looked at me funny because I had no preconceptions of not being willing to work. "What you and Sid do on the weekends has nothing to do with your job here." From the way that he was talking I began to understand that he had a lot of bad experiences with previous drivers. "Do we understand each other?" His question caught me off guard because I was still deep in thought wondering about the problems with prior drivers and if they drove the car that I drove.

"Ah, ah, no sir," I blurted out caught off guard consumed in thought about the other drivers. "What ever you want me to do, I'll do."

"Good, I'm glad we understand each other." He began and sent a mouthful of spit to the pavement. "Anyway, I've got to get these other guys lined out, you'll be with me today. Wait by that truck and I'll be back in a minute." I could hear the chatter in the break room become quiet when Joe walked in.

I walked over to the bucket truck that he had pointed towards to wait. I could not help but to think that I had put myself in one heck of a position. I am twenty six years old, stood about six foot tall and was reasonably fit at two hundred pounds. I had had many years of working on the various farms around my hometown in northwest Oklahoma. Everywhere I went people told me that I was a good-looking kid, something like a cross between Tom Cruise and Tom Hanks. I had dark bushy eyebrows that my last ex-girlfriend said was very sexy. But she was the reason that I had moved into Tulsa, Oklahoma because she had broken up with me after a three-year relationship. When I saw the ad in the paper for a race driver and a security installer, I decided that I had to apply. I had grown up driving the dirt tracks around since I was old enough to sit behind the wheel of one.

"Are you ready to go?" Joe asked as he appeared out from the row of trucks and woke me out of my thoughts.

"Sure," I said and jumped into the truck. I was curious about what they would have me doing, but whatever it was I knew that I would be able to handle it because I had spent the last couple of years building houses with my girlfriends dad and her brothers.

Our day was fairly light, we had several stops to make to do maintenance work and perform systems checks on several systems. Joe proved to be the quiet type and he was not being forthcoming with much information about his boss Sidney and if he knew anything about his racecar. The only thing that he knew was that Sidney had spent a lot of his personal money on the racecars and this was the first year that he had tried to race on asphalt tracks and supposedly had developed a brand new car. I think that Joe got tired of talking and kept me about thirty feet up in the air working out of the bucket for the majority of the afternoon.

Sidney came by one morning while we were checking out of the warehouse and was making conversation with a couple of other crews before they left. I waved at him as Joe motioned for me to get into the truck. The second Joe started the truck, the two-way dispatch radio came to life. "Joe, hold up Sidney wants to see you."

"Crap, what the hell does he want?" Joe asked sounding and acting as if he was upset. We both watched as Sidney lumbered his big body toward us. "He might have a heart attack before he gets here." Joe said pulling out of the parking space and moving to meet him.

"Oh hell," Sidney said between gasps for air, "let me catch my breath."

"Sidney you need a little exercise," Joe teased jokingly.

"Funny man," Sidney said regaining his composure before continuing, "I'm going to need Ricky tomorrow and the rest of the week." Joe reacted by shaking his head and acted like he was upset.

"You can't take my man." Joe said flatly his stare looking as he was piercing holes through him.

"I knew that Ricky was going to be a good hand." Sidney laughed at Joe's reaction. "But I'm going to need him two to three days a week for a while, its racing season." I was thinking overhearing the conversation that it was strange that I had not heard from Sidney much during the week, but today was Wednesday and that would mean that I would have the rest of the week off. Maybe I would get to drive the car again and find out more about it.

"He seems to be a natural at installing this stuff." Joe said referring to me and it made me feel good that he would tell Sidney that I was working out well.

"Ricky I'll see you here around noon," Sidney said to me giving me a little two-finger salute for what I thought was Joe's benefit. I knew that Sidney wanted me to do something with the car but it was odd that he would want me on Wednesday when the races were not until Saturday. "You might want to pack some things for a few days," he said with a big smile on his face, "we're going to Texas."

Joe and I had finished our job at the high-rise apartment and Joe had call from dispatch that Sidney was going to meet us for lunch. For some reason Joe instinctively knew that Sidney had a little barbeque place that he regularly at lunch at and was just a little way from where we were.

At lunch Joe and Sidney talked about all the places that they had but in security systems and I could see Sidney's face light up when he talked about his new video security equipment. "I just love the new stuff," Sidney said in between bites of his sandwich. "You get video, audio and it can give you security alerts." Sidney was visibly impressed with his self and took another big bite out of his sandwich.

"I feel like some kind of frigging private detective when I install one of those systems." Joe agreed with Sidney before adding, "we put one in a store hallway and I'll be damned if a damn near naked girl came out of the bathroom putting her clothes on as she ran."

"But what you didn't see," Sidney was laughing so hard that his words were coming out in stucco fashion, "that sorry little boyfriend of hers coming out of that store room pulling his pants up." I was laughing so hard that my side was hurting.

"What do you think about my car?" Sidney asked nonchalantly as he stared out the big window of the Kenworth onto the road that stretched out before us as we headed toward Texas.

"It's a great car." I said curiously not sure where he wanted the conversation to go. But I had many questions about the car and I was not willing to say too much because I didn't want to loose the privilege of driving his car and I knew how suspicious he could be. I was finally making some good money that I could use to dig myself out of the financial hole I was in.

"But aren't you curious about what makes it tick?" He asked giving me an invitation to ask my questions and I knew that I had to be content with waiting on him to tell me about the car in his timing not mine.

"Yes," I said trying to sound coy, "but I know that you will tell me when you feel comfortable." He scared me as I remembered him talking about the government and the oil companies and the things that they could do.

"I want you to know something," he turned serious and deliberate before continuing, "because you are driving my car, people could assume that you are involved." He paused and took a deep breath. "It's just not fair to you to have you involved in something that you don't know anything about." He glanced at me and I knew that he was watching every move I made for my reaction. "But, I think that if you do everything that I say, we'll have no problems and no one will ever know anything about what really makes this car tick." I knew that there was something different about the car.

"I knew that there was something different about the car," I responded not knowing what to say.

"I think I can trust enough to tell you about the car, but it will change your life forever." He stated flatly sounding very serious. "I know this, since this technology has come into existence there have been people killed, companies burned, companies bankrupted and the people hunted down and strange accidents have happened to them, so I know that should it get out that we were using it, somebody would be very interested."

I sat dumbfounded, listening to him express his concerns about his car and its technology. "How do you think they could find out about it?" I asked knowing that my voice was weak and that I must of sounded scared.

"Look kid," Sidney was very clear and deliberate now, "you don't have to do this. If you're scared we will call it quits now." I appreciated his openness but I needed this job and I loved driving his car. Most importantly I needed the money. I didn't know what else I could do to make the kind of money that I was making now.

"I don't know what you're asking of me?" I asked him to explain himself.

"Well, hopefully there will be no risk," he began twisting in his chair before continuing, "if you can handle things as well as you did last weekend." I appreciated the compliment but I was beginning to believe that he was over blowing the danger of the exposure of the technological workings of the car, but on the other hand if he was right we both could be in for it.

"I've been wondering why you have decided to try out the technology in a race car?" I questioned his logic knowing that since we were having this discussion, I needed to get all the cards on the table.

"Let me tell you," Sidney began swallowing hard before continuing, "I have sponsored a race car for the last five years in preparation for this year." He drew a deep breath and exhaled through his nose making a wheezing sound as he did. "I just need your help to finish developing the engine. Then we are going to take this thing to the big time." He smiled with a great deal of satisfaction as I could see the gleam in his eyes as he thought about how he was going to do.

I didn't know what to think. He certainly had prepared and was very conscientious about letting anyone know anything about the car. "I think that I, I, I" I stuttered remembering how the car accelerated down the straightaway on the racetrack and knowing that if I declined his offer I would never feel that feeling again. "I think that I'll join you." I said meekly not knowing what my decision would bring.

"Good," Sidney smiled widely and extended his hand to me as he checked the road ahead with one eye. "I will do the best I can for you and make it worth your while."

He was rubbing his fingers together in a gesture to express that I would be making some good money and smiled. "To begin with, what you say to making fifty thousand a year, plus making half of what you make on the track." I couldn't believe my ears and my mind was spinning for all the things that I could get with that kind of money. "And you won't have to put up with that goof ball Joe anymore." I could see satisfaction flash across his face. I was overwhelmed. I had no idea of what I was getting paid for but I guess I had signed in for it.

I pushed the car up to eighty miles an hour and discovered that I loved driving on the half-mile oval. On the quarter mile oval it seemed like you were making turns all the time. It felt good to be back in the car again and since there was no one around we were running in silent mode without the gas motor running and I loved the way that the car sounded and handled without the motor running. It was odd, but it was fast. I rounded the outside curve and revved it. It was so smooth. I hadn't remembered it being so smooth the last time that I drove it. As I drove I started thinking how nice it would be to have a car that you could run on the street. You could run down the interstate in peace in quiet and no one would know that you didn't have a motor sucking gas. He was sitting on a gold mine and he was too scared to cash it in.

"Okay," Sidney's voice boomed in my headset, "let's bring it in." I headed down the straightaway and thought I would really leg it out. I was going about one twenty and smashed the accelerator to the floor. The tires spun and the rear end fish tailed, it scared me so badly that I let off of it in amazement.

"Sidney," I shouted as I climbed out of the cockpit of the car, "I don't know what kind of motor you have in his car, but you are sitting on a gold mine." I couldn't help but let my enthusiasm show.

Sidney smiled at me in a semi laugh, "You just don't know what you are saying." He slapped me on the back as we walked out of the trailer. "I saw that little move you made back there on the straightaway. You didn't think it was going to jump up out from under you, did you?" He asked as we raised the ramps and locked the rear doors.

"Sidney," I pleaded, "do you know what it would be like with that motor in a Cadillac. Man, you could cruise down the road." He laughed as we drove away from the racetrack.

"You don't understand," Sidney laughed and slapped the steering wheel of the truck. "If we tried to sell these motors we both would be dead within minutes." My enthusiasm died as his suspiciousness and fear resurfaced. "We have to do this right and then we could still end up dead over it." Dead, what was he talking about, dead.

"You don't think they would kill us over this do you?" I asked getting excited.

"Who knows," he gestured shrugging his shoulders, "you know when I was a kid. We would have inventors who would invent internal combustion motors that would get a hundred miles to the gallon of gas." He paused and took a deep breath. "When they submitted the paperwork for a patent, it got lost and somehow someone ran them off the road on their way home and they would never be heard from again. That was nineteen fifty six. What do you think that they would do now?" He blew a big exhale of a breath and shook his head before continuing, "then we have our friends at the oil companies who I think killed that woman who was just trying to blow the whistle on them." I remembered that story where she was going to meet a reporter and was ran over by a hit and run driver. It could have been murder but the news people reported that it was a drunk driver that ran up on the sidewalk. I was beginning to understand his point of view.

"I remember the case," I said in an attempt to interject some reality into the conversation, "but they said that it was a drunk driver."

"I guess that you believe the news media." He stated flatly like there was no hope for me. "They only spread the lies of the government and the people controlling them." There he goes again with the conspiracy stuff again I thought and I was beginning to believe he has some valid concerns.

"I know that bad stuff can happen to good people, but you think that it is probable." I tried to sound like I was laughing it off but it didn't come out right.

"You're laughing now but you wait," he began becoming serious, "but you wait until the plan comes together. We will have so many people following us that we won't be able to count them all." We stopped the truck at the motel and when I started to get out. "I'll see you in a couple of hours," he began climbing out of the truck, "I've got something to show you." Now I wondered what else he had up his sleeve. He had a plan. He certainly didn't share any plan with me before I made a commitment to join him in his big plan.

"Come on," Sidney shouted through the door of my motel. I opened the door of my room and found Sidney dressed in complete cowboy garb complete with the boots and white cowboy hat.

"What's up the cowboy hat?" I asked laughing at the way that he looked.

"When you go to Fort Worth you have to look the part," he laughed as he spoke as we were walking out of the motel. I wondered where we were going because we didn't have a car or truck here other than the Kenworth. "Come on," he said pointing to a black Suburban parked under the canopy of the hotel.

We drove through town and pulled up in the stockyards district. There was so much that I wanted to ask him, but he jumped out of the truck and was nearly running through the stockyards. The Fort Worth Stockyards were the actual old stockyards that had been converted into a collage of quaint shops and restaurants. And if I knew Sidney he would know just where to get the best food in the whole state of Texas. He charged through the door of a place that had longhorn bull heads mounted on the walls. The place was smoky and had overstuffed booths made of the spotted hides of real longhorn cattle.

"This is one of the best kept secrets in all of Texas," I could see the pleasure on Sidney's face as he spoke, "they have the best steaks and food is to die for." As we sat down at one of the booths reminded myself that I wanted to ask him more about his plan and how I fit into it. He really played the part of a fat cat cowboy and talked about how good his steak was and the next great place that we were going to eat while we were in the area of Dallas and Fort Worth.

It was late when we left the stockyards and Sidney had had a few too many beers with his steak and asked me to drive. "Take us to right here," he said pointing to the coordinates on the global positioning system as he pushed in the information. All I could tell about the location that he identified was that it was thirty seven point three miles from where we were and it was east.

I pulled up to a condominium complex that was somewhere in Irving, Texas. Sidney had fallen asleep and was snoring loudly. I didn't know why we were here, we were staying at a nice hotel in across town. "Sidney," I began giving him a little shake on the shoulder. "We are here."

"Good, good," Sidney began returning to full consciousness. "I've got something to show you." He was nearly sprinting out of the truck and making his way through the darkness of the area. I followed him down the sidewalk for what seemed to be a long ways and I could see that we were coming to the end of the complex. "I selected this place special." He began sounding like he was a running out of breath, "I wanted a place that was secluded and yet in the middle of everything." He walked down the sidewalk toward the house. He pressed the doorbell and a voice came on and said, "Welcome Mister Cain, all secure." I could hear the mechanism unlocking the door making a series of clicking sounds. I started to say something about the lock, but I should have expected that he had a security system on the apartment, but why weren't we staying here instead of the motel.

"Ricky," Sidney began walking in the apartment and as he did lights came on and I could hear the air conditioning kick on, "this is a safe house that I have just in case someone gets to chasing us we can come here and no one will know that we are here." Safe house, what would he need a safe house for but then I remembered how fearful he was. "I've got several of these in almost every city that has a race track near by. I need to show you where they are as we go through the season. It was a nice sized apartment and as you walked in the kitchen dining room area was on one side of the room and on the other side of the room was a black leather couch and chair, television enclosed in an armoire that looked like it had never been opened.

"What do you think about the place?" He asked stepping to the hall and flicking on the light it's a two bed two bath, the bedroom in the back is the master bedroom." He walked as the talked with a little nervous energy, barely turning on the lights in the bathroom and bedroom before turning them off. "I've got about a month's worth of food in here and most importantly." He walked toward an inside door and opened it. When he did the light in the garage came on to revel a black Corvette sitting in the garage with a layer of dust on it.

"Let's go," he said closing the door and watching the light go out. "I've got this place wired up to make it sound like someone lives here. He lights come on and off, you and hear the sound of water running and even people talking to each other and on the phone." I had heard of some on the security procedures before, but this was more than I had ever seen or heard of. "People in this complex don't have a clue that no one lives there but they always send invitations to the diners and mixers that they have here. I hope we won't need a place like this, but I'm afraid that we might." He closed the door and grabbed me by the hand. "Computer, this is Ricky, scan him to let him in. Ricky, push the door bell with your thumb." I obediently complied. In a minute the computer said, "Welcome Ricky, you are now logged into the system, I have houses all over and you can get into them without me being around." He laughed as we walked back toward the truck and added, "Of course you have to know where they are." Good point, I thought, since he was so paranoid he had taken a lot of precautions.

This was the first time that he mentioned "the plan." The more that I thought about it, the more curious I was about the plan and where I fit into it. But I liked the pay and the way that he treated me. He bought every meal, paid for the hotel room and split the purse with me on everything that we won. This race on Saturday was a big one. Second place should pay ten or twelve thousand and I could really use my cut of that.

He had the truck parked in his spot since we got there on Thursday and I took my little drive. I figured that he would want to get out to the track early but he didn't act like he was in any kind of a hurry.

"Come on," Sidney was a little extra jolly for some reason as we prepared to go to the racetrack. It was strange especially since I hadn't seen him since we got back to hotel early Friday morning. "We've got a race to win," he blurted out before catching himself, "or come in second." I was excited too. On this half-mile track the speeds could get up to one sixty or better and the way that the car handled on the track, it was going to be a real fun race.

"I can't wait to run in this race," I said as we started for the racetrack. "By the way, I knocked on your room door yesterday morning and you must have been gone." I was stating the obvious in hopes that he would tell me what he was up to. In fact, I felt

I needed an explanation since I was sticking my neck into a ring that I didn't know anything about and he ups and disappears for a whole day. At first I thought that he might have found him a woman or something, but I watched the parking lot all day and the Suburban was not in the parking lot at anytime.

"I had some business to take care of," he sounded uncomfortable when he spoke and it made me wonder even more. "I didn't figure that you would want to be involved in the boring business side of things." He laughed uneasily at his effort explain himself. But I was uneasy with his answer and I wondered if I should inquire further. Since he was so paranoid I thought I should be just as paranoid with him. I had just about made my mind up to question him. "No," he began sounding resolved, "I need to tell you what I was up to. I have a supplier down here that machines part of my electric motor. I spread out the manufacturing to different machine shops so that no one will have a blue print of the complete motor." He smiled at how his plan had come together and added, "except me of course." I had to laugh with him and that was a beautiful plan. "I don't mind telling you the plan, but it's going to take awhile. Maybe we can have time when we go to Iowa next week." I liked his new found openness.

"I just would like to know as much as I can about "the plan," I sound even more put out than I wanted to. "I might even be able to help, you know."

"I know, I know," Sidney began as we pulled onto the racetrack ground, "but I haven't trusted anyone like this since my wife died." I could see where he could have made such a mistake, but I needed to know.

"Now just let the track guide you." Sidney's last words of advice were as I moved into position in the starting lineup for the heat race. I could feel the anxiety build in me. This was the big time. The same track that some NASCAR races were held on. It seemed an eternity since I had taken my practice laps two days ago. I was assigned to line in the fifth row on the inside because of some sort of number drawing system that the track officials had worked out, supposedly to give everyone a fair shake in the heat race. There were twenty cars in the heat race but it qualified the top five for the feature.

Finally, we started moving around the pace lap. It was a lot different being back in the pack than on the outside poll like I was on the last race. I felt packed in between the cars. Boom, the car behind me bumped me in the back, like I could go anywhere. He was so close that I couldn't make out his car number on his hood. "Okay, you sucker, I'll show you a little something about racing when we take the green," I said under my breath but I knew that he couldn't hear me over the roar of the cars.

I could see the pace car head off onto pit road and I knew that the cars on the poll would be pulling away and I would get my opportunity to make my move. I was going over a hundred when I finally past the green flag and pushed on past the hundred and the speedometer kept climbing as we rounded the first turn. I figured that the drivers ahead of me in the outside groove would attempt to get into low groove to get around the curve at a faster sped. But I knew that I could get around the curve just as fast in the high groove and maybe I would have some clear track ahead of me so I could power down the straightaway.

It worked. I screeched the tires a little and I slid a little closer to the wall than I would have liked, but I past two cars in one move. I was really liking the larger track, the speeds that you could run made it easier to pass and it gave the other cars more room to spread out.

The number twelve car directly ahead of me dipped close to the seven car that was on the inside of him and when he did I moved along side of him, making it three abreast going into the turn. I hoped to be able to slingshot out of the turn and power down the straightaway but the three car was in front of me and wasn't going to give up his position without a fight because every time I pushed close to the wall in an effort to get around him he would block me. I was getting very nervous with all three of us heading down the straightaway and pushing the three car and the fifty one. I hoped that they enjoyed their minute of glory blocking me and the other drivers and I was beginning to think that I needed to spin one of them out but I couldn't do anything until I got out of the predicament that I was in. I looked next to me and there didn't appear to be more than six inches between me and the nine car next to me.

The next turn was approaching and we were still running three abreast. I knew the closer we got to the turn, the chances were much greater that we could have a big wreck and I knew that since I was on the outside near the wall that I would be the one in the squeeze. I could see the lead car start into the turn, it was him, one car behind him then the three and fifty one then the three of us abreast. In ten laps I didn't see how I was going to get out of this mess and break into a position that I could pass.

We were about a third of the way into the turn when the fifty one car ahead of us started to spin out and crashed into the three car. When he did he must havc slowed a bit and the fifty one shot ahead and I followed him on through the turn. I could hear another crash behind me but when I glanced in the rear view I couldn't see anything. Finally, things settled down where we were running single file and I was resting a little easier. The next few laps went by in a blur and it was strange that I didn't have anyone trying to pass me from behind or I just didn't care about them because I was pushing the fifty one car and he was making it hard on me with all his blocking moves. I noticed that he had figured out that I could take the curves a little higher in the groove than other and he would block me for as long as he could and dive to the bottom to power down the straight. I knew that I could pass him if I was ready when he dived to the bottom, I could take him going from the low groove to the high and then power down the straight. But, I had to fake him out by staying low and making him think that I wasn't going to try to pass him there.

I pushed to his bumper and tapped him a little just to make sure that he was going to take my fake. He pulled into the middle of the track and I wondered what in the world he was doing and I backed off a little. As the curve approached he moved back down into the low groove and I sensed my opportunity. I smashed the accelerator and the car quivered a little from the power and I slid close to the outside wall and powered out of the curve, down the straightaway.

I was surprised to see the white flag as I passed the starting point. I was at least in third position but I wanted to come in first in the heat race but if the other drivers were anything like the fifty one driver I wasn't going to get very far. I pulled up on the bumper of the seven car and decided that I had enough room down the straightaway to try to pass him before the curve. I hit the gas and pulled out to go around and he followed me, blocking me. I decided that I would hold him near the outside wall knowing that he would have to make a move before the curve. If he dipped low, I could stay high or vice versa but I was counting on him going low and I could get around by moving to the middle position.

He acted like he was going to try to block me all the way through the curve but when he started slowing he dipped down into the curve and I followed him part of the way and flew by him actually forcing him lower into the curve than he wanted to go. I powered down the straightaway and took the checkered flag in third place. I was disappointed. These drivers were a lot better at blocking than I had ever encountered.

"My God, that was a beautiful race," Sidney was elated as I began climbing out of the car after parking it inside the trailer. "I thought that you were going to crash for sure." He said handing me a bottle of water.

"I can't imagine what the fifty lap feature is going to be like." I began as I unzipped my suit and loosened it up some.

"Don't worry about it," Sidney slapped me on the back so hard that I nearly choked on the water I was drinking. "You'll have fifty laps to make things up." I found my chair and realized that I was exhausted when I sat down.

"I think that these guys are a lot different drivers than what we have in Oklahoma," I began thinking about the race. "I thought that guy was going to put me in the wall."

"I don't know how you got out of that," Sidney cut in, "you should have heard the track announcer. He said that this race was the most exciting that he had seen in awhile." Sidney was ecstatic as he finished closing the trailer and took his seat. "He must have called our number twenty times." I found that odd, but of course when I am in the car I couldn't hear what the announcer is saying.

"I think the car is running fine," I began before finishing my bottle of water, "we just need to gas it up and we should be ready for the next race." My voice broke a little as I spoke and I realized that I was exhausted.

We settled in to watching the rest of the races. There were four other heat races and that would mean twenty five cars in the feature. Sidney seemed to remember every move that I made on the track. Sidney was very complimentary about my driving and what he called my guts when I was willing to go three abreast on the outside on the wall. As we watched the races two or three drivers tried the three abreast move and one of them caused a big pile up. What got me is the way that nearly all the drivers were bent on blocking anybody that was trying to pass, even cars that had been lapped. I began to notice their blocking motions and was trying to think up a way of thwarting their intentions. What I hated was when two cars ran abreast at the same speed effectively blocking everyone behind. I knew that if I could get them single file, I would have no problem passing them and in this racecar.

"Is there anything that we need to do on the car?" Sidney asked as the second heat race was finishing.

"I don't think so," I began thinking about the way the car handled and it's performance. "I think that the tires should be good and if we fuel it up I think that it will be good." I was mentally going through the checklist of everything that could be improved on the car.

I pulled out on the track to line up in my spot. I was in seventeenth on the outside. Evidently, all the cars that finished in first place in their heat race were in a drawing to see which one would be in which position. Then in second, third, fourth and finally fifth until all the positions were selected. I knew from the seventeenth position to get to the front of the pack that I was going to have to press the race from the very beginning. I had the motor to do it and I felt confident in my abilities to drive it, but I didn't know how the rest of the drivers were going to take to my plan.

We lined up and the pace car had us moving down the back straightaway. I hated this part of the race, especially, starting from this far back in the pack. I was actually closer to the back of the pack than the front. At this rate I would be lucky if I broke into the top ten and made any kind of a payday. As we eased around the last curve to head down the straightaway and the start of the race I firmly made my mind up that I was going to be aggressive from the start of the race.

I could see that the leading cars were already into the first curve before we even passed the flag stand. I felt like the drivers in front of me forgot that we were supposed to be in a race instead of plodding along at sixty miles an hour. Stupid, stupid, stupid,

I thought as we plodded around the curve and headed down the straightaway. I could see that the lead cars were a full straightaway length ahead of me. But I did notice that the smallest of opening coming open between the five car and the three cars ahead of me. I eased in between them forcing the three car closer to the wall than the apparently wanted and he backed off and let me have his position. The ten and nineteen cars were directly ahead of me now and the five was on my left. I bumped the rear bumper of the nineteen car and he moved close to the ten car as we approached the next curve. I jumped to pass them going three abreast along the wall. When I pulled out of the curve I was ahead of both the ten and nineteen and staring into the rear bumper of the six and twenty two cars. The six was on the inside and moving ahead of the twenty two. I thought if I could force the twenty two off of him some I could slip in between them and I might have to give him a little push to get him close enough to the wall to push myself in between them. I moved into position and the six car slid close to the twenty two making is impossible for me to get by. I was in the middle of the track directly behind the two cars now I and had no idea of how that I could get by them.

When we headed into the turn the six dove to the low groove leaving a gap between him and the twenty two. I saw my opportunity and pressed into the gap. The twenty two reacted by side swiping me a little bit and I almost over reacted and pushed him into the wall a little. He backed off completely then and I was able to pass both him and the six. I was proud of myself. I was making up ground and at least the rest of the cars had fanned out in single file and I was in eleventh place. I was feeling a little more confident when I heard a big boom on the track behind me and the yellow flag was being waved. I moved close to the forty nine car ahead of me and slowed to maintain my speed behind him. Yellow flags were sometimes a good thing, but most of the time they gave the other drivers a chance to close their distance and calm down a bit before the race started again.

I saw the green flag waving from the flag stand and I knew that I needed to keep pressing and pulled into the high groove next to the forty nine car and was pulling into the curve when I started into the curve I felt a push from the back. I steered quickly as the push had put me into a skid and the skid just kept getting worse as the car that hit me was continuing to push me toward the wall. Boom, my rear hit the wall and I shot into the infield. When I hit the grass of the infield the tires caught and the car started rolling. When I came to a stop the car was upside down and I unsnapped my harness and began trying to crawl out of the car.

I finally crawled out of the car and just sat there leaning up against the wrecked car. I was taking my helmet off when the track officials got over to me in their pickup sized fire truck. They jumped out of the truck and ran to me.

"Are you all right?" One asked as he leaned next to me. "Come on," he began grabbing me by the shoulder, "we've got to get you away from this car." My heart sank, I knew that Sidney was going to be upset, if I just punctured a radiator last time, what was he going to think about this.

When I stood up, I could hear the crowd roar and clap around me. The track announcer boomed over the loud speaker, "He's all right folks, walking under his own power." The ambulance pulled up and a man and a woman jumped out and ran to me.

"Are you all right?" the man asked. He wore glasses and had a little chubby face. The woman grabbed my arm, pulled my glove off and was taking my pulse. She was a young blond, that had a heart shaped face with beautiful deep set eyes. I was real curious to find out what she looked like without her jumpsuit on but I did catch the name on her chest. Carrie.

"Ricky," I heard the out of breath familiar voice of Sidney as he rushed toward us. "Are you all right?"

"He's fine," Carrie said breaking in and standing up to meet him, "he's just a little shaken up." I really liked the sound of her voice. "Do you want to ride with us to get checked out?" She asked turning to me and extending her hand to help me stand up.
"You ran a good exciting race Ricky," Carrie said giving me a little wink that perplexed me, "I'll bet the twenty two car gets a big fine for what he did to you." I started to feel better immediately, I noticed that she was a little shorter than I was and I guessed her to be five-two or three.

"I think that I'll ride back with them," I said turning to Sidney and she guided me into the ambulance. She climbed into the back of ambulance with me and directed me to set on the gurney.

"I appreciate your help, Carrie," I began as her partner started the ambulance and headed back to the aid station. "I'll bet you meet a lot of guys like that."

"Oh, I don't have a hard time meeting guys," she laughed before adding, "but I do have a hard time keeping them around." I was surprised that my little pass was actually caught and returned. Now for the next step.

"How about giving me your phone number?" I asked gingerly hoping for a positive result. "I would like to get to know you." She laughed moving her hand to her face and blushing a little.

"You don't want my number," she responded quickly, "race drivers have plenty of groupies that are more than eager to give you their numbers." Oh, no I thought, she must have had a relationship with a race driver sometime in her past.

"Well, I think that you are a very special person and any one that would hurt you, doesn't deserve you." I was calm and was thinking that a relationship with her probably would not work anyway. She must live around the Dallas – Fort Worth area and we lived around Tulsa the distance alone was just too much.

"Well aren't you sweet," She smiled at me as we arrived at the first aid station. "You want to come in and let us check you out?" She asked with that big smile on her face and a little glint in her eye.

"Sure," I heard myself saying but I knew that I had to get back and help Sidney load the car before he blew a gasket in his head, "but I can't stay long." I followed her into the aid station and she motioned for me to set down on the gurney. The first aid station looked to be like a small shack barely big enough to have a desk and a gurney side by side. It looked like it the back had a bathroom and a wash up area next to it. It was a very non descript place, white frame building, white paint of the walls. I could have been a small office building that had been moved to the race track.

"You all right Ricky?" Sidney charged in the door and nearly hugged me. Where did that come from, I thought. He should be taking care of the car and getting it loaded into the trailer.

"I'm okay, I think, Carrie just wanted to check me out a little." I smiled at her as I spoke and she smiled back. Sidney had a strange look on his face that slowly turned to a smile.

We started walking down pit road, Sidney was uneasy and was very anxious. "Ricky, they found the motor. The sons of bitches took pictures of it before they allowed the wrecker drivers to haul it back to the pit." He had a right to be excited, his worst fear was realized.

"Good race Ricky," someone shouted from the pits as we walked toward our truck and place on pit road. "You didn't deserve what he did to you." That made me feel better, but it didn't change much. Then another someone shouted out similar sentiments. And another, nearly every pit position that we passed had something to say about the race or about how exciting it was to watch me. Sidney was quiet as we walked but I could tell that he enjoyed the comments as well, but it didn't change the fact that the track officials had taken pictures of his differential.

"Aw shit," Sidney began as we neared the car was so wrecked that you couldn't even tell that it started out the evening as a Camaro and there was a crowd of people standing around the car at the end of the trailer. "Listen just tell them that you didn't know anything about it. Okay." I understood what he meant and I really didn't know anything about the rear end.

"Mr. Cain, I'm Jonas Clark and I'm one of the track officials." He began looking at some of the papers on his clipboard. "Do you wish to file a formal complaint on the twenty two car?" His question hung in the air and I could tell that Sidney was a little confused.

"No, no," Sidney stroked his chin, "I'm just thankful that Jimmy is all right and that he didn't get hurt." I could tell that he just wanted to get this whole thing over with and get out of here and hope that they won't say anything about the rear end.

"We are not going to allow that kind of driving around here," Mr. Clark had finished writing on his clip board and was looking a little disgusted that Sidney didn't want to file sanctions against the twenty two. "The next thing is there is an abnormality with your car. Can you explain these pictures of your rear end?" I knew that Sidney was the man to answer those questions, so I opened the trailer doors and let the ramps down. I could tell that Sidney was trying to explain how the rear end was a rear drive transmission and I could tell that he was not getting to far with Mr. Clark. I pulled the wench cable out and hooked it to the car and Sidney was still going at it with Mr. Clark.

"Okay, you do what you have to do." Sidney told Mr. Clark and I could tell that he was glad that I had the car loaded and the truck closed up. “Look I just can’t wait around here, I’ve got a wrecked car and a hurt driver and we need to get home.”

“Ricky, hand me that impact wrench,” Sidney said from underneath the car as we working to remove the twisted metal from the car. I was surprised that Sidney had taken it so well that I had wrecked his car. And the closer we got to lifting the body off the frame meant that I would be getting a good look at his infamous motor that he wanted no one to see.

“Have you heard anything from that Clark guy and the track officials in Texas?” I asked handing him the wrench and continued to work on the wiring harness that I was attaching to the firewall.

“He called me the other day and I told him that it was an automatic transmission for a rear wheel drive from a foreign car and it gave the car better traction.” He smiled at his ability to dazzle them with his bull because they must have accepted the story. “They were more upset that it was not any kind of standard equipment on the Camaro but they didn’t have rules on the transmissions or rear ends only the motors.” He laughed before adding, “The trick was to get it the hell out of there before they wanted to break into the transmission at the racetrack.”

“I think I’m clear up here,” I said checking all the connections over one last time turning the conversation back to the work I was doing.

“Hit that wench real easy,” Sidney slid out from under the car and just laid there as I touched the button on the wench in a series of little bumps. In a second the whole body broke free and was suspended from the overhead wench. “Okay, take her on up.”
He bellowed and I pressed the button on the winch and raised the body about four feet in the air. “Off with the old and on with the new.” He smiled and was actually easy about the work. And I could see why he liked working in his shop, it was completely

decked out with all the equipment that any commercial shop would have, right down to the gray painted floor. He had an area along the wall that had what looked to be milling equipment and along the back wall he had a bench with wrenches attached to the wall on a pegboard. Everything was so neat and clean it was hard to believe that he used the shop for anything that had anything to do with dirt. But when the car popped off the frame, a load of dirt shook loose.

"Let me back the trailer in here and we can go ahead and haul it out of here." Sidney disappeared going for the trailer and I moved the car body into position. It gave me a chance to check out his motor. It sort of looked like two automatic transmissions stuck together face to face where the torque converters were supposed to be. Each end of it had a drive shaft that went to each of the rear tires similar to a front wheel drive set up but without the steering joints. On the front where the drive shaft connects it was puzzling because it didn't look like it connected to anything.

"That is a beautiful thing is it not?" Sidney suddenly appeared from nowhere. "I left my keys on the bench." He explained approaching me. "I'll bet that you want to know what makes it tick." I was hopeful that I was going to get an explanation.

"So this is what makes this car tick." I was acting dumb in hopes that he would elaborate.

"Come here," he said motioning me over to the workbench. "Let me show you something." He picked up to pieces of metal and handed them to me. "Here put these two pieces of metal together." I took the pieces of metal which looked like ordinary pieces of metal and tried to put them together flat side to flat side. They would get to about a half-inch of each other and there was a resistance that forces them apart. "Now you take that same principle and magnify it a million times and you have an idea of what makes this motor work." He smiled with a great deal of satisfaction as he took the magnets from my hands. "The trouble is this technology has been kept under wraps for over a hundred years." He was plum giddy. "But, I figured it out. It took me years, but I figured it out." I couldn't comprehend what he was talking about because the concept was so foreign to me.

"So what makes it go?" I asked not understanding anything that he said and he looked at me like I was crazy. "How much gas does it use?"

"That's the beauty of it." He looked at me like I had lost my mind and was shaking his head as if he didn't realize that I could be so slow. "It doesn't use gas. It's fully self-contained. That's why the oil companies and the government would not want this motor on the market and the government works for the oil companies they are all in it together." I was beginning to understand his concerns. The more I thought about it the impact on the economy of would be huge. "Let me tell you a story. In nineteen ninety eight a man out of Ohio named Randy Myers was offered a billion dollars to sale his hydrogen car, which didn't need gas or anything but water. It was a fascinating invention but after he turned them down, they poisoned him and broke into his house and stole all of his equipment including the Doon buggy that he was adapting to run on his fuel." He took a deep breath and exhaled turning to me gleaming before continuing, "Old Randy didn't have a plan and he didn't have the money to market his invention to the public, but I do." He was absolutely gloating in his own satisfaction.

"I'm beginning to understand why you are so careful not to let anyone know about this motor until you are ready." I wasn't sure what I was saying but I was drawn across the room to look at the motor again. Sidney just followed me toward it.

"You see this?" He asked pointing to the big hump in the center of the motor. "That is the rotor it spins at thousands of revolutions per minute and it has a gear reduction to make it suitable for highway speeds." He tapped on the gear reduction part that the axle shafts extended from. I could see how he had attempted to make the motor look like an old transaxle like out of an old Volkswagen or something. The drive shaft from the transmission connected to a rectangular box connected to the front of the motor.

"If that's true," I was still puzzled. "What does the motor do?" He smiled at me wiping his hands or a grease rag. "It makes a loud noise and makes us legal to run on the track." He laughed slapping me on the shoulder. "Do you see why I said that you had the fastest car out there?" He was laughing so hard now that he could barely stand up. I knew the car would run, but I had no idea that it was as fast as he thought that it was.

"I just couldn't imagine this car in something that you could drive on the road." I said thinking about great it would be just to be able to drive anywhere at anytime and not have to worry about buying gas or anything.

"You just wait," Sidney began showing a great deal of satisfaction, "that is the beauty of my plan. I'm trying to get this thing retrofitted to go in cars and trucks and if everything works out all right, there will be so many out there that they won't be anything that they can do about it." I knew that he had a plan and I was curious about it, but if I questioned him about it he would get suspicious of me.

"I knew you said that you had a plan," I began sounding excited to be a part of the plan. "And I guess that you know what you are doing but to sell the motor without advertising it." My question turned his demeanor somber.

"I've got it all worked out," he laughed and added, "I hope. But if I can get five or six thousand of these units in the hands of the general public their will be no way they can put the genie back in the bottle." He was right, if it could be done. People would beat down the door to get one of these motors, especially with gas around three bucks a gallon.

We arrived at the racetrack in Iowa on Wednesday like we did in Texas. Surprisingly we had heard not anything from the track officials in Texas. I was thinking that Sidney was just playing some sort of game with this race thing, but I didn't know his plan. On Thursday we got out to the track so I could make my hot laps and I hoped that we could run with the motor off like we did in Texas. But when we got there a couple of other cars were on the track.

"Damn," Sidney began, "we are going to have to use the gas motor." I could tell that he was real disappointed.

This track was a three eighth mile oval that had long sweeping turns on the ends. It meant that we would be able to get around the corners a little faster and that there would be more opportunity to pass.

Sidney looked like he was really enjoying himself up here in Iowa. For the first time since I had been with him he was glad handing everyone. Passing out his cards to his company in an effort to make sure that every car owner, every driver and crew chief knew who he was and most importantly what his company did.

I was getting ready to pull the car out to for the first race and for the first time since we started together, I hadn't seen Sidney since we got to the track. But I was not going to let his absence keep me from driving in the race. I opened the doors, let the ramps down and was in the process of pulling out the screens when he showed up. I wanted to ask him where in the hell he had been but he pitched in and started helping me.

"I'm sorry I'm late," Sidney began in between his gasps for air. He was sweating and out of breath. "I got tied up with the guys from the seventy one car. They say that they are going to beat your ass out there on the track." He was smiling, jovial and so much at ease that I couldn't believe that he was the same man. I jumped into the car and started backing out of the trailer. He stopped me as I had the car on the ground. "Now, just get out there and have fun. We are going to the steak house tonight and meet up with the rest of the drivers." Was this a total different man? In Texas and even in Oklahoma he was so secretive, so paranoid that he looked behind every tree, but here, he was friends with everyone.

I didn't have any trouble winning my heat race. The feature race had thirty cars and was thirty laps. I didn't know what kind of payday second place would have but it was the first time that everything went according to plan. I was beginning to see why Sidney was in such a good mood, these people were different. They didn't try to block my attempts to pass just because you were behind them as they did in Texas.

"That was a great race." Sidney said as I pulled onto the trailer.

"I couldn't believe that things worked out like they were supposed to for the first time since we started this." I said taking my suit off and locking my helmet in the cabinet.

"You drive one hell of a race," Sidney was giddy about something and I didn't think that the race had anything to do with it. "Let's go," he said slapping me on the back, "we've got one hell of a party to go to." I didn't know if I liked the idea of partying with an old man or not, but I assumed that if the other race drivers were going to be there it might be a good time.

We raced back to the hotel to change. Sidney emerged in his cowboy outfit, complete with his cowboy hat and I thought

I would be out of place in my jeans and the tee shirt that had a picture of a racecar with the number twenty six on it. We arrived at the steakhouse club and it reminded me of a big barn. Inside Sidney whispered to the doorman something over the sound of the band. We followed the doorman to a table where several other people were sitting. "Hey, Sidney," someone yelled over the sound of the band, "you've finally got a driver that you can win with." They slapped him on the back made room for us at the table.

"My God son," someone was saying as they grabbed my hand, "you are about one of the gutsy-est drivers that I have ever seen." I remembered what he was talking about. In the race I had slid in and out of between two cars and had been three abreast a couple of times. I had wanted to win this race and probably could have verily easily but of course, I had to settle for second.

"So Sidney how's the new motor coming?" someone asked and immediately my ears went on alert.

"It's going good." Sidney began, "I hope to be able to start taking orders for it when we come back in August." Wow, that was news to me. Orders! August! I didn't even know that we would be back here in August and certainly didn't know that he would be taking orders for any of the motors.

One of the waitresses sat some beer down in front of us and I saw Sidney hand her a hundred dollar bill and tell her to set everybody up. There must have been twenty people sitting at the table and I was surprised because he never had seen him in such a good humor before.

"Hi, I'm Jimmy Williams," he began getting my attention by tapping me on the shoulder. "You liked to have scared the shit out of me when you came around me on that curve." He was smiling as he spoke and his weathered, tanned face was staring at me. He was a little taller than me but the hair around his blue Ford cap was salt and pepper gray. It took me a moment as I wondered what in the world he was talking about. "I was driving the eight car, red mustang." And I suddenly did remember a time when I passed a car by starting low in the curve at then veering into the high groove to pass and then back into the low in front of the car. I didn't remember anything special about it and thought that I left the car plenty of room.

"Well, I, I," I stammered to think of something to say, "Well thank you, I hope that I didn't cut you off or anything."

"No, no, I had plenty of room," he began, "but I just had never seen anyone drive like you did on that track." I could tell that he was impressed and I appreciated what he had to say. This was one thing that I missed from my dirt track days, after the race, just getting together with several of the other drivers and shooting the bull about the race and who did what and who got suckered or just flat out ran.

"Let me tell you," I began nearly having to shout over the now very loud band, "In Texas they crashed me for much less."

"That was last year wasn't it Ricky," Sidney appeared from nowhere and cut me off. "And the guy did send us a letter of apology. He said that he just meant to bump you and got hit himself at the same time that he bumped you." It was weird that Sidney would want to limit the information about our prior races, but I decided that I had to play along. But he was different up here in Iowa, he didn't talk about the motor anywhere but here and it seemed that everyone knew about it.

"You were quite the party pooper last night." Sidney was surprisingly alert for a man that was so drunk at three o'clock in the morning when we got back to the hotel.

"I was more interested in checking out those women on the dance floor." I said slipping on my shirt and grabbing my jacket, but really I wasn't. He was so drunk that it was embarrassing me and I had moved away from him. I remembered one time where he was talking so loud that the waitress came over and told him that he was drowning out the band.

"Bullshit," he spit out laughing, "you weren't within ten feet of a girl all night." He had me on that one. I had slipped away from everyone and called Carrie hoping that she would have time to talk. It was so hard to hold a conversation with her without talking about racing but as she said, "there has to be more to a person than racing because racing was not going to last forever." I knew that I didn't have a relationship with her but I wanted to give our relationship a chance by not muddying with water with picking up groupies that Sidney seemed to be interested in tonight. But things had grown very confusing working for Sidney Cain. First, he wanted to keep everything about the motor secret. He had established a network safe houses, what for, I hadn't a clue. He then was talking it up to all these racecar owners like he was trying to sell the thing to them.

"I thought you were keeping the motor secret." I jabbed at him verbally wanting to let him know that I noticed his turn in disclosure.

"It's all a part of the plan." He jested slapping me on the back then reiterating, "It's all a part of the plan." He was really proud of his plan, but I was getting tired of hearing about it and especially being left in the dark about it.

"Do you ever think that you will ever be able to give me the plan?" I knew that I sounded a little more disturbed than I was. His face became serious for a second.

"I'm sorry," he began slowly as his whole demeanor had changed, "I have a couple of places where at the end of the race season we are going to sell the motor to some of the race car owners. I would like to have about five or six thousand of the motors in the hands of the public before we go public. Anyway these guys know that I'm developing a motor but they think that it is a gas motor." He was very calculating in his words and manner. I was beginning to appreciate his plan. If someone was going try to close the operation down before it got started having a bunch of them all ready in the market before anyone knew about it would be a good way to thwart their efforts.

My face flushed with excitement when we pulled in to Las Vegas. I had never been to Vegas before and knew that I would have a lot of time to ply my luck at the casinos. Sidney had a strange way of choosing his racetracks. First Oklahoma, then Texas and then Iowa, how we ended up in Las Vegas was a surprise to me. But I didn't ask questions. Vegas had always been a money town. If Sidney wanted to sell his motor to people who didn't ask a lot of questions this would be the place. I was surprised when we parked the truck and trailer in the back parking lot of one of the casinos.

"Ricky, let's go get something to eat," Sidney shouted as he pounded on my door. I had stretched across the bed and apparently passed out asleep.

"Just a minute," I shouted back coming to my senses; I struggled to my feet and watched as Sidney opened to door of my room. I was puzzled because I had watched when we checked in and he didn't get a key to my room.

"Don't you just love electronics?" He asked smiling holding what looked like a PDA with a connection that hooked to the lock on my door. He looked so satisfied with himself. "You know this place is a security heaven. All the new goodies get checked out here before they go the market." He disconnected the door lock attachment to his PDA. "Take a look at this." He withdrew the stylus and tapped the screen a few times. "There, what do you think about that?" I took the PDA and noticed that is was displaying a surveillance picture of the truck in the parking lot.

"Wow," I uttered amazed at the detail of the images. "You can read the lettering on the back of the truck easily."

"If someone messes with this truck," Sidney smirked taking the PDA from me. "I'll have them identified and the police after them before they get out of the parking lot."
He gave the PDA a couple more taps with the stylus and slid it into his pocket. "Man this is Vegas. I love this place." I was amazed that he seemed so happy to be here. He could live anywhere he wanted, why not here.

Knock, knock, knock the sound came through the door. "Those are my buddies," Sidney moved to open the door as I hurriedly buckled my pants and attempted to make myself presentable.

"You ready Sid?" One the two men standing outside my door asked. They were dressed in all black, in what looked to by a tuxedo shirt of some kind. I ran to the bathroom to comb my hair and I heard Sidney talking to the two men. One was a little taller than the other and the shorter one seemed to be of Hispanic descent but I didn't pick up an accent in their conversation.

When I emerged from the room, the two men and Sid was still talking in the hall but they quickly looked me over and the taller one said to Sid, "Look Sid you have a good time, the boss said the he would take care of everything for you. We have to get back to work." I watched as they walked away from us.

"What was that all about?" I asked Sid because they were acting like they didn't want to be around me.

"Oh, that's nothing." Sidney began as we started walking down the hall toward the casino. "I helped those guys design this security system." He paused as a man dressed in a red Hawaiian shirt and a blond woman passed us in the hall. Sidney acted like he didn't want anyone to overhear anything that he was saying. We stepped into the elevator and he continued. "Those guys are so good that the government consults with them about the latest in technology." He was wearing a special grin that I hadn't seen before but I could tell that he was very pleased that he knew those men. "All I can tell you is that if you ever get into a real bind." He swallowed hard before continuing. "Those guys are the ones to get a hold of." He smiled a self-satisfied smile and the elevator stopped on the ground floor. "Are you ready to get one of the best steaks in the world?" He asked as we stepped off the elevator.

I pushed the accelerator down and the car responded by nearly jumping out from under me. I loved driving the racecar without the gas motor running. It was like it was pure power as a pushed it along the racetrack. Sidney wasn't very talkative this morning. I lost about sixty bucks playing the slots and decided that I was going to bed; I had no clue when Sidney turned in, if he ever did. The last time I saw him, he was in the poker room and appeared to be having a good time. My mind jerked back to the present when the rear end got a little loose in turn three.

"All right settle down," Sidney was calm as he spoke, but I was concentrating on why the back-end craw-fished on turn three. Then I glanced at the speedometer, one sixty, no wonder. But without the gas motor running the car was so smooth that I couldn't sense how fast I was going. "We got some people setting up in the stands; you better start the motor and bring it on in." Sidney sounded excited now and I could hear it in his voice.

I obediently cranked the motor as I passed the stands and I noticed four men running down the stairs of the stands. I knew that the paranoid Sidney would not like this. I turned down pit road. "Aw shit," Sidney shouted over the headset. "The bastards are coming across the track." There was a dreary silence on the airway. "Pull it into the trailer. Those bastards are running across the infield."

I pulled the car into the trailer and I could hear the hydraulic ramps closing before I had a chance to get out. "Hey, let me get out." I said into the headset but he must have not heard me because I heard the doors being shut and locked. I had that sinking feeling of being trapped. Then I started hearing voices outside the trailer.

"Man, that is some kind of car that you have there mister." I heard one of the four men say to Sidney.

"It does all right." Sidney replied obviously downplaying the car.

"What kind of motor are you running?" I heard another of them ask. I knew that was the question that Sidney did not want to answer. "He must have been pushing one fifty or more out there."

"Guys, I've got to get going," Sidney stated flatly.

"Aren't you going to let your driver out of the trailer?" Another one of them asked, but Sidney didn't answer and I could hear movement outside the trailer.

"Hey, I think that we ought to make get some bets down on this car for the race Saturday." I heard some other voices agree with him and the motor of the tractor crank to life.

"Let me get out of here and I will get you out of there." Sidney said over the headset and if I hadn't have had it in my hand I might not have heard him. I wanted to reply and tell him to let me out of there but I knew that it wouldn't do any good with those kids anywhere close around.

We had driven for what I considered to be a long ways before I felt the truck turn off the highway and come to a stop. "I'm glad that you finally decided to stop." I said about half joking with Sidney. He clearly did not take it well.

"Man I got some good video of you before those kids showed up." Sidney was concerned and looked disappointed. "I'm about halfway thinking that we ought to just get out of here, but if we do those damn kids will be running their mouths." I could tell that he was thinking verbally in an effort to determine the best course of action. I knew that I had better keep my mouth shut knowing that anything I said was going to be wrong.

"If we run and leave town," I was cautious as I spoke, "they will know that something is up." I was thinking that I had said something wrong because he was crunching his cigar and tapping the steering wheel.

"Okay, but we will probably have to work half the night." Sidney was disappointed and he acted like he had something better to do than work on the car all night. "I had a plan for this but I didn't think that we would have to put it into action this soon in the season." He paused and I could tell that he was in deep thought. "I've got to have more video." He looked dejected, before adding, "Things were just going so good until those punks showed up."

It was late in the night when we finished changing out the electrical motor with the geared differential and I couldn't help but think that the car would not perform nearly as well and the rear end would not be nearly as heavy, so my ability to maneuver through the corners would not be as good. We pulled the truck back on the lot at the casino and I watched as Sidney enabled the security system.

"Watch this," Sidney smiled as we were walking away from the truck. We were about twenty feet from the truck when he stopped and turned to me. "Now, walk towards the truck and see what happens." He chuckled to himself in a self satisfied way. I thought I might be in for a show and gingerly moved towards the truck.

I was about ten feet from the truck and it started talking. "Halt, you are not to come any closer to the truck. If you do I will notify the police." That was impressive I thought as I obeyed what the truck had said.

"Move a little closer," Sidney laughed coaxing me.

I stepped about two steps closer and the whole area lit up like it was daylight.

"Your picture has been taken and forwarded to the police department. If you touch the truck you will be shocked and immobilized until the police arrive. If you have been drinking or have a history of having heart problems you may die. Do not come any closer to the truck." The truck sounded very serious and intimidating.

"It sounds like it could really shock someone," I sounded more surprised than overwhelmed like I truly was. I couldn't even see where the lights had come from, the voice the threat of being shocked, the picture being taken and being sent to the police department.

"Oh, it will really shock you." Sidney smiled before continuing, "It will knock you on your ass. I don't advise you to try it. You see why I don't worry about the truck too much when I park it somewhere." I could tell that he was more than satisfied with his security system. "Not only that, I have multiple levels of security on this truck, if they do happen to get by this level of security, the truck locks up and won't move, start or do anything." I had to hurry to catch up to him as the truck had started returning to normal and Sidney seemed to be sprinting towards the hotel.

"Well, what did you think of the security system?" Sidney asked as he opened the door of the hotel and didn't appear too interested in my answer.

"It was absolutely amazing." I responded stepping into the elevator that just magically opened as we stepped up to it and Sidney looked into the camera and gave it a little salute. I caught the gesture and was a little puzzled about it and assumed that we were on camera and someone upstairs was watching.

After my first lap around the track, I had to go back to the pit and take the restrictor off the engine so I could run more than three thousand revolutions per minute. I was doing good to get it up to seventy miles an hour. The car handled very differently without the weight in the back, and it didn't seem to have the power that it did with the electric motor. I knew that there would be no way that I was going to win this race. Running the motor at seven and eight thousand revolutions per minute made the car much noisier and it definitely didn't handle as well. I gunned it through turn three and tried to move from the low groove to the high groove like I had done so easily with the other motor and the rear end got loose and I almost lost it. Without my little extra advantage in the turns this race was not looking good.

When I pulled into the pits, a golf cart pulled up to our pit area as if to meet me, I glanced at Sidney and he didn't give me indication that something was wrong so I pulled over and parked. "Shut it off," the track official yelled over the sound of the motor. He was an older man with graying hair and a protruding belly. "Get on out," he motioned to me as he spoke, "we've got to do an inspection on your car. We've got reports that you guys are running something illegal here."

"What do you mean we're running something illegal here," Sidney was turning red in the face and I knew that if I didn't get out of the car in a hurry and calm him down there would be no telling what he would say. The track official and Sidney had moved to the back of the car and I couldn't make out what they were saying.

"Let me tell you one damn thing," Sidney bellowed as he waved his finger in the face of the track official. "You better have something to go on to inspect my car than just the hunch of a frigging busy body." The track official stared at him for a minute and I could tell that Sidney was getting to him.

"What do you need to look at?" I asked stepping in between him and Sidney in hopes of breaking the tension. "It's okay, you can look at anything that you want, and we are doing nothing wrong." I was trying to reassure Sidney as well as the track official.

"Sidney, would you get me the gas can while he looks the car over?" I knew that as hot tempered as Sidney was if I didn't get them apart it was not going to be pretty when he started going over the car. Sidney must have gotten the message and walked off towards the trailer and the track official followed me to the front of the car and I unclipped the hood.

"What did you want to look at?" I asked as I held the hood up for him. He produced a clipboard from the golf cart.

"Who built the motor?" he asked giving it a look over.

"Rossi, I think out of Dallas," I answered, "I could ask Sidney but he is not in a very good mood right now." I was trying to lighten the mood a little more, but he looked at me and snickered a little. He quickly stuck his head into the cockpit of the car and began looking around.

"This is nice, here," He said as he was looking over all the switches on the dash panel. I hoped that he would not know what he was looking at because it took me a long time to figure out what each one of them did. Then he started getting close to the two way radio switch. I knew that if he flicked that switch the radio would buzz and he would really have something to disqualify us on. Just then I saw Sidney approaching the car with the gas can.

"Here Sidney, let me get that," I grabbed the helmet off the top of the car and quickly moved to meet Sidney and nodded at him about the helmet. He didn't say anything but quickly turned and headed back into the trailer. He had made it a few steps and I heard the radio buzz. I just started the gas into the car.

"Is that a standard six speed transmission that you're running there?" he asked pulling out of the cockpit.

"Oh, yes, yes, it is." I said dropping the gas can and moving to meet him and sounding a little more eager than I wanted to.

"You've got a couple of extra switches in there that don't seem to go to anything," he was puzzled but not overly upset, but I knew that I was going to have to give him a good explanation.

"We have them in there when we have the cameras in there," I was being cool and I could tell that he was buying it. "We use them when we are studying a track and trying to decide how to drive it." He puckered his face and started nodding his head.

"Jack it up there and let me take a look underneath it." Evidently he was satisfied with everything that he had seen to this point. I quickly jacked up the left side of the car and handed him the creeper. He looked as if he was not to happy to crawl under the car, but he slowly laid down on the creeper and rolled underneath the car. I could feel him pull on things underneath the car, but was not interested in looking over his shoulder.

"Looks like everything is good under here," he said rolling out from under the car, "but it looks like you all have been working on the rear end."

"Yes sir," I began quickly trying to cut him off, "we experimented with an automatic a couple of races, but it didn't work out as well as we wanted so we went back to the old standard." He smiled as he took his time returning to his feet and I noticed that his face had flushed red in the process.

He returned to his clipboard and withdrew a pen from his shirt pocket and began writing. "It looks like you all have a very fine car here, all the safety equipment checks out and I didn't see anything illegal in your running equipment." He jotted some things down and handed it to me, "Sign here, it looks like you're good to race." I quickly signed his paper and watched as he tore me off a copy and handed it to me. "You have a good race, you hear." He said as he drove off in his golf cart.

I gunned the motor and spun out a little in the first turn of the race. For some reason we drew the third heat race and I lined up in the third position right behind the pole sitter. I knew that if I had my electric motor that I would have no problem in winning from this position. Sidney was so pissed over the inspection that he yelled at me; "You go out there and beat those sons-a-bitches." And I was hoping that I would be able to at least try to win this race instead of coming in second in the feature.

I pushed the car into turn two and gunned it down the straightaway and but some distance between me and the fourteen car next to me, but the seventy one car who had been in the pole position was trying to get out of the high groove in front of me. I knew that if I let him I would have a hard time passing him when I could force him to fall in behind me now. I crowded the rear bumper of the two car in front of me in hopes of forcing the fourteen behind me. He slacked to the side of me where I could see the front of his car through my passenger side window and I smiled to myself because I knew that I had him because we were heading into the three turn. I bumped the seventy one car in front of me in hopes that he would take the hint and pick it up a bit. He hugged the low groove around the turn and I slid into the high groove and smashed the accelerator to power through the turn and down the straight away. In the past I would have had no trouble passing him but I didn't know now.

I knew that I had to crowd the fourteen car to my side and I slid in front of him and he bumped me a little to show me his displeasure. I was at the apex of the turn now and I shower down on the gas. The car twisted a little then held traction and settled into the high groove. I just held the car steady as we shot down the straightaway. The seventy one slid next to me in an attempt to block me from passing and to give him a better opportunity to make turn three and spin me out in the turn.

I pressed the motor to its limits and I was worrying about it blowing up, but the seventy one was trying to cram me into the wall. I knew that he was going to hold his position into the turn and force me into the wall. I saw him coming towards me to push me closer to the wall. I knew that I had to do something drastic to prevent it. I tapped the brakes slowing enough that as he pushed I wasn't there for him to push against and he nearly hit the wall himself. I pushed hard into the low groove and moved around him before the turn. He bumped me from behind a couple of times but he was not going to be able to catch me before the end of the race.

I was actually surprised that the car handled so well, without the added weight of the electric motor and I cruised to the checkered flag in the heat race.

Sidney was looking perturbed as I pulled into the pit. He was sitting on the stool flopping a grease rag from one hand and pulling it through the other. He was still sitting there when I climbed out of the car.

"What's up with you?" I had noticed that he had been acting more than a little weird since the inspector went over the car. I grabbed a bottle of water and sat down on my stool.

"I'm thinking that we might have to make a change in the plan." Sidney was very deliberate with his words but since I didn't know the plan I couldn't comment on it much. "I just don't like those sons-a-bitches sticking their nose in my business."

"Hey, they didn't find anything, so what's the problem?" I asked shrugging my shoulders.

"The problem is that we got people talking about us." He glared at me, "What do you think, that that inspector just decided to inspect our car just for grins. Somebody told them something." He slapped his knee.

"But they can't prove anything," I pleaded.

"But where there's smoke there's fire." he reiterated. "Those damn kids have been blabbing their mouths and somebody has been listening." He shook his head and got up and walked into the trailer.

I started the feature on the inside of the fourth row, and I couldn't get my mind off of how Sidney was reacting. I was having the time of my life. I was driving a car that I could only dream of driving and working for a guy that treated me more like a son than someone who worked for him. I wanted to have a good showing in this race. The stands were full and this being Vegas they were taking bets on us and after the heat race the numbers were looking pretty good. I was also worried about his "change in plans" comment, what did he mean by that. But, I did understand that the kids that caught us on the race track did catch us running with the gas motor off and it could raise suspension, but I did think that Sidney was over reacting.

I was starting in the inside on the third row for the fifty lap feature. I knew that I wanted to win but I was more than a little curious about Sidney's change in the plan. I saw green flag wave and the pace car pull off into pit road and knew that the race would soon be on. I braced myself as I eased on the accelerator to close the gap between me and the ninety one car in front of me. I played with the accelerator a little pushing down to charge and then backing off because I really had no place to go.

I had maintained my position throughout the race and hadn't had to make too much of a move, but all the way I was studying the drivers in front of me. The six car in the lead was very fast but he slowed a little more than necessary in the curves and powered out down the straight away very well. I hoped that I would get the chance to test his car and try to take him for the lead, but I had three cars ahead of me and the ninety one was doing a very good job of blocking me.

As we slowed to ease into the curve, I pressured the ninety one and forced my car into the middle between the five car and him. He reacted by giving room but bumped me to let me know of his displeasure and then bumped me in the rear bumper in what I considered to be an attempt to spin me out. I just eased out on the straight away and ran away from him. The five car dove into the turn and I had to take the middle groove which without my added weight in the rear end would make my move very risky considering my speed and momentum going into the corner could cause me to spin out.

I felt the rear end get a little loose but it held and I was in the driver's seat to pass the five car down the straight. I was in second place with two laps to go. The number two car, I had learned from laps of studying him that he was really fast down the straight but was very leery of the turns. I had to use that to my advantage but I didn't know if I had the motor to catch him or not. I was running out of race. I had to try. I only had a turn and a half left before the checkered flag.

The second he dove into the turn, I accelerated and moved into the middle groove and prayed that I could hold traction long enough to get by him. The car shuttered a little under the power of the motor and the rear end became squirrelly and I had to adjust the steering a little fearful that an over steer would send me into the wall. I saw him look over at me as I pulled next to him and I knew that he was doing everything that he could do to stay ahead of me and get down the straight away. It seemed like it was taking forever for me to pass him. For the first time since I've been racing with Sidney, I was in first place and I planned to stay there.

Chapter Three

"Ricky, hand me that impact wrench," Sidney said from underneath the car as we working to remove the twisted metal from the car. I was surprised that Sidney had taken it so well that I had wrecked his car. And the closer we got to lifting the body off the frame meant that I would be getting a good look at his infamous motor that he wanted no one to see.

"Have you heard anything from that Clark guy and the track officials in Texas?" I asked handing him the wrench and continued to work on the wiring harness that I was attaching to the firewall.

"He called me the other day and I told him that it was an automatic transmission for a rear wheel drive from a foreign car and it gave the car better traction." He smiled at his ability to dazzle them with his bull because they must have accepted the story. "They were more upset that it was not any kind of standard equipment on the Camaro but they didn't have rules on the transmissions or rear ends only the motors." He laughed before adding, "The trick was to get it the hell out of there before they wanted to break into the transmission at the racetrack."

"I think I'm clear up here," I said checking all the connections over one last time turning the conversation back to the work I was doing.

"Hit that wench real easy," Sidney slid out from under the car and just laid there as I touched the button on the wench in a series of little bumps. In a second the whole body broke free and was suspended from the overhead wench. "Okay, take her on up."

He bellowed and I pressed the button on the winch and raised the body about four feet in the air. "Off with the old and on with the new." He smiled and was actually easy about the work. And I could see why he liked working in his shop, it was completely decked out with all the equipment that any commercial shop would have, right down to the gray painted floor. He had an area along the wall that had what looked to be milling equipment and along the back wall he had a bench with wrenches attached to the wall on a pegboard. Everything was so neat and clean it was hard to believe that he used the shop for anything that had anything to do with dirt. But when the car popped off the frame, a load of dirt shook loose.

"Let me back the trailer in here and we can go ahead and haul it out of here." Sidney disappeared going for the trailer and I moved the car body into position. It gave me a chance to check out his motor. It sort of looked like two automatic transmissions stuck together face to face where the torque converters were supposed to be. Each end of it had a drive shaft that went to each of the rear tires similar to a front wheel drive set up but without the steering joints. On the front where the drive shaft connects it was puzzling because it didn't look like it connected to anything.

"That is a beautiful thing is it not?" Sidney suddenly appeared from nowhere. "I left my keys on the bench." He explained approaching me. "I'll bet that you want to know what makes it tick." I was hopeful that I was going to get an explanation.

"So this is what makes this car tick." I was acting dumb in hopes that he would elaborate.

"Come here," he said motioning me over to the workbench. "Let me show you something." He picked up to pieces of metal and handed them to me. "Here put these two pieces of metal together." I took the pieces of metal which looked like ordinary pieces of metal and tried to put them together flat side to flat side. They would get to about a half-inch of each other and there was a resistance that forces them apart. "Now you take that same principle and magnify it a million times and you have an idea of what makes this motor work." He smiled with a great deal of satisfaction as he took the magnets from my hands. "The trouble is this technology has been kept under wraps for over a hundred years." He was plum giddy. "But, I figured it out. It took me years, but I figured it out." I couldn't comprehend what he was talking about because the concept was so foreign to me.

"So what makes it go?" I asked not understanding anything that he said and he looked at me like I was crazy.

"How much gas does it use?"

"That's the beauty of it." He looked at me like I had lost my mind and was shaking his head as if he didn't realize that I could be so slow. "It doesn't use gas. It's fully self-contained. That's why the oil companies and the government would not want this motor on the market and the government works for the oil companies they are all in it together." I was beginning to understand his concerns. The more I thought about it the impact on the economy of would be huge. "Let me tell you a story. In nineteen ninety eight a man out of Ohio named Stanley Myers was offered a billion dollars to sale his hydrogen car, which didn't need gas or anything but water. It was a fascinating invention but after he turned them down, they poisoned him and broke into his house and stole all of his equipment including the Doon buggy that he was adapting to run on his fuel." He took a deep breath and exhaled turning to me gleaming before continuing, "Old Stanley didn't have a plan and he didn't have the money to market his invention to the public, but I do." He was absolutely gloating in his own satisfaction.

"I'm beginning to understand why you are so careful not to let anyone know about this motor until you are ready." I wasn't sure what I was saying but I was drawn across the room to look at the motor again. Sidney just followed me toward it. "You see this?" He asked pointing to the big hump in the center of the motor. "That is the rotor it spins at thousands of revolutions per minute and it has a gear reduction to make it suitable for highway speeds." He tapped on the gear reduction part that the axle shafts extended from. I could see how he had attempted to make the motor look like an old transaxle like out of an old Volkswagen or something. The drive shaft from the transmission connected to a rectangular box connected to the front of the motor.

"If that's true," I was still puzzled. "What does the motor do?" He smiled at me wiping his hands or a grease rag.

"It makes a loud noise and makes us legal to run on the track."

He laughed slapping me on the shoulder. "Do you see why I said that you had the fastest car out there?" He was laughing so hard now that he could barely stand up. I knew the car would run, but I had no idea that it was as fast as he thought that it was.

"I just couldn't imagine this car in something that you could drive on the road." I said thinking about great it would be just to be able to drive anywhere at anytime and not have to worry about buying gas or anything. "You just wait," Sidney began showing a great deal of satisfaction, "that is the beauty of my plan. I'm trying to get this thing retrofitted to go in cars and trucks and if everything works out all right, there will be so many out there that they won't be anything that they can do about it." I knew that he had a plan and I was curious about it, but if I questioned him about it he would get suspicious of me.

"I knew you said that you had a plan," I began sounding excited to be a part of the plan. "And I guess that you know what you are doing but to sell the motor without advertising it."

My question turned his demeanor somber.

"I've got it all worked out," he laughed and added, "I hope. But if I can get five or six thousand of these units in the hands of the general public their will be no way they can put the genie back in the bottle." He was right, if it could be done.

People would beat down the door to get one of these motors, especially with gas around three bucks a gallon.

We arrived at the racetrack in Iowa on Wednesday like we did in Texas. Surprisingly we had heard not anything from the track officials in Texas. I was thinking that Sidney was just playing some sort of game with this race thing, but I didn't know his plan. On Thursday we got out to the track so I could make my hot laps and I hoped that we could run with the motor off like we did in Texas. But when we got there a couple of other cars were on the track.

"Damn," Sidney began, "we are going to have to use the gas motor." I could tell that he was real disappointed.

This track was a three eighth mile oval that had long sweeping turns on the ends. It meant that we would be able to get around the corners a little faster and that there would be more opportunity to pass.

Sidney looked like he was really enjoying himself up here in Iowa. For the first time since I had been with him he was glad handing everyone. Passing out his cards to his company in an effort to make sure that every car owner, every driver and crew chief knew who he was and most importantly what his company did.

I was getting ready to pull the car out to for the first race and for the first time since we started together, I hadn't seen Sidney since we got to the track. But I was not going to let his absence keep me from driving in the race. I opened the doors, let the ramps down and was in the process of pulling out the screens when he showed up. I wanted to ask him where in the hell he had been but he pitched in and started helping me.

"I'm sorry I'm late," Sidney began in between his gasps for air.

He was sweating and out of breath. "I got tied up with the guys from the seventy one car. They say that they are going to beat your ass out there on the track." He was smiling, jovial and so much at ease that I couldn't believe that he was the same man. I jumped into the car and started backing out of the trailer. He stopped me as I had the car on the ground. "Now, just get out there and have fun. We are going to the steak house tonight and meet up with the rest of the drivers." Was this a total different man? In Texas and even in Oklahoma he was so secretive, so paranoid that he looked behind every tree, but here, he was friends with everyone.

I didn't have any trouble winning my heat race. The feature race had thirty cars and was thirty laps. I didn't know what kind of payday second place would have but it was the first time that everything went according to plan. I was beginning to see why Sidney was in such a good mood, these people were different. They didn't try to block my attempts to pass just because you were behind them as they did in Texas.

"That was a great race." Sidney said as I pulled onto the trailer.

"I couldn't believe that things worked out like they were supposed to for the first time since we started this." I said taking my suit off and locking my helmet in the cabinet.

"You drive one hell of a race," Sidney was giddy about something and I didn't think that the race had anything to do with it. "Let's go," he said slapping me on the back, "we've got one hell of a party to go to." I didn't know if I liked the idea of partying with an old man or not, but I assumed that if the other race drivers were going to be there it might be a good time.

We raced back to the hotel to change. Sidney emerged in his cowboy outfit, complete with his cowboy hat and I thought I would be out of place in my jeans and the tee shirt that had a picture of a racecar with the number twenty six on it.

We arrived at the steakhouse club and it reminded me of a big barn. Inside Sidney whispered to the doorman something over the sound of the band. We followed the doorman to a table where several other people were sitting. "Hey, Sidney," someone yelled over the sound of the band, "you've finally got a driver that you can win with." They slapped him on the back made room for us at the table.

"My God son," someone was saying as they grabbed my hand, "you are about one of the gutsy-est drivers that I have ever seen." I remembered what he was talking about. In the race I had slid in and out of between two cars and had been three abreast a couple of times. I had wanted to win this race and probably could have verily easily but of course, I had to settle for second.

"So Sidney how's the new motor coming?" someone asked and immediately my ears went on alert.

"It's going good." Sidney began, "I hope to be able to start taking orders for it when we come back in August." Wow, that was news to me. Orders! August! I didn't even know that we would be back here in August and certainly didn't know that he would be taking orders for any of the motors.

One of the waitresses sat some beer down in front of us and I saw Sidney hand her a hundred dollar bill and tell her to set everybody up. There must have been twenty people sitting at the table and I was surprised because he never had seen him in such a good humor before.

"Hi, I'm Jimmy Williams," he began getting my attention by tapping me on the shoulder. "You liked to have scared the shit out of me when you came around me on that curve." He was smiling as he spoke and his weathered, tanned face was staring at me. He was a little taller than me but the hair around his blue Ford cap was salt and pepper gray. It took me a moment as I wondered what in the world he was talking about. "I was driving the eight car, red mustang." And I suddenly did remember a time when I passed a car by starting low in the curve at then veering into the high groove to pass and then back into the low in front of the car. I didn't remember anything special about it and thought that I left the car plenty of room.

"Well, I, I," I stammered to think of something to say, "Well thank you, I hope that I didn't cut you off or anything." "No, no, I had plenty of room," he began, "but I just had never seen anyone drive like you did on that track." I could tell that he was impressed and I appreciated what he had to say.

This was one thing that I missed from my dirt track days, after the race, just getting together with several of the other drivers and shooting the bull about the race and who did what and who got suckered or just flat out ran.

"Let me tell you," I began nearly having to shout over the now very loud band, "In Texas they crashed me for much less."

"That was last year wasn't it Ricky," Sidney appeared from nowhere and cut me off. "And the guy did send us a letter of apology. He said that he just meant to bump you and got hit himself at the same time that he bumped you." It was weird that Sidney would want to limit the information about our prior races, but I decided that I had to play along. But he was different up here in Iowa, he didn't talk about the motor anywhere but here and it seemed that everyone knew about it.

"You were quite the party pooper last night." Sidney was surprisingly alert for a man that was so drunk at three o'clock in the morning when we got back to the hotel.

"I was more interested in checking out those women on the dance floor." I said slipping on my shirt and grabbing my jacket, but really I wasn't. He was so drunk that it was embarrassing me and I had moved away from him. I remembered one time where he was talking so loud that the waitress came over and told him that he was drowning out the band.

"Bullshit," he spit out laughing, "you weren't within ten feet of a girl all night." He had me on that one. I had slipped away from everyone and called Carrie hoping that she would have time to talk. It was so hard to hold a conversation with her without talking about racing but as she said, "there has to be more to a person than racing because racing was not going to last forever." I knew that I didn't have a relationship with her but I wanted to give our relationship a chance by not muddying with water with picking up a groupies that Sidney seemed to be interested in tonight. But things had grown very confusing working for Sidney Cain. First, he wanted to keep everything about the motor secret. He had established a network safe houses, what for, I hadn't a clue. He then was talking it up to all these racecar owners like he was trying to sell the thing to them.

"I thought you were keeping the motor secret." I jabbed at him verbally wanting to let him know that I noticed his turn in disclosure.

"It's all a part of the plan." He jested slapping me on the back then reiterating, "It's all a part of the plan." He was really proud of his plan, but I was getting tired of hearing about it and especially being left in the dark about it.

"Do you ever think that you will ever be able to give me the plan?" I knew that I sounded a little more disturbed than I was. His face became serious for a second "I'm sorry," he began slowly as his whole demeanor had changed, "I have a couple of places where at the end of the race season we are going to sell the motor to some of the race car owners. I would like to have about five or six thousand of the motors in the hands of the public before we go public.

Anyway these guys know that I'm developing a motor but they think that it is a gas motor." He was very calculating in his words and manner. I was beginning to appreciate his plan. If someone was going try to close the operation down before it got started having a bunch of them all ready in the market before anyone knew about it would be a good way to thwart their efforts.

My face flushed with excitement when we pulled in to Las Vegas. I had never been to Vegas before and knew that I would have a lot of time to ply my luck at the casinos. Sidney had a strange way of choosing his racetracks. First Oklahoma, then Texas and then Iowa, how we ended up in Las Vegas was a surprise to me. But I didn't ask questions. Vegas had always been a money town. If Sidney wanted to sell his motor to people who didn't ask a lot of questions this would be the place. I was surprised when we parked the truck and trailer in the back parking lot of one of the casinos.

"Ricky, let's go get something to eat," Sidney shouted as he pounded on my door. I had stretched across the bed and apparently passed out asleep.

"Just a minute," I shouted back coming to my senses; I struggled to my feet and watched as Sidney opened to door of my room. I was puzzled because I had watched when we checked in and he didn't get a key to my room.

"Don't you just love electronics?" He asked smiling holding what looked like a PDA with a connection that hooked to the lock on my door. He looked so satisfied with himself.

"You know this place is a security heaven. All the new goodies get checked out here before they go the market." He disconnected the door lock attachment to his PDA. "Take a look at this." He withdrew the stylus and tapped the screen a few times. "There, what do you think about that?" I took the PDA and noticed that is was displaying a surveillance picture of the truck in the parking lot.

"Wow," I uttered amazed at the detail of the images.

"You can read the lettering on the back of the truck easily."

"If someone messes with this truck," Sidney smirked taking the PDA from me. "I'll have them identified and the police after them before they get out of the parking lot."

He gave the PDA a couple more taps with the stylus and slid it into his pocket. "Man this is Vegas. I love this place." I was amazed that he seemed so happy to be here. He could live anywhere he wanted, why not here.

Knock, knock, knock the sound came through the door.

"Those are my buddies," Sidney moved to open the door as I hurriedly buckled my pants and attempted to make myself presentable.

"You ready Sid?" One the two men standing outside my door asked. They were dressed in all black, in what looked to by a tuxedo shirt of some kind. I ran to the bathroom to comb my hair and I heard Sidney talking to the two men. One was a little taller than the other and the shorter one seemed to be of Hispanic descent but I didn't pick up an accent in their conversation.

When I emerged from the room, the two men and Sid was still talking in the hall but they quickly looked me over and the taller one said to Sid, "Look Sid you have a good time, the boss said the he would take care of everything for you. We have to get back to work." I watched as they walked away from us.

"What was that all about?" I asked Sid because they were acting like they didn't want to be around me.

"Oh, that's nothing." Sidney began as we started walking down the hall toward the casino. "I helped those guys design this security system." He paused as a man dressed in a red Hawaiian shirt and a blond woman passed us in the hall.

Sidney acted like he didn't want anyone to overhear anything that he was saying. We stepped into the elevator and he continued. "Those guys are so good that the government consults with them about the latest in technology." He was wearing a special grin that I hadn't seen before but I could tell that he was very pleased that he knew those men. "All I can tell you is that if you ever get into a real bind." He swallowed hard before continuing. "Those guys are the ones to get a hold of."

He smiled a self-satisfied smile and the elevator stopped on the ground floor. "Are you ready to get one of the best steaks in the world?" He asked as we stepped off the elevator. I pushed the accelerator down and the car responded by nearly jumping out from under me. I loved driving the racecar without the gas motor running. It was like it was pure power as a pushed it along the racetrack. Sidney wasn't very talkative this morning. I lost about sixty bucks playing the slots and decided that I was going to bed; I had no clue when Sidney turned in, if he ever did. The last time I saw him, he was in the poker room and appeared to be having a good time. My mind jerked back to the present when the rear end got a little loose in turn three.

"All right settle down," Sidney was calm as he spoke, but I was concentrating on why the back-end craw-fished on turn three. Then I glanced at the speedometer, one sixty, no wonder. But without the gas motor running the car was so smooth that I couldn't sense how fast I was going. "We got some people setting up in the stands; you better start the motor and bring it on in." Sidney sounded excited now and I could hear it in his voice.

I obediently cranked the motor as I passed the stands and I noticed four men running down the stairs of the stands. I knew that the paranoid Sidney would not like this. I turned down pit road. "Aw shit," Sidney shouted over the headset.

"The bastards are coming across the track." There was a dreary silence on the airway. "Pull it into the trailer. Those bastards are running across the infield."

I pulled the car into the trailer and I could hear the hydraulic ramps closing before I had a chance to get out. "Hey, let me get out." I said into the headset but he must have not heard me because I heard the doors being shut and locked. I had that sinking feeling of being trapped. Then I started hearing voices outside the trailer.

"Man, that is some kind of car that you have there mister." I heard one of the four men say to Sidney.

"It does all right." Sidney replied obviously downplaying the car.

"What kind of motor are you running?" I heard another of them ask. I knew that was the question that Sidney did not want to answer. "He must have been pushing one fifty or more out there."

"Guys, I've got to get going," Sidney stated flatly.

"Aren't you going to let your driver out of the trailer?"

Another one of them asked, but Sidney didn't answer and I could hear movement outside the trailer.

"Hey, I think that we ought to make get some bets down on this car for the race Saturday." I heard some other voices agree with him and the motor of the tractor crank to life.

"Let me get out of here and I will get you out of there."

Sidney said over the headset and if I hadn't have had it in my hand I might not have heard him. I wanted to reply and tell him to let me out of there but I knew that it wouldn't do any good with those kids anywhere close around.

We had driven for what I considered to be a long ways before I felt the truck turn off the highway and come to a stop.

"I'm glad that you finally decided to stop." I said about half joking with Sidney. He clearly did not take it well.

"Man I got some good video of you before those kids showed up." Sidney was concerned and looked disappointed.

"I'm about halfway thinking that we ought to just get out of here, but if we do those damn kids will be running their mouths."

I could tell that he was thinking verbally in an effort to determine the best course of action. I knew that I had better keep my mouth shut knowing that anything I said was going to be wrong.

"If we run and leave town," I was cautious as I spoke, "they will know that something is up." I was thinking that I had said something wrong because he was crunching his cigar and tapping the steering wheel.

"Okay, but we will probably have to work half the night." Sidney was disappointed and he acted like he had something better to do than work on the car all night. "I had a plan for this but I didn't think that we would have to put it into action this soon in the season." He paused and I could tell that he was in deep thought. "I've got to have more video." He looked dejected, before adding, "Things were just going so good until those punks showed up."

It was late in the night when we finished changing out the electrical motor with the geared differential and I couldn't help but think that the car would not perform nearly as well and the rear end would not be nearly as heavy, so my ability to maneuver through the corners would not be as good. We pulled the truck back on the lot at the casino and I watched as Sidney enabled the security system.

"Watch this," Sidney smiled as we were walking away from the truck. We were about twenty feet from the truck when he stopped and turned to me. "Now, walk towards the truck and see what happens." He chuckled to himself in a self satisfied way. I thought I might be in for a show and gingerly moved towards the truck.

I was about ten feet from the truck and it started talking.

"Halt, you are not to come any closer to the truck. If you do I will notify the police." That was impressive I thought as I obeyed what the truck had said. "Move a little closer," Sidney laughed coaxing me.

I stepped about two steps closer and the whole area lit up like it was daylight. "Your picture has been taken and forwarded to the police department. If you touch the truck you will be shocked and immobilized until the police arrive. If you have been drinking or have a history of having heart problems you may die. Do not come any closer to the truck." The truck sounded very serious and intimidating.

"It sounds like it could really shock someone," I sounded more surprised than overwhelmed like I truly was. I couldn't even see where the lights had come from, the voice the threat of being shocked, the picture being taken and being sent to the police department.

"Oh, it will really shock you." Sidney smiled before continuing, "It will knock you on your ass. I don't advise you to try it. You see why I don't worry about the truck too much when I park it somewhere." I could tell that he was more than satisfied with his security system. "Not only that, I have multiple levels of security on this truck, if they do happen to get by this level of security, the truck locks up and won't move, start or do anything." I had to hurry to catch up to him as the truck had started returning to normal and Sidney seemed to be sprinting towards the hotel.

"Well, what did you think of the security system?"

Sidney asked as he opened the door of the hotel and didn't appear too interested in my answer.

"It was absolutely amazing." I responded stepping into the elevator that just magically opened as we stepped up to it and Sidney looked into the camera and gave it a little salute. I caught the gesture and was a little puzzled about it and assumed that we were on camera and someone upstairs was watching.

After my first lap around the track, I had to go back to the pit and take the restrictor off the engine so I could run more than three thousand revolutions per minute. I was doing good to get it up to seventy miles an hour. The car handled very differently without the weight in the back, and it didn't seem to have the power that it did with the electric motor. I knew that there would be no way that I was going to win this race.

Running the motor at seven and eight thousand revolutions per minute made the car much noisier and it definitely didn't handle as well. I gunned it through turn three and tried to move from the low groove to the high groove like I had done so easily with the other motor and the rear end got loose and I almost lost it. Without my little extra advantage in the turns this race was not looking good.

When I pulled into the pits, a golf cart pulled up to our pit area as if to meet me, I glanced at Sidney and he didn't givex me indication that something was wrong so I pulled over and parked. "Shut it off," the track official yelled over the sound of the motor. He was an older man with graying hair and a protruding belly. "Get on out," he motioned to me as he spoke, "we've got to do an inspection on your car. We've got reports that you guys are running something illegal here."

"What do you mean we're running something illegal here," Sidney was turning red in the face and I knew that if I didn't get out of the car in a hurry and calm him down there would be no telling what he would say. The track official and Sidney had moved to the back of the car and I couldn't make out what they were saying.

"Let me tell you one damn thing," Sidney bellowed as he waved his finger in the face of the track official. "You better have something to go on to inspect my car than just the hunch of a frigging busy body." The track official stared at him for a minute and I could tell that Sidney was getting to him.

"What do you need to look at?" I asked stepping in between him and Sidney in hopes of breaking the tension. "It's okay, you can look at anything that you want, and we are doing nothing wrong." I was trying to reassure Sidney as well as the track official.

"Sidney, would you get me the gas can while he looks the car over?" I knew that as hot tempered as Sidney was if I didn't get them apart it was not going to be pretty when he started going over the car. Sidney must have gotten the message and walked off towards the trailer and the track official followed me to the front of the car and I unclipped the hood.

"What did you want to look at?" I asked as I held the hood up for him. He produced a clipboard from the golf cart.

"Who built the motor?" he asked giving it a look over.

"Rossi, I think out of Dallas," I answered, "I could ask Sidney but he is not in a very good mood right now." I was trying to lighten the mood a little more, but he looked at me and snickered a little. He quickly stuck his head into the cockpit of the car and began looking around.

"This is nice, here," He said as he was looking over all the switches on the dash panel. I hoped that he would not know what he was looking at because it took me a long time to figure out what each one of them did. Then he started getting close to the two way radio switch. I knew that if he flicked that switch the radio would buzz and he would really have something to disqualify us on. Just then I saw Sidney approaching the car with the gas can.

"Here Sidney, let me get that," I grabbed the helmet off the top of the car and quickly moved to meet Sidney and nodded at him about the helmet. He didn't say anything but quickly turned and headed back into the trailer. He had made it a few steps and I heard the radio buzz. I just started the gas into the car.

"Is that a standard six speed transmission that you're running there?" he asked pulling out of the cockpit.

"Oh, yes, yes, it is." I said dropping the gas can and moving to meet him and sounding a little more eager than I wanted to.

"You've got a couple of extra switches in there that don't seem to go to anything," he was puzzled but not overly upset, but I knew that I was going to have to give him a good explanation.

"We have them in there when we have the cameras in there," I was being cool and I could tell that he was buying it.

"We use them when we are studying a track and trying to decide how to drive it." He puckered his face and started nodding his head.

"Jack it up there and let me take a look underneath it."

Evidently he was satisfied with everything that he had seen to this point. I quickly jacked up the left side of the car and handed him the creeper. He looked as if he was not to happy to crawl under the car, but he slowly laid down on the creeper and rolled underneath the car. I could feel him pull on things underneath the car, but was not interested in looking over his shoulder.

"Looks like everything is good under here," he said rolling out from under the car, "but it looks like you all have been working on the rear end."

"Yes sir," I began quickly trying to cut him off, "we experimented with an automatic a couple of races, but it didn't work out as well as we wanted so we went back to the old standard." He smiled as he took his time returning to his feet and I noticed that his face had flushed red in the process.

He returned to his clipboard and withdrew a pen from his shirt pocket and began writing. “It looks like you all have a very fine car here, all the safety equipment checks out and I didn’t see anything illegal in your running equipment.” He jotted some things down and handed it to me, “Sign here, it looks like you’re good to race.” I quickly signed his paper and watched as he tore me off a copy and handed it to me. “You have a good race, you here.” He said as he drove off in his golf cart.

I gunned the motor and spun out a little in the first turn of the race. For some reason we drew the third heat race and I lined up in the third position right behind the pole sitter. I knew that if I had my electric motor that I would have no problem in winning from this position. Sidney was so pissed over the inspection that he yelled at me; “You go out there and beat those sons-a-bitches.” And I was hoping that I would be able to at least try to win this race instead of coming in second in the feature.

I pushed the car into turn two and gunned it down the straightaway and but some distance between me and the fourteen car next to me, but the seventy one car who had been in the pole position was trying to get out of the high groove in front of me. I knew that if I let him I would have a hard time passing him when I could force him to fall in behind me now. I crowded the rear bumper of the two car in front of me in hopes of forcing the fourteen behind me. He slacked to the side of me where I could see the front of his car through my passenger side window and I smiled to myself because I knew that I had him because we were heading into the three turn. I bumped the seventy one car in front of me in hopes that he would take the hint and pick it up a bit. He hugged the low groove around the turn and I slid into the high groove and smashed the accelerator to power through the turn and down the straight away. In the past I would have had no trouble passing him but I didn't know now.

I knew that I had to crowd the fourteen car to my side and I slid in front of him and he bumped me a little to show me his displeasure. I was at the apex of the turn now and I shower down on the gas. The car twisted a little then held traction and settled into the high groove. I just held the car steady as we shot down the straightaway. The seventy one slid next to me in an attempt to block me from passing and to give him a better opportunity to make turn three and spin me out in the turn.

I pressed the motor to it's limits and I was worrying about it blowing up, but the seventy one was trying to cram me into the wall. I knew that he was going to hold his position into the turn and force me into the wall. I saw him coming towards me to push me closer to the wall. I knew that I had to do something drastic to prevent it. I tapped the brakes slowing enough that as he pushed I wasn't there for him to push against and he nearly hit the wall himself. I pushed hard into the low groove and moved around him before the turn. He bumped me from behind a couple of times but he was not going to be able to catch me before the end of the race.

I was actually surprised that the car handled so well, without the added weight of the electric motor and I cruised to the checkered flag in the heat race.

Sidney was looking perturbed as I pulled into the pit.

He was sitting on the stool flopping a grease rag from one hand and pulling it through the other. He was still sitting there when I climbed out of the car.

"What's up with you?" I had noticed that he had been acting more than a little weird since the inspector went over the car. I grabbed a bottle of water and sat down on my stool.

"I'm thinking that we might have to make a change in the plan." Sidney was very deliberate with his words but since I didn't know the plan I couldn't comment on it much. "I just don't like those sons-a-bitches sticking their nose in my business."

"Hey, they didn't find anything, so what's the problem?" I asked shrugging my shoulders.

"The problem is that we got people talking about us."

He glared at me, "What do you think, that that inspector just decided to inspect our car just for grins. Somebody told them something." He slapped his knee.

"But they can't prove anything," I pleaded.

"But where there's smoke there's fire." he reiterated.

"Those damn kids have been blabbing their mouths and somebody has been listening." He shook his head and got up and walked into the trailer.

I started the feature on the inside of the fourth row, and I couldn't get my mind off of how Sidney was reacting. I was having the time of my life. I was driving a car that I could only dream of driving and working for a guy that treated me more like a son than someone who worked for him. I wanted to have a good showing in this race. The stands were full and this being Vegas they were taking bets on us and after the heat race the numbers were looking pretty good. I was also worried about his "change in plans" comment, what did he mean by that. But, I did understand that the kids that caught us on the race track did catch us running with the gas motor off and it could raise suspension, but I did think that Sidney was over reacting.

I was starting in the inside on the third row for the fifty lap feature. I knew that I wanted to win but I was more than a little curious about Sidney's change in the plan. I saw green flag wave and the pace car pull off into pit road and knew that the race would soon be on. I braced myself as I eased on the accelerator to close the gap between me and the ninety one car in front of me. I played with the accelerator a little pushing down to charge and then backing off because I really had no place to go.

I had maintained my position throughout the race and hadn't had to make too much of a move, but all the way I was studying the drivers in front of me. The six car in the lead was very fast but he slowed a little more than necessary in the curves and powered out down the straight away very well. I hoped that I would get the chance to test his car and try to take him for the lead, but I had three cars ahead of me and the ninety one was doing a very good job of blocking me.

As we slowed to ease into the curve, I pressured the ninety one and forced my car into the middle between the five car and him. He reacted by giving room but bumped me to let me know of his displeasure and then bumped me in the rear bumper in what I considered to be an attempt to spin me out. I just eased out on the straight away and ran away from him.

The five car dove into the turn and I had to take the middle groove which without my added weight in the rear end would make my move very risky considering my speed and momentum going into the corner could cause me to spin out.

I felt the rear end get a little loose but it held and I was in the driver's seat to pass the five car down the straight. I was in second place with two laps to go. The number two car, I had learned from laps of studying him that he was really fast down the straight but was very leery of the turns. I had to use that to my advantage but I didn't know if I had the motor to catch him or not. I was running out of race. I had to try. I only had a turn and a half left before the checkered flag.

The second he dove into the turn, I accelerated and moved into the middle groove and prayed that I could hold traction long enough to get by him. The car shuttered a little under the power of the motor and the rear end became squirrelly and I had to adjust the steering a little fearful that an over steer would send me into the wall. I saw him look over at me as I pulled next to him and I knew that he was doing everything that he could do to stay ahead of me and get down the straight away. It seemed like it was taking forever for me to pass him. For the first time since I've been racing with Sidney, I was in first place and I planned to stay there.

Chapter Four

"And now ladies and gentlemen," Sidney began as he moved the microphone closer to his mouth and righted himself to his tallest structure. He looked nervous tonight for some reason but this was his first sales pitch of the new motor to his selected group of clientele. He had rented the banquet hall at the hotel we had stayed in while in Des Moines. It was a big room that had stadium like seating and the stage was elevated in the center of the room. I was an elegant room with hanging globes hanging from the ceiling. It looked like they had concerts from time to time. "This is the moment that I have been waiting for, for more than twenty years. This new motor will revolutionize the world and you are going to get the first chance at it. Without further a due, let me show you how it works. Somebody get the lights." The lights quickly diminished and on the screen I saw a picture of me driving the twenty six car on the track here in Des Moines. I got a thrill from watching it because it was the first time that I got to drive the car without that gas motor running. Then the screen switched to an in cab camera that displayed the gas motors statistics and the speedometer was indicating that I was doing one hundred forty five. "Now watch this," Sidney interrupted the video and I saw myself reach to the dash and start the gas motor. "The car was never running on the gas motor but on my motor, an electric motor. I want you to know the characteristics of this motor. This motor produces over five hundred horsepower and the best part is that it uses no gas." He let the words have a little time to sink into the crowd and they responded with a rumble of conversation among themselves. I noticed that the people in the in room were really expressing their interest in the motor. "Now this is the beautiful part," Sidney began before shouting to the back of the room, "somebody hit the lights. This motor is adaptable to go in most any vehicle." Sidney motioned for me to go get the car. "We have it in a Corvette and we want to bring it in and show it to you." Sidney's voice was fading away as I stepped to the next room and to get the car. I pulled the car into the front of the big screen and popped the hood before I got out. "Well here it is guys come take a look at it." Sidney barely got the words out of his mouth before the crowd suddenly jammed around the car. "The motor," Sydney tried to say something but the noise of the crowd drowned him out. I was having a hard time getting the doors open far enough for me to get out. Some big guy saw my predicament and began moving the others out of the way of the door.

"Wait a minute," he shouted taking authority over the situation, "let the guy get out of the car. I want to talk to him." That would be me that he wanted to talk to and I was confused why would he want to talk to me, but the crowd moved enough to let me out and he grabbed my hand and pulled me out of the car.

"Thanks," I began getting to my feet but he didn't let go of my hand and he was pulling me away from the crowd and I was becoming a little concerned.

"This motor," he began looking intently into my eyes with a stare that looked could have burned holes in me. "What does it run on? How can it produce five hundred horsepower and still," his mind was running fast with questions and I could tell that he wanted answers. He stood over six feet and looked like he spent a lot of time in the gym because his arms and chest were very muscular. He had red hair that was cut in a crew cut that topped his square face with inset eyes. He had that ruddy freckled complexion that red headed people have. I was hoping that he was going to let me go soon because I had to get to the order table and help Sidney take orders.

"I'll tell you Sidney will answer all your questions," I started to try to move toward the table but he blocked me.

"I've heard enough about the motor and I'm going to buy one of them and if I like it, I will buy more." He began reaching for my hand again, "I wanted to offer you a chance to drive for me next year. I think that you are one exciting driver and I could use a driver like you. Here's my card, call me when you get a chance." I glanced at the card before putting it in my pocket, Randy Morgan it read before he continued, "by the way, I'm Randy Morgan of R and M Racing." I was surprised and flattered but I knew that I had to get to the table to help Sydney take orders for the motor.

"Thank you, I appreciate your offer," I began trying to move away from him, "I have to help Sidney take orders and it looked like he was busy.

It was early in the morning when I drove the car out of the convention center. Sydney had insisted that I drive the car away from there and he would call me on the cell phone to tell me where to meet the truck. He had gotten better on his paranoia and suspiciousness since we stopped racing about midway through the season. He said that he had all the film on the car that he needed. My job was just to take the car on a drive down the interstate toward Kansas City and he would let me know where I would meet up with him. I had long decided that I would not question his directions because I knew how careful that he was.

I was enjoying driving around town and was taking the loop around town just to kill some time to allow Sidney to get in the truck and get ahead of me. Just running the Corvette on the electric motor was fun. I was running along doing the speed limit and it was so smooth that it was unbelievable, but I knew that at any second I could smash this motor and hit at least one hundred fifty or more in no time.

I was thinking that this had been a very successful meeting. I didn't know how many motors that he sold but I knew that it was quite a few. He had said that he would like to have five or six thousand of them on the street before taking the motor to the public.

I was just sliding effortlessly through the light traffic on the highway at that time of the morning, when I noticed that a car was behind me and making every move that I did on the highway. I decided that I would slow down and act like I was going to take the next exit off the highway. I had my turn signal on and the car had pulled into the exit lane behind me and turned their signal on as well. I slowed like I was going to get off at the exit but when I got to the exit I accelerated back to highway speed, but I was surprised because the car that was behind me got off at the exit. I breathed a sigh of relief and quickly got off at the next exit and headed toward Kansas City.

After about thirty minutes I got a text message from Sydney. "Make sure you are not followed; go to the safe house at Grand Avenue. Park the car inside the garage and wait for instructions." He had given me a bunch of codes and addresses of where the safe houses were but I didn't see a need to use the safe houses now. Then a second text message came through, "Make sure that you don't have a tracker on you or the car." Wow, I thought, those people seemed so nice at the meeting, trackers; Sidney thinks that I might have a tracker on the car. I was about fifteen miles outside of town when I saw a car come up behind me approaching really fast and then slowed quickly to meet my speed.

Sidney had given me plenty of instruction on how to search a car for a tracking bug without readily being noticed. I pulled over to the side of the road just to see what the car behind me would do and whoever it was stopped behind me as well. It was about two thirty in the morning on a cold early November night and I wasn't going to take any chances about the intentions of the car behind me. It was close enough now that I could tell that it was a Suburban of some kind that was dark in color.

I hammered the car and quickly jumped my speed from a sitting still to over a hundred in what seemed like two seconds and I was putting a lot of distance between me and the Suburban that appeared to be tracking me. I saw the signs that there was a truck stop six miles ahead and I hoped I could get there and get the tracking bugs off the car before my company could find me.

I pulled into the truck stop knowing that I had to get out among the trucks out of the lights of the car parking lot. I pulled in between a couple of trucks that were running and the drivers were obviously sleeping. I parked and opened the trunk and retrieved the bug detector. When I turned it on, it acted like it was going crazy and I immediately thought that I might have more than one but on the car. I found three tracking bugs on the frame underneath the wheel wells but I kept getting a signal and finally determined that it was coming from me. I emptied my pockets and found a strange looking quarter that I didn't remember having in my pocket before. I wondered if that Randy guy that I got the card from could have slipped it into my pocket. I found his card in my pocket and tossed it on the ground.

I was leaving the parking lot and rolled the window down and pulled up next to a truck that was leaving the parking lot and tossed the magnetic tracking bugs into the wheel of the truck. I watched as the truck turned onto the highway and accelerated on the on ramp. I was looking for the Suburban but didn't see it at all and before I left the parking lot of the truck stop I flipped the tracking bug that looked like a quarter onto the parking lot. I was more than a little scared to get back on the highway until I saw the Suburban turn onto the on ramp from under the highway and follow the truck. I immediately felt better. I fought the urge to call Carrie as I was driving but I was concerned that I might get her involved and I was scared that with all the things that Sidney had told me about how a person could be tracked on a cell phone. I did hope that I would get to the Dallas area so that I could at least call her and maybe take her out or something.

It was four thirty in the morning when I pulled into the garage of the safe house after checking for bugs at least three more times just to make sure. I wondered what happened to Sidney but couldn't really worry about it now because I was so tired that I collapsed on the bed.

When I woke up the next morning, my phone was beeping that I had a message and I knew that Sidney would be freaking out to know that I got there safely. "I'm glad you finally made it, call me when you get up." The message from Sidney read. I pushed the number on my cell phone that automatically connected me to Sidney.

"It's about time you got up; did you have a bad night?" Sidney asked as I realized that he didn't know about my encounter with the Suburban.

"Sidney, where did you go last night?" I asked not giving him any time to answer. "Somebody put tracking bugs on the car last night, three of them to be exact, and they even slipped one on me." I was getting excited as I was now fully awake and feeling the adrenaline of the night before.

"Are you sure that you got to the house without anyone tracking you?" he asked sounding very concerned.

"Oh, yeah," I began letting my excitement spill over in my voice, "I made absolutely sure that no one was following me long before I pulled into the driveway of the condo complex." I could hear that he was just as excited or more anxious that I was but all of this time I thought that he was suspicious and paranoid and now it looked like he had good reason.

"Good," he said flatly, "here's what we are going to do. I want you to stay there for two or three days. I will text you when to leave. Flush that phone and get the new one. I will text you instructions on it. You did good now relax and I will see you in a few days." Sidney's voice turned to strict and concise details all the emotions was gone. He was pure logical and deliberate in his instructions. He didn't even give me time to say goodbye. He just hung up like he was dismissing me. He wasn't even curious about what I had been through the night before but he had been preparing me for nights just like that one ever since I had known him.

It seemed a shame to flush my new phone, Sidney had always said that the only phone that he would ever use was a pre-paid one because they were untraceable, and supposedly he says. He was into all the new electronic technology and he says that he could intercept the signal and trace it that way but I didn't know anything about it but I'm sure that someone out there would know something about it. I thought about it for a second before I flushed the phone. I would lose all contact with him if I flushed the phone, but I knew that I had to and trust that he could get in touch with me when he wanted to. I stood there above the toilet preparing to flush the phone and remembered that he knew that I was in the house and when I had got there. I smiled to myself as I let the phone slip from my fingers into the water and watched as the water carried it off.

Beep, beep, beep came the sound from the other room and I ran in there frantically looking for the source of the sound. I found the new phone in a drawer in the kitchen; Sidney had already sent a text to the new phone. "Get some sleep", it read, "tonight head toward Denver, will text routing, stay in the car. Will provide info for morning. Paint car with white water paint."

I couldn't believe what I was reading, he was telling me to get some sleep and then telling me to paint the car. I shook my head at what I was seeing, but I knew that I had to get busy. In the garage I found everything that I needed to paint the car and I decided that I had better do it now to give the paint plenty of time to dry.

I pulled out of the complex at dusk and quickly found the interstate and clicked on the cruise control. I set it at about five miles an hour faster than the speed limit. I had the radio on and I was getting comfortable that no one was following me. I had just noticed the sign that said that interstate eighty to Denver was about three miles ahead and my phone started beeping. I quickly opened the phone and Sidney's message read, "Take I35 south to I70." I acknowledged the message by shaking my head for some reason, even though I knew that it was shorter to take interstate eighty through to Denver. I couldn't understand why he wanted me to go to Denver, we had never raced there and as far as I knew there. I stopped at a truck stop and bought another cell phone that I could use to call Carrie with. I knew that she was attracted to me but I really didn't know what I was going to talk about if I didn't talk about racing. Then I knew that he would not want me to talking to Carrie or telling her about anything that we were doing. I had bought the 500 hundred minute card and the headset that went with the phone. I was getting ready to call her because I knew that Sidney would not be calling me all night long. I dialed the number.

"Hi, Carrie, this is Ricky I hope that you have time to talk to me tonight." I began excitedly, "it looks like I'm going to be driving most of the night and nothing would please me more than to talk to you." I realized that that I was dumping a lot on her in a few short moments but I didn't care. I really wanted to talk to her and I wanted her to know it.

"Ricky," she began slowly, "I'll talk to you for a while but you'll have to call me back in about 15 minutes." She sounded hurried and short in her response, but she did say that I could call her back. I gunned the motor in response in my excitement.

We talked into the night. I was careful to be the one that asked the questions and avoid talking about racing. I got to know more about her than almost anybody knew. She was working as an EMT while she was going to school to be a registered nurse. She was living in an apartment with a roommate who was also going to nursing school. All was not peaceful in the apartment because the other girl had a boyfriend and was not there that much and was not living up to her responsibilities in paying half of the rent and utilities. From time to time she would try to ask something about me and it made me uncomfortable and I would turn the question back to her.

I had talked to her for about 2 hours before I wished her a good night and allowed her voice to slip from my ear. It had been exhilarating to talk to her. She loved to laugh and I loved to make her laugh. It was a laugh that warmed my heart. And through it all I had never said anything about racing. I was proud of myself.

I was starting to get worried because morning was fast approaching and I was only about halfway across Kansas and I had not heard anything from Sidney and most importantly I hadn't seen anyone that was the least bit interested in me. I tried to stay close to the trucks but some of them couldn't travel at the speed that I wanted to travel, but some of them did and we were able to cover some ground.

Beep, my phone went off, I knew that Sidney had some new instructions for me. "Park the car in the lot. Walk to hotel, check in under the name James Lee. Map and codes to follow."

I glanced at the map and I didn't recognize the area of town the he wanted me to be in so I sent it by Bluetooth to the navigation system in the car. When it popped up on the screen in the car I understood where he wanted me to go.

It was after ten in the morning when I pulled into a mini-storage, punched the codes into the entry gate keypad and the gate opened. I knew that I was in the right place. I noticed all the security cameras around the mini-storage and wondered if Sidney's company might have installed the system. Number fifty seven was a big double car garage type storage unit. I hit the code on the door and it readily opened.

The phone was ringing wildly, waking me up from a deep sleep. "Hello," I said into the phone and was surprised at how my voice broke.

"You better wake up," Sidney sounded more light hearted than usual, "your dinner is on it's way up to you. You have any problems last night?" he asked.

"No, no," I responded, "I just had a nice drive." I was fully awake now and felt well rested and I was glad that he had dinner being sent up because I was hungry. I heard a knock on the door and someone shouted, "Room Service." "That was quick," I said to Sidney over the phone, "I think that my dinner is here." I started to respond to the room service guy but Sidney interrupted me.

"Don't say anything, let me check it out." Sidney sounded concerned and I could hear him clicking the keys of a keyboard. "Okay, it's okay," he was much more relaxed, "put your pants on and give her a good tip." I knew that he was watching me and it wouldn't surprise me if he didn't have a camera in the hotel room.

He was right, the girl that was bringing me my dinner was a pretty and blond hair and a pretty smile. "Good evening Mr. Lee," she said flashing her smile and flicking her hair and lifting the lid off of a huge steak with all the fixings. "Would you like to sign this?" she asked handing me the ticket, "this will charge it to your room." I smiled at her remembering what Sidney had said and added a ten dollar tip to the ticket. As I did it, I wondered how long it would take for him to find out about it.

I had barely finished my dinner, when I got a text message from Sidney. "Ten dollars, I hope that she was that good. Head to Las Vegas. Instructions will follow." I knew that Sidney was on top of his game but how in the world did he know things so fast. I headed out of the hotel and I thought that it was a little darker that I would have liked, but the night air felt good and I decided that I would jog down the road just in case someone might be watching. I started that I would use the normal miss direction when you are trying avoiding being detected. I jogged up to the McDonalds and went in to watch the traffic. I saw nothing out of the ordinary. The road was mostly deserted but I wanted to make sure that I was not being followed. Sidney's suspiciousness had infected me. Then I remembered that my phone had all the information about where the car and all anyone had to do was to get to me and they could find the car. When I left McDonald's I decided to continue my jog down the road this time. I never saw anyone or any car or truck that showed any interest in me or what I was doing. I ran past the mini-storage for about a half a mile and then turned around like I was going back to the hotel. But when I got to the mini-storage I turned in and quickly hit the code and watched the gate open. I watched it as it closed behind me and still no one was interested in me.

I jumped in the car and pulled out of there feeling so good that no one was watching me or following me, but I knew that after the demonstration in Las Vegas that I would probably have to do this same thing all over again. As I drove I couldn't help but think that Sidney knew every move that I made. He had to have the car rigged with some kind of tracker like those other guys planted on the car but his bug had to be so good that the bug detector that I used didn't pick it up. Then he was able to see almost everything that I was doing in the motel and on the highway outside of the mini-storage he could see that I was running.

I had to get all that cloak and dagger stuff out of my head, I had a good night of driving ahead of me and I was going to enjoy it as much as possible. I cranked up the country music and accelerated toward Las Vegas. I had about seven hundred and fifty miles to cover before morning and I hoped that I could talk to Carrie again for awhile as I drove, but I didn't know whether or not I should call or not.

I studied that cover of the phone because I didn't know whether or not I should call her again so quick or not. I hit the button to call her and hoped for the best.

"Hello," Just hearing her voice made my heart skip a beat.

"This is Ricky again," I began, "I just wanted to call and see how your day went."

We talked about her classes and the problems that she had with her roommate and I found out that she was not really happy with me not having any way to better myself at this time. But I tried to tell her that I didn't know what I was doing from one day to the next at this point in my life. While we were deep in conversation the phone suddenly went dead. I figured that we might have been cut off because I was out in the middle of nowhere. But I didn't know.

I had driven about six hundred miles and I was way off in the middle of nowhere in Utah and I was really getting into the cruising of the car. Listening to the country music from one of the big stations in Texas and something caught my attention on the side of the road up ahead. In this area of Utah there would be no telling what you could run into and I'm sure that people broke down on the side of the highway. I watched intently at the two little red lights that ahead of me that was getting closer and closer with each passing second.

I recognized the truck as a dark colored Suburban and instantly chills swept down my spine. I wanted to smash the accelerator and just run away from them and leave them in the dust but I knew that if I did there would be a cop over the next little hill and he would have a field day with writing me tickets. Then I wouldn't want to hit a deer or something at that speed, it could make things very messy. I pushed the accelerator up to ninety and the car responded instantly and acted like it wanted more.

I kept checking my rearview and I could see lights approaching me from the rear and they were getting closer and closer. I knew that since I had only a hundred and thirty or so miles to get to Las Vegas they must have help ahead since they were not interested in trying to catch up to me. Maybe they didn't want to stop me and steal the car, but just follow me and see where I parked I knew that was just a fantasy.

I thought about what I should do, if they had help up ahead, every second I could be moving into a trap. I checked the GPS map and Cedar City was coming up in about ten miles and if I was chasing somebody and was going to set a trap for them it would be after I past Cedar City because there was no other way to get to Las Vegas. According to the map there were a couple of other routes available but they would be out in the middle of nowhere.

I decided that I would send Sidney a text message to let him know that I had company. "Have company following me. Any suggestions?" I didn't know if he might even be up but it was worth the chance.

I was getting nervous because I hadn't heard from Sidney and I was sure that if I got outside of town very far my cell phone would go dead. I nervously flipped open my phone hoping for a message from Sidney. There were now two sets of lights behind me and my attention had turned to the closeness of the approaching vehicles.

Beep, my phone went off and in my excitement I nearly dropped the phone. I flipped it open to read Sidney's message. "No state troopers on duty this hour. Run off and leave them. See you at the casino." A wave of peaceful excitement flushed over me because I had always wanted to run this car at all out speeds. I pressed the accelerator and the car responded and soon I was traveling at more than one hundred fifty miles an hour. At this rate it would not take long to cover the miles I needed to cover to get to Las Vegas.

I was about ten miles outside of Saint George and I noticed that there were cars in the road up ahead. I hadn't seen anything in my rear view mirror since I had heard from Sidney and I picked up the pace. I couldn't help but feel like a kid in the candy store, I had a car that would go two hundred miles an hour plus and I hated that there were people up ahead that wanted to stop me.

I had my bright lights on and I could see that they had two Suburban's parked in a vee fashion similar to what police road blocks looked like. I could see flashing lights like they could have been police of some sort. But I had to trust Sidney that no troopers were on duty tonight and what state troopers drove Suburban's. I was going too fast and I knew that I was going to have to make a decision fast. If they parked to close to the center of the road I could pass them on the shoulder and if they tried to block more of the shoulder I would have the center of the road.

I could see up ahead that I might have enough room to slip between the center of the Suburbans. I slammed on the brakes and I was going a lot faster than I thought I was. I wanted to glance at the speedometer but I didn't have time as the car was now creeching on the highway and I used the skid to line up the car to get through the road blocking Suburbans.

Whroom, I lined the car up and smashed the accelerator as I passed between the Suburbans. I could see the Suburbans spin around in the road to give chase. But I was so far ahead of them that it was no use, I had them beat. I felt like I had won a race or something.

"It's about frigging time," Sidney greeted me under the canopy of the casino, "did you have any more trouble?" he asked getting in the car with me and motioning for me to pull out of the casino.

"They tried to stop me back there a ways," I began following the directions that Sidney was motioning to me, "but I just blew right on by them." I was smiling and I watched as Sidney smiled as well. Sidney directed me to the back of the casino and I was half expecting to see the truck back there somewhere, but he was directing me into a garage at the casino. As we pulled up he dialed a number on his cell phone and the garage door opened. There was a big number five emblazoned on the outside of the door and I guessed that they must keep these garages for VIP's or something because as the door opened I could see that the garage was big enough to hold a limousine or something.

"Come on," Sidney began getting out of the car, "I'll bet that you are ready to get something to eat and get to bed." We were locking down the garage door from the inside and I could see that Sidney was turning on electronic devices. When he finished he held the walk out door for me and I noticed that it was one of the barrier doors that was on the safe house. Dynamite might open it but that was about all that I knew of that would do it.

It felt so good to be out of the car and walking down the hallway towards the casino, Sidney seemed giddy and was continually rubbing my shoulder like he was hugging me as we walked. "Are you ready for some steak and eggs?" he asked.

I truly enjoyed seeing Sidney again and it seemed like we talked for hours before I finally got up to the room and crashed into the bed. I had fleeting thoughts of my night of evading whoever it was that was chasing me. Sidney had tried to teach me about all the technology and most importantly how I could beat it if I found someone using it against me. I had a lot of questions. How did they know I was going to Las Vegas? How did they know what route I would be taking? Who was it that was messing with me? I realized that I didn't have answers and I just faded into a deep sleep worried about what was going to happen at the exhibition tonight.

Sidney was shaking my shoulder and it took me what seemed to be a long time before I returned to consciousness. "Come on, Ricky, we've got things to do." Sidney prodded now pulling my arm to get me up. "We've got to get the car ready for the sales pitch." I lunged forward and sat up in the bed. "I'll be back in thirty minutes."

Sidney was talking to someone on the phone as I was getting out of the bed about some sort of a glass shield. I was hopeful that he would do something different to keep people from getting around the car. I glanced at the clock and figured that I had about two hours before the start of the presentation. I wanted to see if I recognized anyone from the Des Moines presentation because it would have to be the people that were after me.

When I walked into the exhibit room there was one of those slow spinning round elevated platforms that they display cars on at the auto shows. I could see the ramps up to put the car on the platform but I didn't see Sidney or anyone else. I opened my phone to call Sidney and he exploded in the back door with a crew of casino employees with some huge pieces of glass.

"Hey Ricky, glad you could join us," Sidney chuckled at his little joke. "let's go get the car." He met up with me as we started the long walk into the bowels of the casino to retrieve the car. "I'll call you guys when we are ready to set the car up on the stage," he said to the casino employees that were helping him and they headed in the direction of the garage. He turned and slapped me on the back as we walked. "Do you know anything about all four of my tires being punctured and a chunk being knocked out of my right mirror housing." He laughed a little and was shaking his head as we walked. "they must have really been after you last night."

"Sidney, how in the world did they know that we were going to Las Vegas next?" I asked as we walked. I was worried that my conversations with Carrie had somehow been the way that I had been detected. Sidney broke out laughing and it took a while for him to regain his composure.

"I told them I was going to Las Vegas," Sidney paused as he watched for my reaction. I was dumbfounded because I realized that he had pretty much set me up. "Don't look so confused, I had faith in you. I knew that they might try to get to you but I knew that you could get by anything that they might try to throw at you." He was smiling as me slapped on the back. "Those were the amateur boys, when the pros get started we will have to get really good." Sidney acted like he had everything under control. "I had to smoke them out, let's go eat dinner before the meeting, and if I'm right we will have a visitor sometime tonight." Sidney was a planner. He planned the racing season. He planned everything about the marketing of his car and if he said that someone would be paying us a visit I was inclined to believe him.

"I can't believe that you put me out there knowing that they would be coming after me." I sounded a little more upset than I actually was but I couldn't phantom him not telling me what was going on. "Look," I said as we sat down at the restaurant in the casino, "let's make a deal, if you know that somebody is going to be after me. Let me in on it. I would like to know if I'm going to have company on the road."

"I can understand why you might me a little upset," Sidney blurted out cutting me off, "but I had to pull a little redirection. If I let the people that are after us just follow us around, we would never know who they are. Not that it makes any difference, but I had to get back to Tulsa. I followed your every move and I even watched you a lot of the way. When you blasted by that roadblock, I thought we were going to lose a big chunk of the car." I knew that I told him about everything that happened but I didn't know that he was watching me all that much.

"Get you a good steak tonight," Sidney sat down at a booth away from the crowd in the restaurant of the casino. "I think that things will get pretty hairy after tonight." Sidney signaled a waiter to come take our order. "After tonight, we are going to have to be really careful. We will not be able to eat in a restaurant like this for a long time." When he said that, it puzzled me. "There are just too many things that a man that has the desire can do to your food as it makes its way to the table." Sidney raised an eyebrow insinuating that he knew that someone would be after us that would be willing to pull out all the stops to get to us. "Do you know that three little grains of something sprinkled on your food is enough to kill you within eight hours." Sidney looked so sad as he talked. "Ricky, I've told you many times that you could back out of this deal anytime that you want. I don't want to get you killed but it could very well happen." I had told him many times that I was in for the long haul and that I would see it through to the end regardless of the outcome.

"Sidney, I've told you time and time again, I am with you," I stated flatly, "but from now on if you think they are coming after me. You let me know. You know that I never so much as went to the bathroom because I didn't know who was after me or how close they were." I was letting my anger get the best of me and it was the first time that I could remember that I let him see that side of me.

"You've got a point," Sidney began, "let me tell you that you were never alone, I had you on video and sometimes audio the whole time." He paused for a moment as he took a look around the room and settled on a couple of men in suits that had just walked in. Audio, oh my God he might know that I was talking to Carrie all those times. "I got it," he said out loud, but I knew that he was not talking to me. He turned back to me and continued, "I have always wondered how quick these guys would get around to us. These are the big boys that I was telling you about. Anyway, don't let these guys bother you." He was whispering as the two men were now standing in front of our table.

"Mr. Sidney Cain I presume," one of the two men pulling something out of his pocket and laying it on the table in front of us, the man with the paper in his hand was older and had close cut graying hair with a bald spot in the middle. He wore a wicked smile on his aging angular face that supported his horn rimmed glasses. The other man was younger and had an over coat that had bulges around the waist and I got the feeling that he was carrying at least one gun beneath that coat. He was muscular and had a square jaw and had a slight but noticeable scar underneath his right eye.

"I would like to introduce myself, I'm James Pritkin, of Pritkin, Neihouse and Cole attorneys," he stated sounding very professional, "we understand that you have developed a very interesting motor, one that doesn't use any gas and we would like to offer you one billion dollars for your motor and all your paperwork on it." I could see Sidney getting mad as his face was flushing.

"Let me tell you one damn thing," Sidney responded getting angry, "you will not treat me like you did Stanley Myers, I am not interested in your money. I want this motor to get out to the public. Your clients had better steal all the money that they can because before long gasoline and petroleum based fuels are going to be as extinct as the dinosaurs that they came from. Let's go Ricky, it is starting to smell around here." He got up and threw his napkin down on the table and was walking away from the table.

"Mr. Cain I have a check for a million dollars as a good faith payment," Mr. Pritkin yelled as I hurried to catch up with Sidney. "Ricky you better stay away from that crazy bastard before he gets you killed." He was shouting at us as we quickly was increasing the distance between us. The last time I looked back he was bouncing his check in one hand into the other and saying something to the other.

"Sidney, are those guys for real?" I asked looking over my shoulder to watch them as they walked away towards the entrance of the casino.

"Oh yeah they're for real," Sidney was more mad than anything, "I expected them to be on us fast but not this fast." We were making our way out of the casino and I didn't know why. "From now on this thing gets real hairy," he was shaking his head as he spoke. “I warned you that this was going to be the most fun of your life didn’t I.” he was somehow giddy about the potential threats that the lawyers and the people they represented presented. “God, I hope they don’t kill us for this, but for now everything is going according to the plan.” Sidney was a little more that self satisfied as he spoke.

“I’m glad that you warned me about all this,” I slapped him on the back as we walked out of the casino and the lawyer and his friend were driving by the front of the casino and were waving at us from the black Suburban. The instant I saw it I was wondering if they were the same guys that were after me on the way here. I was thinking about Sidney’s plan, I didn’t know much about it, but so far he seemed to have an answer for everything. “I just didn’t believe it when you did, but I’m glad that you did.” I tried to make it a joke and he smiled a little but I didn’t think that he thought my comments were all that funny. We walked into a steakhouse a few doors down from the casino.

“You’ll like this place,” Sidney said as we sat down at a table, “It’s not a plush as the casino but they have good food.” As he spoke I remembered the little out of the way places that he liked to eat when I first hooked up with him on the racing circuit.

“I know that you know what you doing, but I want to know something and I’m almost afraid to tell you,” I began settling in to my chair and checking out the menu that the waitress had handed us when we sat down as Sidney stared at me waiting on me “but my worry is that I don’t and if I get stopped or captured or the car gets stolen, what happens then and what happens to my girlfriend that I have been talking to on the nights that I have been driving.” My concerns hit him like a sledge hammer.

“After tonight,” Sidney began, “we, we, well hell,” I could see that he was thinking and laying out in his mind the plans for the next step in the big plan. “I’ll tell you what, tonight,” he paused apparently continuing to flesh out the alterations in the plan. “Okay,” he continued, “this is what we are going to do. Tonight we are just going to show the video and not show the car. In the morning, we are going to get another white Corvette and you are going to start driving it home. I'm going to stay here and change the motor out of the Corvette and put it in a Suburban.” He paused again and I was thinking that there would be no need for me to provide a diversion if we were going to change the motor out of the Corvette.

“Let me suggest something,” I broke into his chain of thought, “if we change the motor out of the Corvette, there would be no need to for me to be a diversion, right?” He looked at me and I think was seeing the logic of my proposal.

“Well you're right,” he responded waiting for the waitress to set the food down in front of us and continued when she was a safe distance away. “you know I think that we need to put some more heat on the situation. I'm calling the news media and having them at the meeting tonight.” His mind was still searching for answers and objectives that he needed to meet. “I'll tell you what, tonight I want you to drive the Corvette, no, no, maybe not. I was thinking that we are going to need tools and to find a Suburban to put the motor in, but I guess that we could just put the motor in the back of the Suburban and drive it away from here. No, that's not going to work. I want you to drive the car out of here tonight while the presentation is going on.” He smiled as his plan was becoming clear. “Yes, that will work, we don't have the vehicles or the tools here, but we do have a water hose and we can change the color of the car.”

I was just letting him talk, I was busy eating, but I liked the plan so far. I was glad that I got a good sleep this morning, because it looked like I would be driving all night again.

"Here's what we'll do," he began, "we'll both go to the presentation and when the lights dim, you slip out and take off in the car." He was excited as he spoke as if he was winning at something. I didn't like the idea too much, if they were willing to kill that Meyers guy in Ohio, why wouldn't they be willing to kill him and he would be left exposed.

"Let's think about doing something else," I began not totally ruling out his plan, "they or whoever they are, they want to get you, me and the car. If you fly out of here in the morning going home, I'll take the car and meet you somewhere." Sidney was stared intently into my eyes, emotionless, and I could tell that he was thinking it over.

"That is a good idea," he began finishing the last bite of his steak, "I can help you better if I could get home and they couldn't get to me at home. I've got enough security around my house that no one could get through it to get to me." He face broke into a big smile, before he continued. "We've got to take this thing underground now. We need to be a mere shadow of their imagination, but one that is going to kick their butt one of these days."

"Ladies and Gentlemen," Sidney began the meeting, "tonight you have the opportunity to buy one of the hottest, the most innovative, the most spectacular motor ever invented. It produces over five hundred horsepower and it uses no fuel. You never have to send the camel jockeys another nickel." I could hear a rumbling of conversation coming from the full house crowd in the casino. There were several television camera crews present and they were pressing to get to the front of the room. "And now let me show you this motor in action." Sidney pressed the button on the multi-media player. I had seen the video before and the room was so intent on the video I thought that it would be a good time to slip out of the room.

I got up from my seat and made my way to the wall aisle. The door was in the back of the room and there were so many people crammed in there I didn't know if I could get out or not.

I had made my way to about twenty feet to from the door and another big bunch of people were pushing their way to get in. I really didn't like being so close to people, there was no telling what someone could slip into my pocket or puncture my skin or something.

"Where you going Rick?" a semi-familiar voice sprang out of the sea of bodies around me. I immediately began looking for the source of the question. "Rick, Rick," he began again, "I'm over here." I looked in his direction and it took me a minute to recognize who was talking to me. It was that Randy Morgan fellow that I had met in Des Moines. Since he was between me and the door I figured that I would respond to him.

"Hey, what are you doing here?" I asked not expecting a truthful answer.

"We just thought we would come down and do a little gambling," he chuckled as he spoke to let me know that he was lying. "You are one hell of a driver, do you still have that card I gave you? I could really use you to drive for me." He was nearly shouting at me over the noise of the crowd as the lights came back up and Sidney once again stepped to the microphone.

"Let me tell you how serious this motor is." Sidney began with his voice showing a little anger. "Tonight a lawyer who represented somebody that didn't want you to know who they were offered me a billion dollars for this motor. But I am for the little guy, Henry Ford wanted to put man on wheels, I want him to drive them for nothing." He went on to give out a web site and a password to order a motor. Then he sat down and started answering questions about the motor and the news media was eating up every word.

"Here let me walk out with you," Randy quickly took my arm and started to follow me out of the room. I didn't like the way that Randy was grasping my arm. "Hey, I just want to talk to you," he shouted as I twisted my arm free and pushed on the crowd in front of me to put some distance between us. I knew that he was following me and I didn't know where to go. I was more floored to find out that it was Randy Morgan that was after me instead of the sinister people that were represented by the lawyer and his crowd.

I broke free into the casino and found myself running on instinct and heading for my room upstairs. I looked through the rows and rows of slot machines. People were everywhere and the noise of the dinging machines were deafening. I slid into an aisle of slot machines and tried to blend in with the players. I saw the men with Randy walking up and down the main aisle. I quickly stuck a five into the machine and hit the button to spin the wheels. I noticed in between the spins on my machine that there were three of them, Randy and two other guys. I half expected to see the guy that was with the lawyer; just thinking about him gave me the creeps. He was just emotion less.

"Ricky," someone said and I nearly jumped out of my skin as they slapped a heavy hand on my shoulder. "We don't want to hurt you?" I recognized the voice to be that of Randy but I didn't even want to look up. "If this motor is as good as Sidney says it is, we want in." He spun me a little on my chair and I was looking at him in the eye. "Do you realize how important a motor like that is? It would change the whole economic system of the whole world." I could tell that Randy was just as fascinated with the possibilities of the motor that Sidney was.

"It is an absolutely the best motor that I have ever driven." I said flatly over the noise of the machines around me. I was looking at the Blackjack table and I was wishing that I had made it over there because it would be a better place to have the confrontation that I was having with Randy. "I'm just the driver and the helper,"

I tried to minimize my role in helping Sidney, "If you want to talk to him, you can get in touch with him on the website that he told you about." I tried to stand up and walk away but he caught the sleeve of my jacket.

"I want to make you a deal," he began reaching into his pocket for something and I was getting very anxious as to what he might bring out. "Here," he said handing me his card again, "you can get me at this number at any time, because I figure that there are powerful forces that will not want Sidney's motor on the market, I am willing to offer you five million dollars if you will bring me the motor if things go bad." I took his card this time not really knowing why.

"Sidney says that he is going to start making deliveries on these motors in a couple of months," I responded slipping his card in my pocket.

"I would be surprised if Sidney was alive in a couple of months." He stated flatly allowing me to stand, before continuing, "and you had better be careful yourself." His words hit me like a ton of bricks as the realization flushed my face. I decided that I had to get back in the room and do what I could to protect Sidney. At least I could give him another pair of eyes to be on the lookout.

I ran back into the meeting room and found that the lights were up and Sidney was speaking about something in the front of the room. The place was quiet and orderly and even the news media was behaving themselves. "I'll tell you how important this invention is," he was answering a question from one of the reporters, "tonight, I was offered one billion dollars for all rights to this invention. Think about that for a minute, there are not very many people that could write a check for a billion dollars and if you owned a gas company would you write that check? I'm not the only one that they have offered a billion dollars to, Randy Meyers invented a way to produce enough hydrogen to run a vehicle and all you would have to put in it was water. They ended up killing him and stealing everything that was in his garage." He took a deep breath and exhaled slowly before continuing, "so if anything happens to me, you know who to tell the authorities who did it." He laughed and a ripple of laughter broke out in the room and he stood to walk out of the side door of the room. Then the news people started chasing him trying to ask him more questions.

I immediately saw the need to try to run interference for him to let him have time to get out of the room. I ran around the assembled moving group of people and caught up with Sidney, he was surprised to see me. "I'll see you upstairs," I shouted as I pushed him through the door and closed it, blocking it to prevent anyone from following him. He looked shocked to see me but complied with what I was telling him.

"The show is over," I shouted to the crowd of people trying to follow Sidney, "the show is over.

Chapter Five

"Pritkin," Herbert shouted from the board room of some building in New York and he was the boss, the final word on what was done and who was going to do it, "get in here. This thing is getting out of control. The frigging news media is trying to take this video national and we have to get it under control." The boss was an older man with white thinning hair that was groomed impeccably over the top of his chubby face. His suit was a crisp dark shinny color that made him sort of glows when you looked at him. Other nondescript executives started taking their chairs around the big shiny conference table. There were eight in all and all represented some of the heads of industry including the news media, the oil and gas industry and other interested parties.

"Let me call this meeting to order," the Herbert began, "we have got another serious threat that we have to deal with. I had Pritkin go out and make him our standard offer, but he refused. So that leaves us with no other choice." His voice fell with the seriousness of his conclusions. "Pritkin, tell them what we know." Pritkin stood to his feet and moved to the multi-media wall of the boardroom.

"This is Mr. Sidney Cain," he began pointing to a picture of Sidney on the monitor. "And this is his friend and driver Ricky Jones. At present Mr. Cain is at his home outside of Tulsa and his driver is in their prototype headed south out of Vegas and we don't know where he's going. The pair first surfaced about ten days ago in Des Moines, Iowa where they put on a sales seminar to some of their race car friends."

"What kind of motor do they have?" one of them shouted the question; he was getting anxious and was tapping his pen into his hand.

"I was getting to that," Pritkin clicked the media device to a picture of the car, "all we know about the car is that it seems to move very fast. He says that it doesn't take any fuel of any kind." A hush fell over the room. "I have a make shift video of his presentation that he put on in Las Vegas. I will show it to you but the video quality is not the best as it was shot through a cell phone." Pritkin was preparing the video to show on the screen, when he stopped and looked intently to the assembled, "before I show you the video, it is deteriorated in a couple of areas but since we had a man at the meeting shooting it on his cell phone, I want you to know what he said. He said that he was taking orders for the motors and would be making deliveries in January. Anyway, here's the video."

He flicked the switch and the video sprang to the screen. All sat motionless while the video played out. When the video played out, Pritkin stood to his feet and waited for the lights to come up. "There are a couple of things about this video that I would like to point out." He began clearing his throat, "did you notice the reference that he made to Randy Meyers. That was messy; we need to prevent something like that happening this time. The public is already clabbering for an investigation in to gas prices and we can't afford for them to become even more suspicious over this guy." He picked up the remote control off of the front of the table. "This is the most troubling part of this morning's briefing is that unlike Randy Myers. Sidney Cain has some money and he is not going to be as easy to deal with. Estimates are that he is worth between three and five hundred million dollars. He has holdings. He is the president of All-Tech Security; he is an electronic engineer and has developed some security equipment. The people in Vegas love him."

"If this guy has so much money," one of the attendees blurted out interrupting Pritkin, "why in the world would he want to develop a motor?" Others began talking to themselves and the chatter escalated until the boss stood and held out his hands.

"Wait a minute, wait a minute," Herbert began slapping the table with his hand to get their attention. "Let Pritkin finish." He paused and motioned for Pritkin to continue.

"Okay," Pritkin took out a laser pointer and was moving it along the statistics on the company. "He has a few private investors in the company but he holds about eighty percent of the company. It looks like everybody that does business with him loves him. He has a fleet of trucks that make installations of security equipment in most states. As I said almost every casino uses him including the ones here on the east coast." Pritkin clicked to the next slide before continuing he cast a worried look to the crowd.

"When I offered him the billion, he didn't even blink an eye in turning me down. I don't know how we are going to get to him, especially if he gets to those bastards at Fox news. We have got to get a lid on this thing soon." Pritkin sounded scared and excited at the same time.

"This guy scares me he could be the one to break our grip on the energy industry, if we don't do something and do it fast. Well, you get the picture." Pritkin turned to glance at the video before continuing his presentation.

"Wait a minute," the boss straightened himself and cast a stern look at the assembled, "this means that we are going to have to pull out all the stops and if you guys don't have the guts for that then we are going to lose everything. If you guys think that we can pussy-foot around with this guy you are wrong." He motioned for Pritkin to continue but he clearly communicated his disgust for the inaction of some of the assembled.

"Let me go on," Pritkin pressed the remote and a picture of a house appeared on the screen. "This is Mr. Cain's house outside of Tulsa. On the outside it looks like a normal house but Fort Knox is less secure than this place." A murmur rose in the room and Pritkin raised his hand to calm the crowd. "But lately he has been spending a lot of time traveling the country. He runs a race car that was the one that we saw in the demo. And that is where Ricky Bristow comes in. Evidently, he has had other drivers prior to this year, but he has really vested his self in him. He doesn't have much of a family left. Both his parents are dead. He has an ex-wife but he doesn't have any children. He has some extended family but he hasn't had any contact with them for years according to the ex-wife." Pritkin drew a deep breath and started shaking his head before continuing. "This is the most puzzling part of the background that we completed on our dynamic duo, they seem to have nowhere to build these motors. There is a big metal building on his place but we were told that he used it to work on his race car. Also, if he is building these motors, he is not personally involved because for the last few months we have a pretty good accountability on his where a bouts and he just hasn't had enough time to build any motors."

"That," one of the men at the table broke in, "might be the way that we attack this guy. We could expose this guy as a hoax, kind of like we did with the cold fusion guys."

"Yeah," another one chided in, "no one has seen the motor, he has not shown anyone the inner workings of the motor." He seemed satisfied with his plan and was nodding his head in the affirmative.

"This guy is not going to be that easy," the boss nearly shouted over the rumble of the others, "this man is a millionaire, he has money and that means that he has power just like we do. But he lives in Tulsa and we have a lot of assets on the ground there too." His smile displayed his satisfaction of his abilities to contain any threat. "Let's let Pritkin finish his background and we'll make a decision on what to do," he paused and motioned for Pritkin to continue.

"As I was saying, they have a lot of vulnerabilities," Pritkin pressed his remote and a list of suggested plans of action that could be taken.

"First, we could debunk the invention as something that is inoperable," he began, "we could demand that he produce a couple of units or his plans for one of the universities to examine and validate his claims of invention." Pritkin paused to catch the response of the board members and he seemed very satisfied with himself.

"Then we could attempt to capture the vehicle that Ricky is driving right now, reports have it that he is headed somewhere south of Vegas, they might be planning another presentation like Des Moines and Vegas in Phoenix." He paused and shook his head, "there was an attempt to stop the car while Ricky was driving to Vegas from Des Moines. Reportedly, they had three SUV's and tried to set up a road block and he blew right by them, he is a race car driver and the motor in the car must be something."

"Okay," the boss broke in, "Pritkin we thank you for all your help but we have some decisions to make. We will let you know if we need you further." He was dismissing him and he knew that they did not want him to know what decisions that they were going to make to handle this threat. A satisfied smile appeared on his face because he knew that he had done a good job for them. He gathered his papers and put his papers into his brief case.

"Men, I believe that this is a serious threat." Pritkin stated as he walked out of the room. They all watched as he left the room.

"Okay," the boss cleared his throat, "what do you guys think?" He asked looking into the open stares of the men sitting around the conference table. "Pritkin is convinced that this guy is a legitimate threat and it looks like we are going to have to do something."

"I think that Pritkin was right, "one of them on the right said, "we can put it out that this invention is a hoax and a scheme to defraud the public."

"That is a good idea," another one chimed in, "maybe we could get the FBI to investigate him, that would give us an opportunity to see exactly what he got."

"I don't think that we ought to get the FBI involved," another broke in, "if we get them involved they might make is prove our allegations before they make a move and I don't think it would be good to have them look into us."

"That's a good point," another man confirmed the others assumptions. "if we were able to get the police on our side we would have better leverage to get at them."

"I've been thinking," another broke in, "if we accuse him have perpetuating a hoax and a fraud then he will have to prove that his motor works in public and we sure don't want that."

"Enough," the boss shouted, "you guys couldn't make up your mind if you had to. I'll tell you what we are going to do. Hugh, get one of your newspaper reporters to write a story that exposes the motor and Sidney Cain as a hoax. Say that you are from automotive research organization or something, make up a good name. James, you get a line on his web site, if someone as much as makes a key stroke on that web site, I want to know about it." The boss was very decisive in assigning duties to his subordinates. "Okay, I'm going to get Pritkin to do deep research on the company. He has to be doing business with some of the businesses that we own and maybe we can pull some of those accounts or something. I want to get someone who can get some black ops people to shadow these men until we decide what we are going to do with them and I say that we meet back here in about a week to see where we are." He stood to his feet and the others stood along with him. "We are going to stop these guys, don't worry about it but we all have to hang together." They all started to walk out of the room, "Wait a minute, wait a minute," the boss called the attention of the group, "these guys are communicating with each other somehow while they are on the road, I want to know how and if we can tap into it."

"I've got a cell company," one of them said, "I'll look into that just let me know when you have them located."

"Ricky where in the hell are you?" Sidney asked over the cell phone.

"You know where in the hell I am," I began knowing that he would have me on some kind of GPS monitoring device and that he would know exactly where I was and what I was doing. "I going to be close to home before long." I was looking forward to being home for a few days.

"I've just got a feeling that things are going to get real hot around here in a very short period of time." Sidney said flatly, "I'm going to text you some new directions and I'll want you to get there as fast as you can. We are going underground for a while." Sidney was suspicious and paranoid which was probably a good thing considering what happened on the way to Vegas.

"Where am I, anyway?" I asked knowing that I was just a little ways outside of Phoenix."

"You are about nine hundred miles to San Antonio. At your present rate of progress you should be able to be there in about twenty hours." Sidney stated flatly. "Okay, don't leave the car without arming the security system and I will be sending you new directions before then. I've got a few loose ends to take care of around here." I didn't know what Sidney was thinking but I didn't like the sound of it. He had always been paranoid but now he sounded like he was running scared.

"Okay, whatever you say," I said trying to be a little jovial, "I'm having a good time and I'll take care of everything with the car. I will get it there." I was having a good time and I knew that Sidney was going to take care of everything, if he could. It was about three in the morning and I was listening to the radio and just cruising down the highway. I was more than vigilant about the other cars on the road. I couldn't wait until I could call Carrie because it had been a couple of days since I talked to her and I was anxious to see how she was doing.

I called her twice and didn't get an answer and I was beginning to think that she was screening her calls and she did not want to talk to me. I knew that I was in trouble with her and probably was not going to live happily ever after with her. I knew that I had to get her off my mind because there was no telling who was going to be coming after me.

The sun had come up and I was a about a hundred miles or so from the Texas line and there was not a lot of traffic on the road. I was somehow uneasy driving in the daylight. It was mid November in southeast New Mexico and I was listening to the scanner and the news talk station when a newsflash alert came on the radio. I sort of figured that somebody escaped from jail or something.

"Attention: we have information that Sidney Cain and Ricky Bristow have defrauded several people in Las Vegas and Des Moines out of millions of dollars on an invention scheme that they had supposedly developed." The radio blared out but they didn't say that the police wanted us for anything. A chill ran down my spine and I grabbed my phone to text Sidney. I held the phone in my hand for an instant wondering if I should call or if I should text. The news was so damning that I figured I had better call. I dialed the number and waited as it began to ring, one, two, three, and I knew that if it went to four the message system would pick up. It started to ring the fourth time and I heard a series of clicks that was really strange. I decided that I would hang up.

For the first time that Sidney and I had been doing this, I was scared and I hated admitting it. Out here in the desert, there was no place to hide. Without any messages from Sidney, I wondered if I needed to take the car underground. I was approaching the Texas line and if the police were going to be looking for a black Corvette. I had an extra set of plates in the back and I had some more of the water color paint. But I needed a place to make the change and to disable the GPS and Sidney's tracking device for fear that someone could be hacking into his system.

I cruised into El Paso and I still hadn't heard anything from Sidney even though it had been a couple of hours or more. I would love to be able to make it to San Antonio because I knew that Sidney had a safe house there and I could hold up there for a long time. I wanted to find a storage building place that didn't have much of a security system. I stopped at a convenience store to check the phone book to find one. I found one that was not too far away and ripped the page out of the phone book to follow the little map on the add.

I turned into the storage building facility and checked in. The woman that I was working the desk was Mexican and I had a hard time communicating with her what I wanted. She finally understood what I wanted and charged me fifty bucks for the month. I didn't have the heart to tell her that I was only going to be there for a few hours. I parked the car, pulled down the overhead door and disconnected all the GPS and tracking devices that Sidney had installed to keep track on me. I had most of the things that I needed to change the color on the car except for the tape and the paper to tape it off. If I could get some tape I could use a newspaper to tape it off before shooting the color to it.

According to Sidney's plan, should something like this happen, I was to let him contact me. I decided that I had to try to walk to a store or something to get some tape, but I hated leaving the car even though it would be locked up in the storage facility.

I had painted the car, changed the plates and changed my driver's license to the fake one that Sidney had made for me. It looked strange seeing my picture with the name Wade Thompson next to it, but if someone was looking for me I would have a much better chance to evade them with the fake driver's license. I had slept the rest of the afternoon to prepare for my five hundred or so mile dash to San Antonio.

I eased the door up on the storage unit slipped out on foot to check out the road and to see if anybody was in the office at the gate. The gate was designed to keep people out and I saw that all that I had to do was push the button and the gate would open. I didn't see anything that seemed out of normal but I watched the traffic flow on the road. I retrieved the car and head out onto the road. I cruised by a drive through and picked up food for the trip. Sidney had always preached to me that I could get almost anything in a drive through and it was the safest way to eat on the road because if someone was trying to follow you they wouldn't have any idea where you were going to stop and they wouldn't have any way to tamper with your food.

I eased out on the interstate and brought the car up to highway speed. The traffic was heavier than I expected and it was mostly trucks, I liked traveling around trucks because the satellite signal could be easily confused. I was wondering why I hadn't heard anything from Sidney. I had done everything that he taught me and I knew that he would be all right even though I hadn't heard anything from him.

I nearly freaked when I saw a state trooper sitting on the side of the road, but when I passed him he didn't even act like he was interested in me. I had about decided that they always sat by the side of the road. In a few moments the pylons in the started taking the left lane out of existence and the road was diverted to a shed that all traffic had to stop at. The border patrol agents were checking every vehicle. I pulled my new identification out and held it out to the agent. I could feel the anxiety building in me as he took it and handed it back to me. "Have a nice night," he said, "that is one nice Vette." He motioned to me with his flashlight and turned to check the next car in line.

"Thanks, I love it," said to him thankful that a big truck had gunned his motor taking off and I eased my accelerator down at the same time, hopeful that he wouldn't recognize the my car was not making any engine sound.

I was trying to listen to the news stations to see if I could find any news about us and what was possibly happening with Sidney. I was searching through the satellite channels when my cell phone started beeping that I had a text message. I was relieved that Sidney was at least all right and he would not be sending me a text if he had been arrested. I checked the text; it was twelve roads of numbers. I recognized the code that Sidney and I had worked out where he buried the numbers of his new phone number and the last two rows of numbers were the date and time that he wanted me to contact him. According to the code he didn't want me to contact him until noon tomorrow and I hoped to be in San Antonio by then.

"Sidney, how in the world are you doing?" I asked excitedly as I answered the phone.

"Good to hear from you," he said with a chill in his voice, "you having any problems?"

"I'm good," I responded taking the minimal approach that he was.

"Code word, blind rooster." He said as he hung up. I enjoyed hearing from him but he worried me his sounding so worried.

Under the blind rooster code word I was supposed to go to the safe house in Key West by using all the travel precautions that he had taught me. I didn't like the idea of going to Key West because there was only one highway in and out of there. But if I knew Sidney he always had a backup plan.

I knew that Sidney would not want me to talk to him from one of his safe houses and stay there for very long. I knew that I would have another long drive ahead of me. I checked my hand held GPS and from San Antonio to Key West it was more than fifteen hundred miles. But since he had a brand new Harley Davidson sitting in the garage and I wanted to take a ride around San Antonio and at least get a meal at a restaurant.

I grabbed my hand held GPS and rolled out of the safe house on the Harley. It was good to be riding a motorcycle again. I was enjoying the warm November afternoon as I drove along Interstate four ten headed toward downtown. My plan was to ride downtown and get something to eat and come back to the safe house but I noticed an area on the GPS called Market Square and thought it would be worth checking out. It was a beautiful group of buildings that was decorated in the Mexican style. It had a brick pave courtyard in between one side that had shops of Mexican merchandise and on the other Mexican restaurants. I decided that I would eat first and went in a restaurant called Mi Tierra it had a big bar on one side and had a counter of bakery goods in the middle of the room. A hostess seated me and a waitress took my order. I took my GPS out of my pocket and began plotting my course to Key West. It was amazing that I felt so comfortable there, I thought about it for a moment and concluded that nobody seemed to notice me at all and were involved in doing their own thing. I didn't know that it was because they were mainly a Mexican population or what but they spoke English well enough for me to talk to them.

As I walked back to the Harley I noticed that the tag on the motorcycle had expired and immediately my anxiety went straight up. The police could stop me at any moment and I had to get back to the safe house north of downtown. I instantly checked my surroundings and saw a San Antonio Police cruiser coming in my direction. I quickly stepped behind the bike to block the officer's view of the bike's license plate and pretended to be checking out something on the back of the bike until they passed. I quickly jumped on the bike and headed toward the Interstate highway headed north.

I knew that I was getting as paranoid and suspicious as Sidney had been before we even started taking the motor to the public. But I felt so good to get back at the safe house. It was in a neighborhood of middle class homes just off the interstate off Rittiman road, the next door neighbor came out of their door and wave at me when I pulled into the driveway. She was an older woman and looked like she dressed in a blue print house dress of some kind. She saw me and waved and then went back into her house. I felt a little relief when she disappeared inside her house. I parked the bike and had to go in the house and open the garage door. As I went in the house, I heard her shouting at me,

"Young man, young man," and in a few minutes she was pounding on the front door. "Young man," she kept shouting and then found the door bell. I didn't want to open the garage with her out there because I didn't want her to see the car. She must have rang the bell for what seemed like thirty minutes or more and I decided that I had to go see what she wanted. I opened the door, "Oh, I'm so glad you came to the door," she was nearly exhausted as she spoke between gasps for air. "I'm Joan Purcell, I live next door,"
Somehow as she spoke I got the feeling that she was just gathering her wind. "I've been noticing that you don't stay around here very much." She cleared her throat and caught a breath, "Who did you say you are?" Her question caught me off guard.

"Ah, ah, I'm Mason Tucker," I responded grabbing at names and all I could think about was the Marshall Tucker band and I knew that I had to say something. She smiled at me and extended her hand even though I hadn't opened the door. I reluctantly opened the glass storm door and took her hand. "I'm just so exhausted, could I come in?" She smiled at me with a twinkle in her eye.

"I'm sorry," I said quickly, stepping out of the house and closing the door behind me, "I've got such a mess in there I wouldn't feel right if anybody saw that mess." I could see from the expression in her face that she clearly didn't like my response.

"Well, ah, ah," I couldn't figure out why she was stammering, "my daughter is looking to buy a house out her close to me, I'm getting older you know."

"Ma'am, I don't know anything about who owns this house," I was lying but I hoped to make it sound good, "the management company just gave me the keys, because the company I work for provides the houses." I could see the questions start forming in her mind and I didn't want to take time to come up with more lies to appease her and get her off my case. "I've got calls I need to make will you please excuse me." I didn't give her time to answer but stepped back in the house and closed the door in her face.

"Mason, Mason," she was shouting but I didn't answer and wished that I had told her that I needed to use the bathroom. Finally she walked away and I was so glad.

I waited about thirty minutes and raised the door on the garage and pushed the motorcycle in. I glanced at the old woman's house and she was talking on the phone with someone and I knew that old women like her kept the police on speed dial. I decided that it was time to go. I jumped in the car and headed toward the interstate. As I approached the on ramp to the interstate I could see two police cars turning down the road that the house was on. I gunned the car and took the four ten loop around the city. I was hoping that she didn't get a chance to catch my license plate number.

It was rush hour and I about halfway wished that I hadn't even opened the door for the busy body, but I was away from her now and I didn't need to be thinking about her.

I pulled into Key West the next afternoon after driving for almost twenty four hours, and I was ready to go to bed. I drove up and down Duval Street just to get a look at the place where I was supposed to be safe for a long period of time. I couldn't believe the people that were waving at me as they walked on the sidewalks of the street. I pulled in the garage of the safe house which was located just a couple of blocks off the beach and I noticed that there was a Hummer sitting in the garage. I was closing the door and the door opened and Sidney was standing there in a panama shirt, he had a big hat on and was wearing a pair of shorts.

"It's about frigging time," he smiled at me and I knew that he was glad to see me as much as I was glad to see him. He came running out and gave me a big hug. He was squeezing me so hard that I was getting uncomfortable. "Well come on," he shouted, "let's get you changed and let's hit the town." After driving more than twenty four hours hitting the town did not sound so good but I hadn't seen Sidney since we left Las Vegas and I had a lot that I wanted to talk over with him.

He had bought me a panama shirt that was similar to his, a pair of shorts and a hat. I emerged from the bedroom surprising feeling better than I thought I would. "Let's go," he was anxious and was rubbing his hands together. "You like sea food; they have the best sea food in the world, right here." Sidney was more than excited and I did my best to get caught up in his mood. "Hey you know why I call this place the blind rooster?" He paused and was smiling at me motioning for me to make a guess. I shook my head that I had no idea of what he was talking about. "Because," he paused continuing to motion for me to make a guess. "It's because even a blind rooster could get laid down here." He broke out in a huge laugh and was bent over and slapping his hands and rubbing them together like he was anticipating something good was going to happen.

We walked out of the house and down the road a piece to a place called Seven Fish which I considered to be a little strange on the outside as it looked like an old filling station or something that had been remodeled into a restaurant. We took a table in the back room of the place and at that time of the afternoon we were the only customers.

"Did you hear that they wanted us for fraud?" I asked as I sat down and my voice echoed a little louder than I would have liked. "I was scared to death that the police would get me on the way down here."

"Don't worry about that stuff," Sidney broke in, "they do the same things over and over again and expect that we are not going to get any smarter." He chuckled to himself, "I filed a law suit against them for slander and libel," he flashed a satisfied grin at me as the waiter came. He took the menus and handed them back to him and apparently ordered for both of us as he spoke to him in French and he quickly disappeared into the back. "I ordered you a great piece of fish and I got us a couple of beers coming. Anyway, on that other deal, right now they are probably shitting a brick back in their ivory tower somewhere."

"I was hoping that you had this thing figured out," I was trying to be jovial and chuckled a little as I spoke, "but that roadblock back there nearly freaked me out."

"We are playing with the big boys now," Sidney was now flat and serious in his speech, "these guys will not stop at anything to stop us. I just hope to stay one step ahead of them. I'm sorry about not being able to talk to you but I had a mobile electronics van outside of my door and I had to jam them to get any kind of a message out. I didn't know whether they would be able to intercept our texts or not but I didn't want to take any chances." The waiter brought our food out to us and it looked so good, a piece of cod or other fish that had been cooked in a marinade of some kind. I quickly cut off a piece and it tasted heavenly.

"My God," I exclaimed, "this is good." I couldn't keep myself from inhaling the food and I felt the gaze of Sidney on me in between bites of his on food.

"My God son," Sidney blurted out, "slow down, we've got time. There are a lot of things that I would like to fill you in about." I didn't realize that I was eating so fast but it had been such I long time since I had anything to eat that wasn't from a drive through.

Sidney laid down his fork and looked me in the eye, "This is getting very intense now," he was very serious in his tone and continued, "Are you still with me? You can quit now and I don't think that they will bother you much." He was chewing on a bite of food and continued looking me in the eye.

"I am with you," I said remembering what he told me about all the money that I was going to make if he could complete his plan and I would never have to worry about money ever again. He promised me a percentage of the take.

"I want you to know that I couldn't do this without you." He was taking a sip of his beer as he spoke. "I've been thinking about it, I have changed my will. You will be my one and only heir. Should things go wrong and they get to me, I want you to be taken care of and I want you to know that I appreciate everything that you do for me." Sidney was nearly crying by the time he finished.

"Are you sure?" I asked surprised of the change in the financial arrangements and I knew that he had a couple relatives from his widow's family but I didn't know anything about him. For the last six or seven months he and I had spent nearly every day together.

"Believe me, I'm sure," he smiled and grabbed me by the shoulder, "I just hope that I don't get you killed. You know that it has already been possible. Thank God that nothing has happened." I knew that Sidney was sincere and I wanted him to know that I appreciated his generosity and his recognition of the spot I was in.

"I am only the driver," I smiled at him, "I don't know anything about anything the motor or the plan and don't want to know."

I pushed my plate back on the table and watched as the waiter quickly picked it up. "Oh, before I forget, the safe house in San Antonio, that old bitty that lives next door, I think called the cops on me. She caught me outside as I parked the motorcycle. Anyway she wants to buy the house." Sidney looked shocked.

"Were you in the right house?" he asked looking serious, "I don't remember a motorcycle at that house."

"What do you mean?" I asked breaking in on his thoughts. "There was a big beautiful Harley in the garage. I wanted to go get something to eat and I didn't want to take the car out in the daylight so I took the Harley." Sidney was nodding his head following my story and my logic for doing what I did. I could tell that he didn't like my answers but there was nothing that I could do about it.

"Man, you do take some chances," Sidney was shaking his head and throwing his napkin on the table. "Let's get out of here. You feel like walking over to Sloppy Joes or do you want to go home and go to bed?" Sidney asked and I could tell that he wanted to go to Sloppy Joes and I nodded my approval of his wishes.

It was late in the night before we got back to the house. Sidney had filled me in on some of the plan and what he was doing about it. He was taking a lot of pleasure in his ability to orchestrate his plan. "They have shown their hand and let me know that they are on to us when they tried to discredit us as a fraud and I had my lawyers ready to file a legal action to prevent it. I think I'm going to send an advertisement to one of the green organizations just to get a rise out of them. I figure that the green organizations were controlled by the same people that were behind trying to get to us. They are like sheep hollering about something they don't know anything about and don't know what to do about it except bitch, but when they get this advertisement it will start them clamoring. I'll bet the bastards raise the gas prices and blame it on something." He had a self satisfied grin on his face.

"Do you really think that the energy people are behind the green people?" I asked surprised as I looked around the bar otherwise known as Sloppy Joes. It was a rustic place that didn't have air conditioning and the bar and all the furnishing were made of ruff hewn wood furniture. The bar itself was in the center of the bar and had a place saved for Ernest Hemingway who was a resident of the Keys who had written several books in the fifties and killed himself in the early sixties. I liked the place because Sidney and I were just sitting there and people weren't interested in us at all, except for a few women that kept staring in our direction. I was beginning to understand what Sidney meant by his "blind rooster" comments.

"Are you checking these women out?" Sidney asked waving at a couple of women that instantly started waving back at us.

"Sid," I began taking a sip of my beer, "how long do you think that we can stay down here?" I asked waving back at one of the girls. I really didn't feel like trying to romance some women as the beer and the full belly were taking their toll on me and I was drifting out of consciousness. I could hear Sidney saying something but I leaned my head back against the chair and went to sleep.

I didn't know how long I had been out, but when I woke up the band was playing and Sidney had three women sitting at the table with us. "My God Sidney how long have I been out?" I asked checking out the women sitting at our table.

"I don't know son," Sidney began, "I wasn't keeping time," he turned to one of the women sitting next to him, "I had other things to worry about." The women were all dressed in bikini tops and looked to have a pair of shorts. They had long hair and sported deep dark tans.

"I think I'm going to go back go to bed." I said as I stood up. I just didn't feel good and my head didn't feel like it could fit on my shoulders.

"Jason, son you're going to be a party pooper," Sidney was surprising me; down here he was open and not concerned about his safety as he was when we were on the race circuit or in Vegas. He stood up and pulled a key from his pocket.

"Your room is at the Southern Most House at the end of the road," Sidney winked at me and I figured that he wanted to entertain one or more of the women that he was buying drinks for at the table. "You can get a cab out there on the street and ride down there; I'll see you in the morning." He handed me the key and the women were kind of shocked and made an "Ah" sound as I started to walk off.

"Wait a minute," one of the women said as she grabbed me by the arm, "I think that you need someone to tuck you in." I smiled at her and thought to myself that if she knew how tired I was she wouldn't be making that assumption. "Besides I wouldn't want you to get lost."

Chapter Six

"I'll tell you this son of a bitch is pissing me off," Herbert shouted as he called the meeting to order. "Has he vanished into thin air?" He looked intently into the faces of the over board members assembled. Herbert's face flushed all the way to the top of his bald head. His chest was heaving forcing his chubby body to tremble under his obvious stress. "Who's got anything to report? What are we going to do about this guy; he's got to be stopped?" He blurted his questions out to the members of the board out of his frustration.

"I had my van outside of his house and we think that the communicated with his driver once," Antonio reported, "but then he disappeared. We attempted to get into his house but the place is like a fortress. Thc house said that it was recording everything that was happening and sending it to the police and I had to pull my people away from there." Antonio sounded like he was intimidated by the security system at the house and he was confused as what to do next. He had thinning black hair that he combed straight back over his head and he wore horn rimmed glasses that overpowered his lean pale face.

"I don't give a shit if the frigging house sends a video to the police," the boss broke in and slapped his hand on the table. "Do you sorry bastards know what is at stake here? We could lose everything. Texaco, Shell, British Petroleum, Conoco/Phillips all could be gone. Millions of people could be out of work. A whole industry in the freaking toilet, and needless to say a big portion of your fortunes will be in the toilet, as well." Herbert was nearly shouting and was standing behind his chair pacing back and forth. His face was beet red and he was panting nearly out of breath.

"Boss," one of them broke in, "I hate to tell you that the charges of that we made up about him being a fraud were met with several legal challenges along with threats to go public."

Hugh stood to his feet and continued, "I don't know how they found our lawyers, but there was four or five them and they weren't playing."

"I don't give a shit how many of them they were," Herbert shouted breaking in as he glared at him, "we can send a million lawyers against them. We've got to stop these guys. We have got to find these guys and we have got to stop them." He slapped the table again and was shaking his head. "Does anybody have any ideas?" he was now sounding exhausted and desperate. "The frigging Europeans have even called me wanting to know what is going on. Bad news travels fast. What are we going to do?" He sounded like he was defeated and exhausted.

"Boss these guys will resurface sooner or later," one of the men at the table attempted to reassure him and continued, " and when they do we'll have some of our guys take them out."

"Joe you can't be that frigging stupid," Herbert said as he began taking his seat, "this is two thousand and seven and the frigging media would be all over it if we did something like we did like that Myers guy. We can't just wait around and do nothing, has anyone got anything else?" His question was met with blank stares.

"I've been looking into his business holdings to see how we could attack him," Price stated calmly. Price was one of the more mild-mannered of the board members. He was younger than most of the men there and didn't like dressing like the rest of the men. He had long hair pulled into a tight pony tail that was salt and peppered colored. He looked like he had stepped from the pages of Gentleman's Quarterly with his mock turtle neck sweater and sport coat.

"Finally, somebody has got something to say, by all means let's hear it." The boss sat down and settled in looking like he was hoping for something good.

"He is probably the premiere security system engineer in the country," he began, "he has systems in all the major casinos, in several government buildings throughout the country, including the FBI, I was amazed that several of my banks were using him or his equipment." As he spoke he suddenly realized that he had the attention of all the men at that table. "I can find nothing in his portfolio of how or where he could build the motors. He has a couple of electronics companies but they produce security equipment. He has a line of home security products that he produces that couples the security system with video recording equipment and it has the ability to operate and fax the police a picture of the person that is breaking into a building. He doesn't advertise all that much but his products are the top of the line and anyone in the security business is well aware of them." He paused and pulled out a file out of his brief case as all in the room watched his every move.

"Have you got more?" Herbert asked while tapping his pen into his hand.

"Do you think that we could buy his company and put him out of business?" Another asked and suffered the astonished stares of the others in the room.

"Are you crazy?" Herbert asked emphatically, "we can't give this bastard any more money, we offered him a billion and he laughed at us." Herbert was definitely frustrated and his face was flushed. "You got anything else?" he motioned to Price to continue.

"I've just got a couple more things that I discovered when I had my people work up the background on him." Price began adjusting his paperwork, "We tried to look into his investments and discover where all his money was. A man that is worth that kind of money has to have it doing something besides sitting in one of your banks. As I said he is the sole owner of his company, All Tech Security, and it does about a hundred million a year, both inside the country and outside. The Japanese and the Chinese have tried to duplicate his products but have had very little success in duplicating them, it seems he has a virus or something that melts his circuitry and they haven't been able to independently produce a duplicate device. We suspect that he has his money out of the country somewhere or in a fictitious name somewhere. As far as we could tell he does not have any money on Wall Street." Price sat down and gathered his papers and calmed himself into his chair.

"Well," Herbert was shaking his head, "we have got to find a way to stop this guy, we've got too much at stake. We can't even find the bastards. I don't think that we have much of a choice. I think that we don't have a choice but to call in one of the black ops teams from out of the country. What do you guys think?" His asked the assembled men sounding like he was desperate and exhausted and at his wits end.

"We've hacked his web site and his security network and just got through it this morning, when I was coming to this meeting they were copying the information." Joe began sounding unsure of his information. "We are trying to get his order list in case he decides to try to ship his motors."

"How would he ship those motors?" Herbert asked sounding suddenly excited, "we own the trucking companies, and we could but an end to this deal pretty quick if he was going to ship them by truck." He was smiling at his assumptions and slapped his hands as the thought about it.

"We don't even know where he is building the motors or how he is doing it," Joe said standing and clearing his throat. "I had the only video that we have of the motor analyzed by some of my company's scientists. They said that it appears to be self contained and they were able to make out the label that was on the top of the casing, it read, "Contents under high pressure, do not attempt to open." I don't know what that means."

"This is one smart son of bitch," Herbert began slamming his fist to the table, "he is not going to let anyone take a look inside his motor. It will probably just blow up in their face."

"Maybe we could set the Product Safety Commission on him," Hugh broke in.

"You dumb ass," Herbert retorted angrily, "a product has to be on the market before the Safety Commission can get involved. This bastard is smart he is not going to do anything to get the government on him, but you know that we might let some of our politicians know that we are interested in finding out where he is now and maybe we could get some help from the FBI."

"Are you sure you want to involve the FBI in this," Price broke in protesting, "they like to ask too many questions." Price was shaking his head showing his disapproval of the plan.

"That settles it," Herbert began, "I'm getting a couple of teams in place to find these guys and to take care of them if need be."

"What do you mean, take care of them?" Price interjected the question breaking into his statement.

"Before we can do anything we have to find them," Herbert began addressing Price's fears, "I'm going to get an electronics team to dissect their web site. I'm going to get a GPS team to find them and I'm going to get a team together to take care of them if need be." Herbert knew that he was going to have to make the decisions because the men at the table did not have the guts to do it. And if anything went wrong, no one would ever be able to trace the authority for the operation back to him."

"So this is going to be Operation Hammer?" Price interjected angrily with his question.

"We weren't given a choice," Herbert glared at him with his answer. "We cannot allow this man to put his motor on the market. And that is the bottom line." His words seemed to chill the men at the table as they all sat with flat expressions and stared in his direction. Price acted as if he was going to say something in protest but Herbert's glare stopped him in his tracks. "What, you've got a better idea, Price," he continued.

"No," Price said meekly, "I just don't want us to make the mistakes that we have in the past." Herbert received his words with a frown and a flushed red face.

"I'll swear we are not going to do anything that would end up with them being dead," Herbert was distinct in his words and the rest of the group seemed to understand that he wasn't playing. That he would do whatever it took to take care of this problem.

"Jason," Joanie asked as she gently stroked my shoulder as I lay in bed with her. It took me a couple of seconds to realize that she was talking to me. Sidney was the master a picking names and how he came up with the name Jason I would never know. I barely remembered that she joined me the night that Sidney and I had went to Sloppy Joe's bar and when I passed out she volunteered to take me to the motel and tuck me in. There was something rejuvenating about seeing her naked and I had no trouble staying up for a while. From that time to this, some three days later except for getting dressed to go out for dinner, there wasn't much need for clothing.

I barely knew anything about Joanie, except that she was a school teacher from Delaware or somewhere in New England. I never asked her for a last name and she never asked for mine. I had thought that might have been married because she definitely knew how to take care of a man. She had a penchant for wanting to sun bath in the nude and every morning we would take one of the rental scooter and find a secluded beach along the east side of the island.

Knock, knock, came the sound on the door. I checked the door and saw Sidney standing outside the door. "Just a minute," I said grabbing a pair of shorts and pulling them on. "Joanie get some clothes on Charlie is at the door." She smiled at me and I watched as her naked but jiggled into the bathroom.

"Hey, Charlie," I said opening the door.

"Jason, we've got a little errand to take care of," he said, he was dressed in white pants and a dark blue Hawaiian shirt that had palm trees all over it.

"Okay, dad," I said thinking about what I need to wear, "are we going to be gone long?" I asked motioning to the bathroom to indicate that Joanie was in the bathroom.

"We may have to be gone for a couple of days," he said it loud enough that Joanie could hear him.

"Oh no," she said flashing us with a vision of her in her bra and panties showing off the smooth curves of her tanned skin.

"I'm sorry dear, but business calls and it waits for no one," he was getting antsy and was tapping his leg. "come on, we've got to go." He said turning to me and I knew that he had something that had to be taken care of, or maybe someone was on to us and the chase was going to be on and was out of the door. I followed Sidney out to the street where he had the Hummer parked.

"We have to drive up to Atlanta," Sidney began, settling himself behind the wheel of the Hummer. "It's about eight hundred miles and we have to be there by midnight," he was easing through down in the Hummer and when he hit the highway he pushed it up to about fifty miles an hour.

"If we are going to get there you better let me drive," I joked checking my watch and discovering that it was a little after eight in the morning, "at this rate we might not get there until tomorrow morning." The look that Sidney gave me made me think that he was not to please with my comments.

"Oh, you're going to drive all right," he smiled, "I've got a lot of work on the computer to do before we get there." He didn't respond by picking up his speed any. "These little towns are nothing but speed traps down here and I sure don't want to get a ticket down here." I was curious about which identity he had for us to use, I still had the Wade Thompson driver's license in my billfold and my real one was in the Corvette in Key West, but I guessed that since it had my picture on it, that it wouldn't make that much difference.

We pulled into the outskirts of Atlanta a little before ten. I had wondered why he wanted to come to Atlanta to make the call to be on the Coast to Coast program with George Nori. He was giving me directions and it looked like we were in a commercial area on the north side of town. He had said that he had done a lot of work in Atlanta and that he had picked out a place that he thought would be good for what he was going to be doing tonight. For most of the trip he had been in the back of the Hummer working on three laptops and a bunch of other electronic equipment that he had back there. He had altered the Hummer into an electronic workstation.

"Well I think that I've got things set up as much as I can for right now." Sidney sounded very satisfied with himself. "I certainly hope that I have taken all the precautions. Well, if they find us tonight we'll have to take some evasive action but I think that we will be able to get away from them." He was not sounding as sure of himself that I would have liked but I knew that he would make if very tough on anybody that tried to get to us. The only thing that I didn't like was that we were in the Hummer and it was a gas burner. It could climb a tree but it loved gas. I didn't know what Sidney had in mind but I trusted that he would have a plan.

"How in the world could they find us?" I asked sounding more ignorant about the electronic array that was in the back of the Hummer.

"Trust me, you don't want to know but I can tell you this," Sidney cleared his throat and hit the keys on one of his computers. "If the sons a bitches find us tonight most importantly I will know it in a matter of seconds and we will have to make a move quickly. This scares me more than anything because if we don't try to get out to the public as much as we can to keep the pressure on them not to do much to us should they catch us." I didn't like how Sidney sounded as he talked about what might happen to us. He was much too concerned and anxious for me.

"They really wouldn't do anything to us, would they?" I asked and my question sounded really stupid. Sidney started laughing.

We had three big motels surrounding us and we were in a residential area that was close to them and had pulled into a garage of a house one street behind the motels.

"Look at this," Sidney was pointing to one of the laptop screens. "I've got us linked up to be originating from Paris, France. We'll, give those bastards something to look at. What I want you to do is." Sidney paused and pulled another laptop from the floor of the Hummer. "I've got it rigged up to pick up all the video feeds up and down the road and all the motels on the street. If anyone comes in our direction we'll know it in a matter of seconds." I looked at the screen as he opened the program and it seemed to have about thirty little two inch pictures on the screen. He must have caught my reaction, "If you see something that you want to check out, all you have to do is click on the picture and it will go full screen." Sidney was definitely good at his electronics and his security gadgets. He was truly amazing.

"Sidney, I don't even know what I'm looking for." I protested as we both stared into the screen of the laptop.

"Most of the time these guys prefer a Suburban or something like that," Sidney began, as he pointed to the screen, "they will usually be three or four men. So they have to have something big enough to carry them all. You're looking for someone that cruises around the motels and don't stay. See anything out of the ordinary?" He asked as I was getting the picture. We were backed into the garage of the house and I didn't know if Sidney owned it or not, but I figured that he did. I assumed that the house was vacant because I didn't see any lights on or anything.

"I'm about to go on the air," he stated flatly, "just keep a look out and let me know if you see anything." Sidney was hitting the keys on the computer and before I knew it he was talking to someone on the phone and had quickly was involved in a conversation with the person. I was sitting in the front seat of the Hummer and Sidney was in the back working his computers and then he started talking to someone. It wasn't quite midnight but I was guessing that he had who he wanted to talk to on the line. He was talking free and easy and telling whoever he was talking to about the motor. To my surprise Sidney was using his real name and telling him about his motor and the website. He kept motioning to me to check my screen. He motioned to me that he was about to go on the air, that was my signal to be quiet. I was amazed at the information that he was talking about on a national radio show, he kept referring to the website and telling everyone that they should check out the video link that would show them the video clip that we used in Des Moines and Las Vegas. He was scheduled to be on the air for an hour and I didn't think that anyone could find us in they could find us in that amount of time.

We were about forty five minutes into the program and he was taking questions from the people listening and there were people clamoring to buy one of the motors and then there were others that were skeptical. Sidney had priced the motor at nine thousand, nine hundred, ninety five dollars and he wasn't playing about the money it was fifty percent down and fifty percent on delivery, but he wouldn't say anything about the projected delivery dates or anything other than he had a way to get it done. He had to deal with several people that had heard the fraud story and were worried that he was going to take off with their money. Sidney was upfront with all of them, he told them if they were not comfortable ordering a motor, then don't order it. The host seemed to think that was funny.

They were on a break and all of a sudden the line to the radio station went dead. Sidney freaked out. "Holy shit," he yelled as he started shutting down his computers, he was staring at the last one, "look at this," he said turning the screen to where I could see it. "The bastards are good," he was pointing to the screen that had a red line on the map of the world that was turning yellow as it came from Paris, France into New York City, he tapped on the screen before continuing, "it would take only a matter of seconds and the bastards would know exactly where we are, or almost. Watch this, I'm going to let them look for us in the Big Apple." Sidney was confident in his abilities with his electronics. "Boom," he hit a key on the keyboard and patiently watched the screen. The yellow line stopped at New York for four or five seconds and then started for the next stop on the screen. Sidney freaked. "How in the hell, did they do that. Get us out of here, now." He shouted and began closing the computers down.

I started the Hummer and pulled onto the road, "Where to?" I asked stopping at a stop light on the main road.

"What are you doing?" Sidney asked excitedly, "We can't stop, even for a second. We have to go." I hadn't seen Sidney this frantic ever. So I decided that I would turn right but just then the yellow light flashed on for the cross road. Then in a second I thought that it would turn green in my lane, but it didn't, it went back to green on the cross road. It was about one in the morning and I didn't see anything on the road so I ran the light. Most big cities had cameras at intersections and I knew that my running the red light might get the police interested in me, but I didn't know what might happen and I wanted to get on the interstate.

"Oh my God," Sidney exclaimed as he continued to watch his computer. "They have found the motels where we were using their wi-fi networks. Oh, I hate that, I hate it, I hate it, I hate it." Sidney had shut down his last computer and was looked with great despair at it as he closed the lid.

"Sidney we are good," I tried to calm him down some, "there is no one on the road and we are almost out of town. We'll be fine." I started seeing some traffic coming from the other direction.

"Shit," Sidney exclaimed, "get off this road and head back into town on the residential roads." From the tone in Sidney's voice I could tell that the shock of being discovered had worn off and now he was a logical and analytical as ever.

It took a while but we finally got down town and he had me pull into a parking garage. "It will take them a while to find us now," Sidney smiled at me, "but they will keep trying." He handed me a ball cap. "From now on you have to wear one of these, and never look up to where they can see your face." He was getting excited now, like he was going to enjoy matching his wits with the best that they could throw against him.

We parked the Hummer on the third level of a parking garage off Peachtree Street in downtown Atlanta and Sidney began backing a backpack with computer and electronic equipment. When I stepped out of the Hummer in Atlanta it was cooler than I would have imagined and I was wishing that I had brought some jeans or something.

"Here, change into these clothes," Sidney said handing me a duffle bag. I zipped it open and found a pair of jeans, a shirt and a jeans jacket. I was chilled and I didn't hesitate to drop my shorts right there and pull on the jeans, shirt and jacket. "Right here we are in a dead area of the surveillance cameras. I'm sure they will try to hack into this system, but this is one of mine." He had a sinister grin on his face, "I'll give them a virus that will melt their ass." He smiled at me as he handed me a back pack full of computer equipment. He had slipped his hat on and started walking down the ramp to the elevator. I didn't know where we were going but I swung my back pack on my back and hurried to catch up with him. "From now on, or once we get to the subway we don't travel together," he was amazing fit for an older man and walked at a fast pace to the elevator. "You know why I chose this place?" he asked as we stepped into the elevator, "Well, I designed the security system and it's connected to the subway and the subway is connected to Amtrak." Sidney had plans and connections all over and this was one of them that was paying off, so far anyway, I thought.

He didn't notice that I had ran the red light when we pulled out of the house and on the street, I figured that I had better tell him. "Sidney, when we were sitting at the stop light back there, it changed to yellow and then it changed back to red." I explained as we walked towards the subway. "I thought that it had to be a mistake so I ran the light."

"Holy shit," Sidney exclaimed slowing his pace, "my God these bastards are good. I've got to think. If they knew that we were in the area, you running the red light would give them an identification ping on us." He was verbalizing his thoughts as he pulled up to a bench near the elevator. "Sooner or later they are going to compromise the safe house in Key West and they will trace you back to San Antonio, all the way back to Vegas." He paused awhile and pulled a small computer from his back pack, then he dug into and produced a fanny pack that I had never seen before. He looked at me and exhaled deeply. "We have got the do some things to cover our ass right now and I am counting on you to take care of things." He looked deeply into my eyes as he pulled on the fanny pack to reveal a Velcro sealed compartment that held a Glock automatic pistol and two extra clips that were preloaded. "Do you know how to use one of these?" he asked pointing to the gun. "I had hoped that this would not be necessary, but we don't have a choice." I didn't like the desperation in his voice as he handed me the fanny pack and the gun.

"I grew up shooting guns," I tried to joke, "but none as good as that one." He continued to seal the Velcro fastening into perfect alignment. "But I'm not really keen on this fanny pack deal." Sidney looked at me like I had lost my mind.

"I will try to find you one of those shoulder bags, would you be happy with that?" I nodded that I would and he continued, "Would this one be good for now?" I again nodded my acceptance. "Good, now," Sidney was stroking his chin deep in thought and then continued, "what I want you to do is to get down there and get that Vette that has my motor in it." Sidney was very deliberate in his words and I was beginning to understand the seriousness of what he was talking about. He unzipped a compartment on his back pack and pulled out a stack of money. There were five bundles of hundred dollar bills that had ten thousand dollar insignias imprinted on them. "Here," he said handing me four of the stacks of money, "I want you to take the train south to Mobile and I want you to buy a Corvette that is about the same body style of the one that we have the motor in." I was thinking how good Sidney's logic sounded. If we had two cars that looked the same they would have a harder time tracking me. "Then when you get to Miami, to park the car in a parking garage off of South Beach and walk to a motel and rent a car, then take off to Key West and get the car." I nodded my head that I understood his plan and it sounded like a good plan to me. "Make sure that you contact me when you get to Miami and before you head to Key West." Sidney was now breathing heavily like he had been working out or something.

"Are you all right?" I asked as I stood and looked at him, "what are you going to do?" I asked showing concern and knowing that we were embarking on a big adventure and I hoped that we would live over it.

"Look," he began, "I'll be all right," he reached into his pocket and produced a chain that had a little pendant attached to it. "Listen, we are dealing with the big boys now and things could get very touchy." He took a deep breath and was shaking his head, "this contains a GPS homing device that only pings when it comes in contact with water. If they should get close to capturing you, swallow it and I will get there as fast as possible." He drew a deep breath and exhaled it slowly. "And I hope to God that it won't be necessary." I understood the seriousness of the matter and I found myself wanting to reassure Sidney but all I could think about was how I muffed things up by running that stupid red light.

"This is all my fault," I began, "I'm so sorry," I tried to say more but he raised his hand and cut me off.

"It was bound to happen sooner or later," he smiled at me before continuing, "but we have to do a little damage control now." He was rubbing his hands together and suddenly a big smile came on his face. "I love this shit," he blurted out, "these sons a bitches don't know how they are dealing with." There was a gleam in his eye as he spoke and he seemed genuinely excited.

"You never did say where you were going." I was letting my curiosity get the best of me.

"I've got some friends in Atlantic City," he had a gleam in his eye as he spoke, "I think I will show these sons a bitches something about electronics." For someone that was nearly in a panic just a few short moments ago he was excited now. "Isn't this fun?" he asked, "you just wait until the hunted become the hunters." He grabbed me and hugged me and it surprised me because he had not been so emotional before.

"Just remember," he began, "don't shoot anyone unless they shoot at you first and wear your fanny pack all the time." I was wondering why in the world he wasn't wearing it if it was so danged important. It made me look like a dork. I figured that I could do it until I met up with him again, maybe he would have me the shoulder bag by then.

"When you get the car, head towards Houston," he was clearly thinking as he spoke, "or Memphis, well anyway I want you to end up in Eureka Springs. I've got a cool place there that has a cave in the side of a mountain." I didn't understand why he was so excited about them hunting us or why he wanted me to go to Eureka Springs with the car, but it really didn't matter to me because I really enjoyed driving that Corvette.

It was about four in the morning when Sidney and I parted company. I went one way and he went the other. He waited until I went down the elevator and then said that he would follow me on the next elevator down. I felt like my security blanket was leaving me as I watched the door close behind me and I descended down the elevator to the subway. I hoped that I could remember everything that he told me.

I found my way to the subway and checked the route that led to the Amtrak station. When I got there I discovered that they didn't have a train to Mobile by looking at the kiosk. I had my choice of Houston, New Orleans, Charleston or Savannah. I thought I would have a better chance of getting to the car quicker if I went to Charleston or Savannah, but I didn't know if I could find another 2002 Corvette there or not. I wanted to do what Sidney told me if I had the chance. Sidney had always had a reason for everything but him not knowing that Amtrak did not go to Mobile puzzled me. Then there were his instructions about buying another car and going by the parking garage and changing the color on it to be some sort of decoy to avoid the people that are watching us. I would do my best, even if I had to paint the car every day I would try to get there without being detected.

I was glad to finally get on the train and to get moving away from there. I could have rode in the coach but the price for a private sleeping berth was not that much more and I decided to get it and I settled in for a good night of sleep. My thoughts drifted to Carrie and the fact that I hadn't been able to talk to her lately. I was hoping that she was still interested in me. I was hoping that when we stopped this running all over the country that I would get the chance to pursue her a little more. Somehow I felt guilty after spending a few days in Key West with another woman. I went to sleep thinking about all the things that had happened since I left the waiting arms and super fine body of Joanie. I had about halfway wanted her to still be there when I got back to Key West. The time we spent together were times that I would always remember. Then I couldn't understand how running a red light would mean so much if someone wanted to watch us. I thought that Sidney was way to paranoid, but being cautious was something that he was always going to be. How could they be watching us on GPS and control the lights in the city of Atlanta at the same time. Sidney never explained that one, but it obviously meant something to him.

"Ten minutes to Savannah," the porter shouted, "Savannah, ten minutes." I quickly jumped from the birth and dressed while shaking the cobwebs from my head.

The train station in Savannah was downtown and I checked my watch and was surprised that it had taken almost six hours to go a little more than three hundred miles. No wonder train travel was not the most popular any more, but it was very comfortable. The trouble was that it was almost four in the afternoon, I had to find a paper and make a deal before I could head to Key West.

The closest thing that I could find was a black Camero and it was even reasonable priced. I called the guy and he agreed to meet me at the bank downtown so that we could get the title notarized. I broke loose the five thousand dollars that he wanted for the car and stashed it in my pocket. The fanny pack looked awkward but it was very useful and it concealed a very nice pistol.

When the guy arrived with the car, we didn't have but about thirty minutes to take care of business before the bank closed. The car looked good and clean but it had some tires that needed attention. Especially on the back which gave me the idea that he might have been a hot rodder of some kind. But the car seemed to run pretty good and I figured that it would make it to Miami. He was acting a little nervous and I didn't know if I trusted him or not. But when I suggested that we go into the bank and do the paperwork, he held the door open for me. When we had finished making the deal as we were walkingback to the car I told him that I would give him a hundred to let me use his tag for the weekend. He readily accepted and I headed for Miami.

Sidney always wanted me to change clothes several times a day when I was on the run especially when I had just had contact with someone who could identify me. Just for safety sake I didn't like shopping at the bigger department stores like Target, Walmart or Kmart because they had so many cameras in their places. Sidney said that damn near anybody could hack into their systems, but I think that it ticked him off because they wouldn't buy his security system. I kept on the lookout for a clothing store of some kind and finally found one in a strip mall on the outside of Savannah. I got a few sets of clothes and headed on to Maimi. I wondered if the people who were chasing us were onto us. I had taken all the precautions that Sidney had taught me about and I certainly hoped that they had not figured out where I was at.

But what about Sidney, he could have went to Philadelphia and then got a taxi to Atlantic City. With his friends at the casinos I was sure that he would be all right. But for some reason I didn't like leaving him alone. I started thinking that the reason that he liked us to be separated was to protect me because he was the one that invented the motor and I really didn't know that much about it. The way that Sidney was advertising the motor on the radio, on the web and to the green community he might create an environment where we would be safe because of the notoriety that he was making from his media appearances.

I parked the car in the parking garage in Miami and took a taxi to the bus stop to catch the bus to Key West. Sidney had wanted me to rent a car but I thought I would have no way to return it so I decided on the bus. I got on the bus with a bunch of other people and some of them were already drunk. It was about eight o'clock in the evening and I looked out of place. Some of them looked like older hippies and others were obviously gay. It had always surprised me who rode a bus.

It was one wild bus ride. For some reason a couple of the stoners thought they could fire up a doobie on the bus and the bus driver had to stop and put them off on one of the keys on the way to Key West. We finally got to Key West just before midnight and I decided that I would walk down to the safe house because the bus station was on the northern end of the island. It proved to be a pretty good little walk and the night life of the city was going strong. I found myself standing out in my khaki Dockers and blue golf shirt so I just wanted to get to the safe house and get out of there but I had some unfinished business with Joanie at the motel. I walked down to the Southern Most House hotel where I had spent a few magical nights and days with Joanie and noticed a car sitting on the street running. I could see from the other side of the street that there were two men inside that appeared to be looking at a computer screen of some kind.

I quickly turned down the road that led to the buoy that was the southernmost point in the United States and I was somehow glad that no one was following me. The other place that we had been was up at Sloppy Joe's bar. I wondered where Sidney had stayed while we were there. I didn't think he stayed at the safe house. I walked down the quiet residential street and was startled a time or two when a dog would start barking at me. Then I started arguing with myself that I didn't know that those people in the car were after me, they could have just been watching a movie or something. Who knows, but I had been around Sidney enough that I was not going to take any chances.

The safe house was on the other side of Duvall Street and I wondered where it would be safe to cross the street. There were four or five businesses on Duvall Street that had live video feeds up twenty four hours a day and I didn't want to get in one of their pictures in case someone was watching. I decided that I would cross Duvall on Truman because I didn't think that there were any video cameras around there. As I crossed the street I could hear several types of music blaring from several bars and people were milling around on the street in varying degrees of drunkenness. I about halfway wanted to join them but I wanted to get out of town while it was still dark.

I cautiously turned the corner that the safe house was on and didn't see anything out of the norm. I walked past the house on the opposite side of the street and didn't see anything that would suggest that anyone watching the house. I decided that I would try it and walked across the street and pushed the code into the lock and the door opened. I didn't even turn on a light, I just went to the garage and pressed the button to open the garage door and jumped into the car.

It felt good to be in the car again and for several blocks I ran without the lights on until I got to the northern end of the island. I wound my way through the residential district. It was about two in the morning but still there was a lot of traffic on the road. I eased out onto the highway and kept a watchful eye out for anything out of the ordinary. The only thing that I didn't like about the keys was that there was only one road in and one road out. It seemed like it would be an easy way to get trapped and I was happy to be getting out of there.

I was listening to the radio and sort of thinking about how far I was going to get before I stopped and what route I would be taking to get to Eureka Springs, Arkansas. I wondered about Sidney and whether or not he had been able to get to Atlantic City safely.

I made my way through one of the keys that prided itself on being a speed trap more than anything else because they reduced the speed limit to thirty five miles an hour and they had the police working twenty four hours a day, seven days a week. When I noticed what I thought was two men sitting in a car along the side of the road and there seemed to be the florescent glow coming from the front seat of the car. It was odd because these guys reminded me of the car that I saw at the Southern Most House when I was thinking about going to see if Joanie was still there.

I eased by them at the snailish pace of thirty miles an hour and was surprised that they didn't seem to pay me a whole lot of attention. I just knew that they would be following me. I pushed on the accelerator on the far side of town when the speed limit began increasing and noticed that I did have a new car following me.

I was approaching the seven mile bridge and I figured that I might as well put some distance between us. I smashed the accelerator and the car lunged forward and in no time I was doing over one hundred and fifty miles an hour. I was going so fast that there were no lights anywhere behind me. By the time I got to the end of the bridge I could see them at the top of the bridge and they looked to be gaining on me fast. I knew for sure that they were chasing me now but I didn't know what I was going to do about it because I had more than sixty miles to go of single lane road with no way of evading anyone very much if I couldn't out run them.

I was just in the middle of thinking that if they had the road blocked up ahead I would have do some evasive driving, when my phone started ringing. It scared the crap out of me. Sidney was the only one that knew my number. I glanced at the phone as I pulled it from my pocket, it was Sidney.

"Ricky, Ricky," Sidney was excited as he spoke into my phone.

"Yes," I replied keeping a watchful eye on the rear view mirror.

"They have got you pegged," he was still excited, "they have the road completely blocked about five miles ahead of you. I want you to pull the car off the road at the bridge you are coming up to." I looked down and I was doing almost a hundred miles an hour and I had to slam on the brakes to pull off the road before I got to the bridge. "Park the car near the water and there should be a guy in a boat waiting on you." I could see the boat waiting in the water just off the boat ramp. I parked the car and locked it up as I saw the pursuing car turning off the highway and coming in my direction. I ran in the direction of the boat. It was a lot bigger boat than I would have thought but Sidney usually went first class if possible, it was about a forty footer that had a big cabin with the controls on top of it. As I got out of the car and engaged the security system, I noticed the Captain shining his light on a dock that was just under the bridge and he moved the boat in the direction of the dock.

I was focused on getting to the boat to and the second I jumped in the boat and the Captain gunned the motor and moved us out of there. Just then there was a huge explosion coming from where the car had been. It lit up the morning sky and I had the sinking feeling that someone had blown up the Corvette and the motor. Then I heard a secondary explosion that was not as loud as the first and I wondered where it would have come from. The Captain turned the boat around and eased past where the car was parked and there were two cars that were ablaze and there were two guys laying on the ground about twenty feet or so from the car. I loved that car and it gave me a sinking feeling watching in burn as we cruised out to sea. I watched as it grew smaller and smaller and finally disappeared in the morning sky.

Chapter Seven

Herbert was angry as he shuffled through the papers and pictures on his desk while he waited on the other members of the board to get settled into their seats. He cleared his throat and shook his head as he prepared to speak. “I’ve got the reports from the people we have in the field, and this has been a miserable day.” He slapped the papers on the desk. “Take a look at is what left of the car and the motor that he supposedly developed.” The picture was of a car that was so burnt that the only recognizable parts were the two pieces of the frame and the rear axle.

“Anyway,” Herbert’s forehead was flushed red, “we had the bastards cornered in Key West and this is how the car ended up. Our guys were nearly killed before the car blew up and the driver got away on a boat. We got what is left of the car and I’ll guarantee you we didn’t get much. Evidently when the motor gets hot, it blows up to.” Herbert grabbed his head as he sat down. “Does anyone have anything good to report?” He asked as he looked into the faces of each person around the room.

“I don’t have anything good to report,” Price said meekly from his chair, “but I do have something. So far we have been able to block most of the people that ordered motors on his web site. We have contacted some of them and none of them have sent any money to Mr. Cain so we can't accuse him of fraud." He cleared his throat and pulled some papers from his brief case before continuing. "We were attempting to shut his web site down and we hit a super virus or something and it melted our main frame so it is still up and running and it doesn't seem that we are going to be able to shut them down." Price sounded defeated and angry at the same time.

"We had people everywhere that they had been from our GPS tracking," Herbert said picking up another stack of papers. "It seems that they checked in separate motels and stayed in Key West for a couple of days, we never found out where they kept their vehicles. But we do know that they had the Hummer at the hotel on the north end of the island at least two nights." Herbert was sounding frustrated. "It is like that frigging Hummer just appeared out of thin air," he was chuckling to himself, "then there is the damn Corvette, it was black and then it was white and we were about to capture the damn thing and this is the only thing that we have left of it." Herbert was over his jovial mood and it had turned to sinicism and now he was just mad. "Damn it, has anybody got anything?" He asked slapping the table and holding up a picture of the burned out car.

"Well this is not good news," Joe began, "but he went on the Coast to Coast program the other night and South Americans and the Iranians got wind of it and I think that they both will have teams over here in a little of no time."

"Oh my God," Hugh blurted out, "this thing is getting out of hand." Hugh had always been one of the more mild mannered members of the board but he sounded like he was upset at the slow progress that was being made on containing this problem.

"Do we even know where they are?" Joe asked flatly.

"Hell no, we don't know where they are." Herbert responded, "The bastard fried our GPS monitor after the car exploded. We have no idea of where either of them is at right now and that worries me a lot. The last known IP address was somewhere outside of London and we know that he is not over there." Herbert was frustrated and he let it show by taking his glasses off and covering his face with his hands.

"What do you think the foreigners are going to do with them?" Hugh interjected with his question.

"I think that they will probably kill them if they can find them." Herbert responded shaking his head. "It is a pity because I would really like to get my hands on one of those motors. I look at it this way, if anyone is going to make a change in the world economy. It might as well be us." He chuckled to himself in a sinister manner and the others joined in with his jovial mood with a little laughter of their own.

"How in the hell are they going to do anything if we can't even find them?" Sammy shouted spoiling the mood. Sammy was one of the older men at the table that had thick gray hair with huge bushy gray eyebrows and horn rimmed glasses that contrasted his chubby pale white face.

"We are glad to have your input Sammy," Herbert joked, "we thought you had drifted off." Sammy had been one of the quieter of the board members and his comments returned the meeting to the reason that they were there. "But you are right; we have to make some decisions about what we are going to do next." Herbert slapped the table out of desperation.

"I think that we need to step back and see if the others can do anything," Price was in deep thought as he stroked his chin.

"Price is right," Hugh chimed in, "we can't be blamed for anything if we don't do anything." Hugh sounded as if he prematurely hoped the problem would be over.

"Bullshit," Herbert snapped, "we have to get that motor. We have to get the plans, the manufacturing facilities and the motors that he has built and ready to ship. Anything less and we lose everything." Herbert outlined the objectives of the assembled board members and punctuated his statements with a slap of his hands. "We have to squash him like a bug." He added, as his face once again flushed.

"So what you are saying is that we have to work against the teams of people that are out there trying to do the same thing that we are." Price glared at him and stroked his chin.

"I think that you have a point," Herbert joined him in thought, "we have to have our guys keep from getting their hands on our dynamic duo all the while we try to get to them." Herbert was nodding his head as he was deep in thought.

"He will feel like he has to get information about the motor out to the public," Joc interjected, "Will we be able to track them then?" He asked holding his hands up in a gesture of desperation.

"I don't think that they will give us another look at them like they did in Key West," Price sounded like he was anticipating what they might do next.

"We have got to keep the lid on this news story," Hugh broke in changing the subject.

"Yes," Herbert concurred, "I want you calling in every favor that you have with the news media and tell them to be on the lookout for any stories about this man and this motor." He drew a deep breath and exhaled slowly.

"So what's our plan?" Sammy asked raising his eyebrows.

"I think that we have to have a GPS team on both of the foreign teams that are going to be after our men." Herbert began slowly obviously thinking as he spoke, before continuing, "Then we have to have our guys ready to move in and get what we need." Herbert spread his hands in a gesture that indicated that he felt he had no other options.

"You know that those guys are not going to give things up easily." Sammy sounded concerned over what might happen.

"Herbert, this could get messy," Price interjected stating the obvious, and then continued, "There could be a trail of dead men left all around the country. Do we want to be involved in an operation that is going to do that?" He asked sitting back in his chair and folding his hands in his lap.

"Well shit Price," Herbert blurted out, "nothing is going to be traced to us. It is just going to be an unfortunate gang war or something." Herbert shrugged his shoulders like he was planning his denial.

"I've got a couple of Senators and Congressmen on my payroll," Sammy interjected, "I think that we need to get the government involved. We could get the FBI to smoke them out." Sammy said coming to life and letting his opinion be heard.

"My God, Sammy," Herbert broke in, "the frigging government would just make things worse. That would take the whole thing public. I can't take anymore of this, let's meet again next week. If we have a week to wait before this whole thing blows up in our face." Herbert stood and held his head low as the other filed out of the room. The others wore grim expressions as they walked passed Herbert.

"Ricky," Sidney began as he called me shortly after the car had blown up and the boat Captain got us out of there as quickly as he could. "I have blacked out their GPS so get the car that you left in Miami and head toward Memphis. I'll try to meet you in Tunica." Sidney sounded like what just happened was nothing and that he wasn't worried about it at all.

"Sidney when that car blew up, there was nothing left." I sounded more than a little concerned because I had been driving that car at over two hundred miles an hour just a short time before. "Did you have some explosives in there somewhere?" I asked letting my concern show in my voice.

"Well, just a little," Sidney confessed, "but you were always safe. Trust me." He sounded jovial as he spoke. "I would never do anything to hurt you but I had to do something to make sure that the motor would not fall into the wrong hands." I could see the logic but I did not like the idea of driving a bomb.

"Look Sidney," I began sounding a little upset over my discovery, "you told me to take the train to Mobile, but the train didn't go to Mobile. You told me to buy a Corvette but I couldn't find one so I bought a Camero and now you tell me that you want me to drive to Memphis. What the hell is going on?" I didn't realize that the longer I spoke the louder my voice became and I was nearly shouting as I asked my question.

"I'm sorry for Christ's sake," Sidney responded calmly, "in the future if I ask you to drive a car that is rigged to blow up; I will tell you before you drive it." He sounded conciliatory but I knew that he would do everything that he could to protect me but it was up to me not to wreck it and set it off accidently. "Look, just drive the Camero or buy you whatever you want and check in at Sam's Town casino in Tunica under the name Bill Withers. Got it?" That was the old Sidney, down to business and just the facts of what he wanted me to do. "Are you going to be all right?" he asked sounding concerned.

"I got it," I responded, "I will see you there in a couple of days." I hung up wanting leave him with the impression that I was ticked by his omission. All in all I knew that Sidney probably just forgot to tell me. Somehow he always had my back. He knew where I was and what was happening ahead of me everywhere I had been. What worried me is that he was not going to be able to track me so easily now that I was not driving a car that had his security system on it. I loved driving across the country but I didn't understand what Sidney was doing. But I knew Sidney well enough that he had a plan and that plan could be very intricate.

"Hello, I would like to check in," I said to the woman behind the hotel desk at Sam's Town, "I believe I have a reservation, the name is Bill Withers." I noticed that the man sitting in the lobby suddenly pulled his cell phone and started making a call as soon as I said the name Bill Withers.

"Enjoy your stay," the desk clerk she flipped over the card holder to reveal the number of the room and nodded to me about the man behind me. She acted like she wanted to tell me more but was quickly approaching me. He wore a stern look on his olive skinned face and wore a sports coat over a dark turtle neck sweater. He had a very fit muscular build and walked in a brisk manner to the desk. As he approached the hotel clerk pushed the key holder into my hand and pushed a nervous grin onto her face. "Enjoy your stay," she said and quickly turned away from me.

"Mr. Withers, "the Arab man said extending his hand.

"No," I responded quickly, "my name is Waters." I brushed by him and walked into the casino. He looked shocked and then smiled as I walked by him to go into the casino. I wanted with every ounce of my being to look around and see if he was following me. I settled into a slot machine where I could glance at the entrance of the casino so I could see if he was following me or watching me. The background noise in the casino was so loud I could barely hear my cell phone ringing.

"My God you are smooth," Sidney exclaimed over the phone. "What did that bastard want?" I could tell from his tone that he was watching me again and it gave me a good feeling to know that I was not alone.

"He asked if I was Mr. Withers," I responded calmly, "and I told him that I was Waters." Sidney started laughing over the phone.

"Go upstairs in the casino and you'll see a sign that will lead you to the rooms." Sidney was back to his old self and I was glad that he was.

I took the escalator that was located towards the back of the casino after the machine stole my twenty dollars that I had stuffed into it. I was about halfway up the escalator and I saw the Arab man standing at the entrance of the casino with three other men. I didn't want them to see me so I stepped up close to that rather large man going up the escalator in front of me. I was afraid to look back at them until the last second to see if they saw me. I knew that the man thought that I was a nut but I didn't care I wanted to be undetected to get up to my room.

I followed the room numbers around to my room number and I noticed that room two zero one three was directly opposite the elevator. It didn't surprise me and because I knew that Sidney knew everything that happened in the casino. I found my room and started to work the key card but a room opened about two doors down and Sidney stepped out in the hall.

"Psst," he signaled in a hushed tone to get my attention and motioned to me to come down his room. I was really glad to see him.

He hugged me excitedly, "God kid, you scared the shit out of me when that guy came up to you downstairs," Sidney caught his breath and was suddenly in a jovial mood. "What did you tell that guy?" he asked stepping back from me.

"He asked if my name with Withers and I told him that my name was Waters." I said flatly. He blurted out laughing.

"Oh my God," he turned to the array of laptop computers that he had arranged on the desk that he had in this room, then continued, "the bastards rang the operator and asked to be connected to Mr. Waters room. They are definitely onto us." He turned to another computer screen. "Look at this," he turned the screen to where I could see it and the four men that I saw at the landing were now at the door of the room that I had the room key to. One of them but something into the key slot that was connected to what looked like a handheld computer or something and before they entered the room two of them pulled guns before they went in the room.

"Who are those guys?" I asked as chills down my back and watched as they left the room looking like they were angry that I was not in the room.

"Evidently we have attracted some foreign talent," he motioned to me as we watched one of the men pull a cell phone and make a call. "Watch this," he said pointing at the man making the phone call. He clicked a screen one of the computers and there was a list of numbers displayed. He studied the screen a minute and shouted. "I got him," he clicked on number being displayed and a conversation in some foreign language emerged from the computer. "I'll have to run this through a translation program, but I should be able to tell you what they are saying in a few minutes."

Sidney was excited about his ability to work his computers and what he could make them do. "Now just keep watching that screen and see what happens." He said as he turned his attention to working on another computer.

I watched the computer as the men took the elevator back to the main floor. I could see them in the elevator and when they stepped out on the main floor it seemed like there were a dozen or more security guards from the casino waiting for them with guns drawn and they led them away in hand cuffs. "You knew that security was going to get those guys, didn't you?" My question was met with a smile.

"Mr. Boyd is a friend." Sidney began, "he wouldn't appreciate people carrying guns in his casino." He laughed before adding, "I think that we had better get the hell out of here until I can figure out where these guys are from and what they want with us." He closed the top of one of the laptops and made a move like he was going to start packing but he thought better of it. "Well," he began obviously thinking to himself, "security is going to hold those guys for a while and we don't know how they knew that we were going to be here. I'll bet that they have some other guys close around somewhere." Sidney sounded like he was a little nervous.

"I think that we need to get the hell out of here," I found myself nearly shouting at Sidney my desires.

"Wait a minute," Sidney began opening one of his computers. "Let me find out what we are dealing with and who we are dealing with." Sidney was typing something into the computer.

"I'm emailing the security people to see what they can tell me about their catch." Sidney waited and pictures of the four men that were after me. "They say that none of them had any identification on them." Sidney began, "that usually means that they are professionals and that means trouble for us. We can't let them get a hold of us." Get a hold of us, what the hell did he mean. I was scared to ask. He typed a little more on the computer and stepped back from it. "I think that I need to go upstairs for a little bit," Sidney sounded concerned about our situation and was moving with a little snap in his step. He opened the connecting room door and turned to me, "why don't you order up some room service and I'll be back in a little while." He checked his computer again and folded one of them underneath his arm and was out the door.

I went into the other room, closed the door and stretched out on the bed. Sidney had perplexed me, I couldn't understand everything that he was concerned about and that concerned me a lot. Before I knew it, I stretched out on the bed and I was out like the light.

"Ricky, Ricky," Sidney was shaking me to consciousness and I slowed responded to him, "Wake up, Ricky," Sidney was sounding frantic before continuing, "we have to get the hell out of here. These sons a' bitches have hacked into the casinos system. I don't know how, but they did it, I've got to figure out how they did it but for right now, we have got to get the hell out of here." Sidney ran back into the other room and I could hear him shutting his computers down and packing them away. I dressed and ran into the other room to find Sidney packing the last of the cases and zipping it up. He extended the handle on one of the travel bags and handed it to me. I knew with all the computer stuff was heavy and I was thankful that the cases had wheels on them.

Sidney opened the door and checked the hallway and stepped out into it, pulling his travel bag. As we made our way down the hall toward the elevator, Sidney would stop and pick something from the walls or the ceiling. Once he laid his travel bag down and stepped on it to retrieve whatever it was from the ceiling fixture. He pushed the button on the elevator. I followed him into the elevator and he opened his hand showing me what he had. "I'll bet that you have never seen anything like this?" he began, "these are miniature cameras that work on a secure Bluetooth frequency, they have a range of about a hundred feet but they can see for a couple of miles with great clarity." I was surprised because they didn't look like anything more than a little piece of plastic with what looked to be a camera lens in the center of them. "I can control the lens remotely from the computer. I don't have these on the market yet, but I guess I should, they really work well." He was smiling a smile of self satisfaction when he was telling me about his newest invention," then suddenly changed the subject, "that damned car you bought, where did you park it?" I didn't know what he was thinking but I knew that he would have a plan to get us by anyone that was watching.

"Won't they be watching us as we leave the hotel?" I asked sounding confused.

"This is what we are going to do." I cleared his throat and began slowly obviously thinking as he spoke. "When we get down here," he paused for a second then looked like a light had come on in his head, and he continued, "I will take the bags and go to the kitchen, I want you to slip into the parking lot through the side door of the hotel, get the car and drive around to the kitchen loading dock and pick me up." His plan sounded simple enough but I didn't understand, if the people that were after us had hacked into the casino's system wouldn't they know where we were because every square inch of the casino property. I knew that I had to trust Sidney.

I left Sidney at the entrance of the kitchen on the far side of the casino and he sort of gave me an idea of where I could get out into the parking garage and get the Camero.

I slipped as inconspicuously as possible through the hallways and kept my ball cap pulled down and forced myself not to look around or look up. I knew that I had to stay focused on just acting normally and not allowing my own anxiety to betray me.

I found the car and opened the door, no one seemed to notice or take notice in any way. I started the car and about halfway expected it to blow up. I picked up Sidney and throw the bags into the trunk, and we headed out into the night.

"Pull into the station up ahead," Sidney said and I was surprised because he had been so quiet since we left the casino. When I stopped, he took the keys to the car and opened the trunk. He came back to the front of the car with the bug sweeper and I was surprised that he found one underneath the front fender well. I watched as he walked to a pickup and said something to the man pumping his gas and I could see him slip the bugs under the rear fender well. Then he calmly waved goodbye to the man and walked easily back to the car. "Wait just a minute," Sidney began, "let's not go anywhere until he starts moving." I didn't know where the man in the truck was going but he jumped in and headed south. "Okay, let's go north into Memphis." Sidney seemed nervous as he spoke, "I think that we have got several people chasing us now." My heart sunk as his words hit me. "It worries me that the bastards might have made us on satellite," Sidney sounded angry and determined at the same time. "If I can get somewhere where I can set up my computers I can smoke their ass but, we've got to get there first." I knew that Sidney was good at what he does with the computer but how he could stop someone watching a satellite was news to me.

"What bothers me," I began expressing my concerns, "is how in the hell did they know that I was going to Sam's Town in Tunica and the name that I was going to check in under the name of Withers?" That little fact had bothered me ever since I got to Tunica, but I didn't know that Sidney was going to be there either. I hoped that he do another one of his little deals to put me out there as a decoy to flush whoever that was after us.

"I wondered how they found out about that as well," he was moving around in his seat as he spoke, then settled down a little and produced a personal computer out of his pocket and then continued. "The only thing that I can think of is that if they were monitoring all the traffic and picked it up off the scanner or something." He was obviously deep in thought when he flipped his phone out and made a call. I wondered who he would be calling at this time of the morning. It was approaching five o'clock in the morning.

"Old Charley must not be out fishing this morning," Sidney sounded like there might me something wrong. "I think that I will call his house and see what his wife has to say." Sidney flicked through his PDA and found the number and punched it in his phone.

"Hello, is this the hospital?" I heard a woman's voice excitedly come over Sidney's phone.

"No, Vivian, this is Sidney. I was trying to get a hold of Charley and he wasn't out on the boat this morning." Sidney was very cautious in his tone, "is he in the hospital?" I could tell that Sidney was very concerned about the man that plunked me out of the situation with when the car blew up.

"Sidney, Charley is in the hospital," she began and I could barely hear what she was saying but I could hear her saying something like some guys beat him up for something. Sidney was very attentive but I couldn't hear much of what he was saying. Soon Sidney tried to console her and let her know that he would do everything he could to help out.

We were approaching Memphis and I had figured that I would take Interstate Forty and head toward home. Sidney was quiet and sullen as I turned onto the highway to go into Arkansas.

"My God these bastards," Sidney sounded like he was very disgusted, "I can't believe that they beat up a little old man just to get some information out of him. I am going to have to deal with these bastards somehow." I knew that Sidney could handle any tracking device or electronic surveillance technique that was on the market but the heavy handed stuff had to be more than he was able to cope with.

"Was that guy a friend of yours?" I asked knowing that he had some connection with him.

"Charley worked with me in my Atlanta office and when he retired he bought a place on the keys and decided that he was going to fish for the rest of his life." Sidney let his pain show through in his words. I fought off the urge to ask the obvious, if they would do that to a boat captain what they would do to us. Sidney sat quietly as I drove and I was more or less scared to say too much.

"Pull into this truck stop ahead. I think that I am going to ship the thousand or so motors that I have ready." That was the first time that Sidney had ever said anything about the motors or how many he had completed or anything about them. He had said in the past that he didn't want me to get hurt, but I didn't understand because that Charley fellow didn't know anything either. "If you'll fill this clunker with gas," Sidney began slowly, "I'll be in the restaurant working on the computer. I think that I can get a secured connection on this Wi-Fi server." I could tell that his mind was racing a thousand miles an hour.

I walked in the restaurant and saw Sidney busily working on his computer and a plate of steak and eggs was sitting across the table from him. He looked up and noticed me and motioned for me to sit down. "I hope that you save one of those motors for me." I began not realizing that the waitress was within earshot. She was a rather plump woman that had darkish straight hair that framed her oval chubby face.

"What kind of motors does he have?" she asked out of nowhere. I was dumbstruck by her question and I knew that I had to make up something because I knew that I could never tell her the truth and I knew that I had to make it good because waitresses like her tended to be nosey.

"Oh, he has a line of race car motors," I responded hesitantly. I was hoping that she didn't want to know more because if she was inquisitive she could end up like Charley.

She started to say something but Sidney cut her off, "Could I get some more coffee?" he asked and I saw the question disappear off of her lips. I watched as she walked away, "you have to be careful what you say. It is stuff like that that could make things bad for her and us." She filled his cup and Sidney shut the lid of his computer when she walked up with his coffee. She acted like she wanted to talk more and neither or us gave her an opportunity and she walked away. "When we leave," he paused and I wondered why because there was no one anywhere around us. "Never mind are you about ready to go?" he asked even though I hadn't eaten but about half of my food.

"My God," Sidney declared as we pulled out on the highway, "I was afraid that you were going to get chatty-kathy with that waitress. Here go north on highway fifty five." He motioned to the road sign ahead.

"I know, but I didn't think that she could hear me." I tried to explain myself but I knew that it didn't make any difference.

"Well it makes little difference now," he quipped sounding somewhat upset, "we have got to get the hell out of here." I didn't like the way that he was acting but I felt that I had to understand what he had at stake.

He had directed me up through Jonesboro and on east on sixty two highway and we seemed to make it without being followed or detected in any way. Sidney for the most part sat quietly clicking on his small little twelve inch laptop. I didn't know what he was doing and he was quiet except to occasionally bitch about the size of the Camero. As we approached Eureka Springs from the east we came through a small town where he found a Wi-Fi hot spot and he had me stop and we went in the little coffee shop and café. He acted like he had been there before, sort of like that little out of the way places that he frequented when we were on the race circuit. When we walked in he ordered a sandwich and sat down and opened the top of his laptop.

"We're going to be here a while," he said to the youngish waitress who seemed more interested in talking to her girlfriend behind the counter. I saw them staring at me and giggling but I guessed them to be high school aged one had deep dark hair that was shoulder length and she wore low cut jeans and a pink top that purposely exposed her belly button ring. The other had short blond hair that was spiked out on her head. Both were pretty in their own way and I wished that I had a little time to spend with them. One thing for sure I was not going to do or say anything to jeopardize their safety like I did that other waitress.

Sidney was feverishly working on his computer when the blond brought our food and sat it down on our table. Sidney didn't even look up. He acted like he was mad about something and I knew that I didn't even want to ask. I decided that I would go out and eat in the car. I picked up my food and he didn't even act like he noticed and I eased out the door. The girls giggled again when I walked out the door carrying my food and drink.

I had backed the car into the parking place and tilted my seat back and was in the middle of taking a nap, when Sidney came out to the car. I checked my watch and discovered that he had been in there for over two hours.

"You are not going to believe what happened," Sidney began settling into the car, "the bastards had hacked my web site and sent everybody that had expressed interest in a motor or a motor dealership a message that I had realized that my invention was not worth pursuing and that any further contact could be an attempt to defraud them." He paused and clicked his seat belt as I pulled back out on the road. "I had to send them a virus to blind them while I re-contacted some of the more serious buyers and they are still with me. I've got the thousand motors that I have ready shipped to them." Sidney seemed satisfied with himself and he started giving me directions to his save house that he had in a cave that he had told me about. I was excited about it when I heard about it and I couldn't wait to see it, but I wondered why Sidney would stop at the little café to make his communications rather than his safe house at Eureka Springs. But I knew that he had his reasons. "We have got to get out of here." He said hurriedly, closing the lid on his laptop. "They have traced us to St. Louis and they only had a couple of other stations to trace to get to us." Sidney motioned me to turn west on the highway toward Eureka Springs.

Sidney motioned for me to pull over at the big Best Western motel on the curve that he knew that it had a Wi-Fi hot spot. He flipped open his laptop and started working on his laptop. "Look at this," he began turning the laptop to where I could see it," isn't that a beautiful house?" He asked pointing to the house on the screen. The house was a two story rock house that looked to have a fireplace on each side of the house and it had a big two car garage on the left side of it. "Some sucker built this place and planned on moving here when he retired but he never retired." Sidney chuckled to himself as he spoke about his acquisition of the house.

"Is this the one that you said had a cave on the grounds?" I asked while I was tapping my fingers on the steering wheel.

"Check out my surveillance cameras," Sidney was pointing to a screen that had ten or twelve small screens. "I tell you a bird can't fly around this place without me knowing it." Sidney was very satisfied over his security system that he had on his house and his enthusiasm shown through as he spoke. "Let me show you how to get there." He motioned for me to head out the highway on the west side of town and when I was outside of town about a mile or so he told me to turn right onto a road called Flat Rock. We traveled about a mile or so down the road and he said to turn into a drive that looked to be grown up on each side of the little pathway that had the stubble of grass growing up between the tire tracks. I kept looking at Sidney as I drove down the bumpy drive. It was very uncharacteristic for Sidney who usually kept things in better shape than this. It was way past nightfall and the November night was darker than usual. I rounded a curve in the drive and instinctively slammed on the brake because a huge wrought iron fence loomed in front of me that had a big M in the center of each half of the gate.

"I do that every time I come over here too," Sidney laughed before adding, "What do you think of the M's?" He asked without giving me a chance to answer before continuing, "I think it was for Marty and Mary or something. I didn't see the need to change it." He clicked on his computer and the gates opened. I could tell that behind the gates the place was well maintained and the drive was even paved to the garage and I noticed that Sidney had the garage opened as well.

"Let me give you a little tour of the place," Sidney sounded very proud of this place as he laid his computer on a table in the garage. I followed him into the house through the kitchen where he flipped on the lights. It was a beautiful kitchen that was trimmed with granite counter tops and stainless steel appliances. We walked past the kitchen into the living room and centered on the far wall was a huge flat panel television and had maroon leather couches and a recliner or two. It was really nice. It was more of a home that I could have ever hoped for, but I noticed that in the picture that it seemed to be built into a solid rock cliff and I suddenly understood why there were not back windows in the living room. "The bedrooms are upstairs." Sidney sounded a little preoccupied about something. "I think that we will be safe here," he swallowed and exhaled hard before adding, "for a while anyway." I knew what that meant. Somehow, at some time, someone would track us down.

Chapter Eight

"Oh my God," Herbert called the meeting to order with a flushed red face and a frantic sound in his voice. "This son of a bitch has ordered a hundred or more of these motors shipped to the public." Herbert collected himself and took a deep breath and exhaled slowly before continuing, "the frigging Arabs made a play for him at a casino in Tunica and he has been on the run ever since. I'm afraid this time that he is gone deep undercover. We are monitoring everything that we can on him but we have nothing." Herbert took his chair as Price, Joe, Sammy, Hugh and Tony settled into their chairs.

"I've got something," Price interjected joyfully in an attempt to change the mood of the room, "We think that he has a property management company that has properties all over the country and we think that he is using some of them to hide in." Herbert took the news with joy.

"Well, thank God," he exclaimed, "that would make a lot of sense. We have got to check out every property to make sure that he is not holed up in one of them." Price smiled at his assumption.

"Well," he uttered regaining the floor, "our last known place that we actually knew where they were was in Tunica about twenty four hours ago. According to my calculations they couldn't have made it more than five or six hundred miles and I really doubt that they would be headed towards their home in Tulsa because they know that someone will be watching their house." Price sounded proud of himself for his accomplishments.

"What are we talking about," Herbert interrupted him with a big smile on his face, "a hundred or more places." Price smiled and walked to the overhead projector and switched it on.

"We actually have fourteen places within the diameter of five or six hundred miles from Tunica." He switched on the graphic and displayed the properties, one in Nashville, Memphis, Jackson, Mississippi, Little Rock, Arkansas, Fort Smith, Arkansas, Eureka Springs, Arkansas, Saint Louis, Missouri, Branson, Missouri and a couple of others that are out in the country. One in Arkansas, one in Missouri and another in Texas that could all be places that he could be hiding or could have at one time or another." Price left his slide projecting on the wall and retook his seat.

"How in the hell did you find about this company?" Sammy sounded amazed by the discovery and continued, "are you certain that this is his company and that he has these properties." Sammy acted as if he didn't believe that Price had come up with such important information.

"First of all we can't be certain of anything until it produces results," Price glared at him while he was responding. "I can tell you that we had people monitoring every communication that we could in Tulsa, Oklahoma. We got a communication on an encrypted email line that we were able to sift through and descramble that was an order a sell on a property in San Antonio. Then we searched all the real estate companies in San Antonio that issued a sell listing for three days around the time that we thought the sell order was communicated. Then we checked gas, electric and water companies for each of these properties and we found a company that had its main office listed in a post office box in Tulsa, Oklahoma." Sammy seemed pleased with his answer and sat back in his chair and Price continued, "then we checked police calls to the addresses in question and we discovered that the police had been called to an address off Rittiman road and when we questioned the next door neighbor she identified our man Ricky as the man that she had called the police about because he was acting strange." Price glared at Herbert as he spoke as if he thought that he was more capable to handling the situation than he was.

"Acting strange," Herbert laughed in response, "no, I would say that you and your team are to be commended. That was masterful investigative talent at its best." Herbert smiled and flashed a devilish grin. "I hope that your reporters won't be reporting any of this in any of your newspapers." The others laughed at his assumption and Price responded by turning beet red in the face.

"My reporters were told that they were working on a special assignment for the editor and I have told all the editors to send the information to me." Price was indignant in his answer and he responded with an angry look.

"Have you sent anybody to any of the places that you have identified as possibilities?" Herbert asked like he was impressed at the dedication that Price had to solving the problem.

"No," Price sounded disgusted as he responded, "it would not be good for me to send one of my reporters to go out there and knock on the door and ask them if they are the bad guys that we are looking for." Price's words were showing his disgust at the stupidity of Herbert's suggestion. "That would only make them run again and we may never get an opportunity to get them then." Price stood and gathered his papers.

"Calm down Price," Sammy jumped in to calm the situation, "Herbert has got people that will check out the places. We are going to get these guys. We are not going to let them put those motors out." Sammy reached over and placed his hand on Price's shoulder. "You and your team have done a masterful job of breaking his real estate holdings. We have to stay calm and let Herbert send in the guys with guns to take care of these people." Price cut him a quick look and then stared at Herbert.

"We will do what we have to do." Herbert began sounding calm and resolute in his tone like he had won something and had finally gotten the upper hand. "I will contact my people and give them the addresses that Price has identified and we will go from there." He smiled to himself as he stroked his chin, and then added, "you know, I think that I will go out there when they find him. I want to talk to this man. I think that he has probably invented the best replacement to the internal combustion engine that we have seen so far and it would be very useful to us to pick his brain, so to speak." Herbert laughed and sickly, evil laugh and the others joined in.

"What are you going to do about the Arabs and the South Americans that are charging around here with guns drawn looking for an opportunity to shoot someone?" Joe rose from his seat a little as he spoke. "This whole thing has gotten to be such a mess; we can't keep the lid on it forever. You know that he sent the movie to the Green Party headquarters and they are all up in arms wanting to get more information about the motor. I'm using everything that I have at my disposal to keep this story off the airways. I'm sure just as Price is with his television people. This story is going to blow and it is going to blow big." Joe had an angry tone in his voice as he spoke. The others were talking like they had the whole thing rapped up and done with but Joe knew different. All they had to do was to get to the right newsperson and this story would be picked up all over the world and then nothing could be done about it.

"Joe, we are going to get these guys," Herbert sounded as if he was trying to calm a school boy instead of Joe, a billionaire and a captain of industry. "Yes, things could go wrong, but then, if they do all we have to do is to leak their whereabouts to our foreign friends and they will be taken care of." Herbert sounded like he thought that things were under control and none of the concerns of the other members of the board were going to bring him down. Joe shook his head and acted like Herbert didn't know what he was talking about and he was going to have to give in to his leadership.

"I just want you all to know that this guy is not going to be as easy to deal with as that Myers guy," Joe knew that their weak spot was what they authorized to happen to Randy Myers. Not that any of them ever thought that they would be held accountable for his murder but he knew that it was something that they would all like to avoid in the future.

"We had no choice," Hugh one of the more mild mannered and quiet members of the board. "Herbert said that we had no choice and we had to do what had to be done or I would have never had voted to poison him." Herbert squirmed in his seat when his name was mentioned in what had become known as the Stanley Myers Affair.

"Let's calm down a little, Hugh," Price interjected, "this is the business that we are in. If we want to continue as leaders of the free world then we have to do things that are not pleasant and that we would not like to do." Price was attempted to reason with Hugh and the other reluctant members of the board that approved the use of violence only as a last resort.

"If I remember correctly, Hugh and I were the only ones that voted against the use of force in the Randy Myers Affair," Sammy stated calmly, "and the rest of you overruled us. You will have to live with that until you go to your grave. I just don't want us to do anything that is absolutely not necessary." Sammy had a regretful tone to his voice.

"We don't need to be pointing fingers," Herbert broke in, "we can't be concerned to what happened in the past. We had to do what we had to do and that is the bottom line. Mr. Myers had plenty of opportunities to play ball but he didn't see the need and that's on him. Not us." Herbert had a way of putting things that made them sound like it was somehow justified what happen to Mr. Myers.

"I agree," Price broke in, "we can't be digging up the past because we made a mistake back then." Price was clearly trying to shift the focus of the conversation.

"I think that we need wait until we have him in our hands before we make a decision," Joe interjected trying to sound calm.

"That's a great idea," Herbert quickly picked up Joe's idea, "we don't have to make a decision on him now, because we are going to get this guy because I want to talk to him. Then we can make a decision as to what to do with him." Herbert sounded pleased with himself in how he had handled the members of the board.

"So what are we going to do now that we have come this far," Sammy interjected sounding like he wanted to understand the decisions. "so far I don't think that we have made any decisions to deal with this problem." Sammy was mocking the group and showing his displeasure with the whole thing.

"Sammy," Herbert addressed him in particular sounding irritated at his assumptions, "if you want to go out there with me to see for yourself what is going on. I'm more than willing to reserve you a seat on my plane." Herbert was adamant that nothing was going to happen that the board had not agreed to. Sammy nodded to him that he would do it by giving him a little salute. "Well, we are adjourned," Herbert raised his hand, "lets meet again in about three days, we ought to have some information about them to talk about then." The members of the board were slow to move out of the room and acted like they were reluctant to make a decision on the problem.

"Ricky get up and let's go to lunch," Sidney yelled from the open bedroom door. It had been late by the time we finally got to bed because Sidney had been running off at the mouth about all the things that could happen and might happen and how he had designed security systems to counter them. He said that there was a passage to town through the cave but it was about a mile through the mountain. I only wished that I could remember everything that he told me.

"It's about time, sleepy head," Sidney blurted out when he saw me on the upstairs landing. I liked the house. It had a master suite on each end of the house, complete with a Jacuzzi tubs and fireplaces in the bedrooms.

"Man, I like this house," I responded to Sidney on my way down the stairs.

"This house is full of surprises," Sidney laughed as started walking out the door. "The first thing that we have to do today is to get rid of that stupid little car." Sidney was in a good mood for some reason. He looked at me hard for a second, "Where's your fanny pack?" He asked placing his hand on his hip. "You have to keep that with you at all times, even when you think that you won't need it." I was about to complain that it made me look like a dork, a nerd or something out of the middle aged set.

"Man can't we find a shoulder holster or something?" I protested. Sidney smiled at me but he didn't respond to me but instead sort of brushed me off.

"I wish I had the balls to go to Tulsa," Sidney laughed at his thought as we walked out to the garage. "Here let me show you how to get into the cave." Sidney walked to a big steel door and punched a code into the lock. "This door will withstand a blast the size of a pound or more of C4, or that is what they say and it is solid rock around it and it is set in reinforced concrete." Sidney was proud of his door and I knew that if he thought it was safe and secure that it must be more than anyone would ever expect.

"You know," I began thinking about his desire to go home, "why don't you check your security systems from your computer and if you don't find anything, I think we could get over there and back without being discovered." I really didn't know what I was talking about and wasn't sure what good going home would but we could get one of the vehicles that he had at the house.

"There are things that I would like to do at home," Sidney surprised me that he would consider going home. "I'll tell you what; we could head in that direction and see what we could find." He was smiling at me and had a twinkle in his eye. "But we are going to have to come back over here; I've got things here that I need." I didn't understand what he thought he needed but that was all right with me.

Sidney didn't want to go to the house during the daylight and we had a few hours to kill and surprisingly he wanted to stop at the Cherokee Casino on the outskirts of town. Sidney got us a room in the hotel and quickly disappeared. I knew that he was probably with his security friends and that he was up to something. I had stretched out on the bed and was watching a movie on the television and was quickly asleep.

"Ricky," Sidney barged into the room, "how much money do you have left?" He asked excitedly. I had laid my fanny pack on the bed as I picked it up; Sidney took it from my hands.

He counted out ten thousand dollars. "I've found us a car," he exclaimed, "It's a Cadillac Escalade, it will be great. Get you something to eat; we'll be ready to leave in a couple of hours." I was happy that he had found a truck for us but I was a little concerned that he was getting something that stood out a little too much. But then again, nobody would really know that we were going to be driving it.

It was dark when we headed down the lane to Sidney's house. He had me drive by once and when he turned around to go back to it he had me pull into a neighbor's house which was a quarter of so miles down the road. He opened the top of his laptop and began clicking away at the keys.

"Whew look at this," he exclaimed turning the screen to where I could see it. There were three Suburban's in the drive and about six men that were running around the house, but it looked like none of them got in and finally they all left. "I wonder what that meant." Sidney asked and continued to click the keys of the computer. "Take a look at this infrared camera that I have set up for the house." I leaned into over to see nothing but an outline of the rooms of the house. "You see, there is no one in my house. Let's go up there." I wondered what in the hell he was thinking because even I knew that if anyone was after us they were sure to be monitoring the house.

I drove up to the garage like I had always done and Sidney hit the keys sending the code to the doors and they opened. I noticed that it looked like someone had been hitting them with a sledge hammer or something but it worked fine. The garage was a little out from the house and Sidney had an underground passageway that led from the garage to the house. When he first showed it to me I accused him of not wanting to get his head wet when it was raining.

"Let me check things out before we go in the house," Sidney was always cautious but now he was even more cautious than I had ever seen him. "The computer says that we had three sets of visitors and all of them tried to get into the house." He was peering into the screen and clicking the keys with unexpected fervor. "Shit, shit, oh my God." I started to say something and he put his hand over his mouth and motioned for me to not say anything. He quietly walked back to the passageway and disappeared. I felt very weird just sitting at the kitchen counter knowing that I should not move or make a sound.

In a few minutes Sidney emerged from the passageway carrying a box with a loop on the top of it. He handed me the cord and sat it down on the counter top. After working the knobs for a little while, he nodded his head. "These bastards are good," Sidney began, "somehow they have got some microphones in the ceiling of the house. I think that I have them jammed right now but we need to find them." Sidney picked up his computer and started walking around the house. "You're going to have to go upstairs in the attic and find them." I started to protest but I understood that we were in this thing together and there was no way that Sidney was going to get up in the attic.

I had spent almost two hours retrieving all the bugs that had been drilled into the attic. Sidney had decided that we could stay at the house that night because they would not be expecting us to be there and he could do something to make them think that the bugs were still working. I knew that the house was safe.

"Ricky," Sidney yelled calling me from my room, "come down here and let me show you my latest commercial." Sidney's house was a beautiful two story that had all the latest security equipment, including cement reinforced walls. He said that he filled the walls with lightweight cement. Then he had his standard security vault doors at each of the openings. I noticed that he didn't have a sliding glass door that went out to the patio and when I asked him about it he said that it was the weakest part of the house and he didn't believe in them. I walked down the stairs having barely pulling my jeans and tee shirt on and found him in the sunken living room stretched out on the black leather sectional couch. "My God," Sidney greeted me as I sat down on the end of it, "do you know that it is past nine in the morning." Sidney was strangely in a good mood as he clicked the remote and the video sprang to the big television screen.

I could see myself on the screen driving the race car around the track. Then it cut away to the video of the Corvette and it showed the pictures of the motor. An announcer broke in and was saying something about a imagining a motor that never had to have fuel of any kind, then it flashed to the web site to get more information about the motor.

Beep, beep, came a sound from one of Sidney's computers on the desk in what looked to have been a dining room at one time but Sidney had made it his office. On each wall he had banks of computers and it sort of surprised me because they were all laptops. He looked startled as he ran to the computers. "What the hell is going on now?" he asked while nearly in a dead run to get to the computers.

"Look at these bastards," Sidney blurted out as he picked up the phone, "I'll get the police to give them a little welcoming." Sidney dialed the number of the police and was telling them what was happening, "Look at that sucker, he's trying to break my door in." Sidney said into the phone, "are you getting this?" He said something in the phone about sending them the uplink. Sidney had been clicking the keys of another one of his computers. "I think I found their vehicle, it's parked along the road about four houses down. In a second I will be sending you their license number." Sidney was smiling as he was giving the police the information. "Holy crap they just broke into the house." Sidney started jumping around like he wanted to do something but there was nothing to he could do.

In a view minutes the two police cars showed up and one policeman was walking up the driveway when he suddenly fell down. "Oh, my God," Sidney exclaimed, "they have just shot a policeman." Sidney turned to me, "they hung up on me, but do you see the kind of people that we are dealing with." Sidney continued to watch the ensuing gun battle that was being played out on his computer.

"Where is that?" I asked as I watched.

"That is Memphis," Sidney said flatly visibly thinking as he continued to watch his computer. "That must mean that they have found my property management company." Sidney moved to another computer and began clicking on the keys. "I need to watch the other properties so I can notify the police if need be." He confused me with that the people that were at the house in Memphis were in a shootout with the Memphis Police. "Here, take this computer and let me know if you see any movement around this house." I recognized the place that he wanted me to monitor was this house. That was scary.

Sidney was becoming frantic as he watched the computers and was making all kinds of guttural sounds. I pulled the computer to the side and began watching the six divided screens on the laptop. "Holy crap, I can't believe this crap," Sidney shouted, "they are down in Jackson too." I knew that he was upset, but I didn't know what he could do about it. "These bastards are going to drive me crazy," as he picked the phone and dialed a number. He was telling the police that a group of three men were breaking into his home. Just them I noticed a van coming down the road in front of Sidney house where we were.

"Hey," I began, "I think that I've got something here, a black van is coming down the road in front of the house and now they look like they are parking." Sidney jumped from his chair and ran to a window and carefully moved the curtains to get a better look. I was trying to magnify on the license plate but it didn't have a license plate. "It doesn't seem to have a license plate either." I exclaimed.

"Holy crap," Sidney uttered beneath his breath and he signaled for me to not say anything, he quickly ran over to the computer that he had given me to monitor and started typing. Then he motioned for me to look at the message that he typed. It read, "We have to get out of here. They have the capability to listen to everything that we do or say. I'm going to the garage. I want you just to watch the computers and not let them in the house." He nodded at me to make sure that I understood. I watched as he gathered up one of the computers and headed to the basement door that led to the tunnel that went out to the garage.

I sat and watched from the big office chair and I couldn't help but notice what was happening on the computer that he had focused on what was happening in Jackson, Mississippi. It looked like the house was surrounded by the police and they were walking the people out that had broke into the house. It was strange to see them with their hands tied behind their backs and walking to the patty wagons quietly. They looked like they were professional people of some kind and the three of them wore sports jackets with a dark shirt under them. One of them looked to have a silver chain that hung from his neck.

Beep, beep, another one of the computer started going off. A big red bar started flashing on the screen and I clicked it. Instantly the house in Eureka Springs came into view and I could see a black Suburban going down the overgrown drive. My interest was absorbed on what was happening at the Eureka Springs house. When they arrived at the gate, they backed off from it and one of them got out of the truck and put something on the gate and then ran back to the car. I could see the explosion and the gate springing free. I was thinking that out there in the woods there would be no one to call like there was in Memphis and Jackson, but I knew that getting into that house would be very difficult even with explosives. When they drove up to the house and got out of the truck somebody started shooting at them. I was able to see one of the guys who was doing the shooting was on the garage but I couldn't see any others. He was a dark skinned foreign looking man that looked like he worked out a lot and he had an angry look on his face.

Soon, I could see that two of the guys in the Suburban were down and the others had scurried away from the truck and had taken defensive positions in the lawn behind some of the statuary and flower beds.

I was so engrossed in watching what was happening in Eureka that I lost focus on what was going on outside, when the doorbell rang. I freaked. I had left my fanny pack in the bedroom and I sure wanted to get my gun. I certainly was going to ignore the door bell but I was going to do what I could to slip to the bedroom to get the gun. I eased out of thc chair and crawled around the corner and into the hall, jumped to my feet and ran to the bedroom to retrieve the gun. I just felt better when I wrapped my hand around it and started back to the front of the house.

Boom, boom, it sounded like they were trying to break the door down. I didn't think that they could break the door down but they were making me so nervous that I didn't know what to do. I stood there holding the gun debating as to whether or not I should try to shoot through the door or not. I was so nervous that I couldn't stand myself. My hands were sweating so bad that I was having a hard time holding onto the gun and I could hear my heart pounding like it wanted to get out of my chest.

Where was Sidney when I needed him? All I could think about was watching the charge that they placed on the gates and watching them blow open. Hoping to God that they would not be putting a charge on the door and blow it apart. My hand was shaking so bad that I couldn't hold the gun up to it anymore and I felt an overwhelming urge to sit down. Boom, Boom, they tried the door again, then I heard a big explosion outside and I almost shot myself out of sheer nervousness. But nothing happened and suddenly the assault on the door stopped.

I finally gathered up the nerve to peer out of the window. I saw a man running towards the van and it looked like it had been hit by something because the whole back part of it was blackened but the front part looked like it was untouched.

Suddenly I heard footsteps coming up the back stairs. My heart skipped a beat, praying beyond measure that it would be Sidney and knowing that I would have to be ready if it wasn't. "Sidney, Sidney is that you?" I shouted my question into the basement.

"Of course it's me," he said almost laughing.

"Someone was beating on the door and I was scared that they were going to bust it down." I was excited and my voice broke as I spoke. Sidney responded by laughing at me.

"There's not a way in hell that they could break that door." Sidney chuckled, "I'll bet they didn't even dent that door." He walked over to the door and opened the door. I nearly fell over. He checked his door and started waving his fist at the disabled van in front of his house.

"Why would you open the door?" I just couldn't believe what he was doing.

"The bastards know that we are here," he quipped with a smile on his face, "I don't know why they would come back and try that crap again." He was laughing and shaking his head as he closed the door. "Poor bastards, they don't even know who they are playing with." I remembered then that I needed to tell him what I saw on the computer.

"That computer," I began pointing to the computer that I had been watching, "it said that there was a security alert and I clicked on it and saw a Suburban pulling into the place at Eureka Springs. There was a shootout and some guys looked like they got shot." I started to feel better knowing that Sidney was back around. He looked at me for a second and then ran to his big chair where the computers were and began working on the keys. I moved over and was watching the whole scene all over again. "Where did that guy come from?" I asked pointing to the man on the roof of the garage.

"Hell if I know," Sidney said as he watched the man that got shot hit the ground in front of the house. "I had better call the Sheriff up there and let him know what is happening." Sidney picked up his phone but rose to see if the van was still parked in front of the house, then dialed the number to the Sheriff.

"I think that I've got everything in place now," Sidney began, "I've got a publicity agency hired to get me on the television and they are going to handle the individual sales. I've just got to get the information out there because if they can snuff out our message they can snuff out us, but we have got to get back up to Eureka Springs so that we can hunker down for a week or two to get the pressure off of us. I think that we are going to get through this just fine." I loved his optimistic attitude but it made me nervous that we had people out there willing to beat our door down.

"I just think that they have found out where we are and where we are going to be," I was apprehensive about what he was saying and I wanted to let it be known. "I, I, I, just think," I could tell by Sidney's expression that the subject was not up for discussion. "Well, I know that you have got a plan and I'm going to trust you." I know that I sounded conciliatory but I couldn't help it.

"I'll explain it all to you when we get settled in up at Eureka," there was a gleam in his eye, "but as soon as those buffoons get there piece of junk out of my front yard we are going to get the hell out of here." I didn't understand but that was not going to change anything. "let's get packed up. I wonder how they found my safe houses. That ticks me off." He still had that gleam in his eye.

We packed the computers and had to make several trips to the truck in the garage and finally were sitting in the garage watching as the wrecker was hooking up the van that sat in front of the house. "What did you do to those guys?" I asked Sidney as he was steadily peering into one of his computers and working the keys. He sort of chuckled at my question.

"Well, I'll tell you," he laughed as he began, "for many years I wanted to develop a machine that would produce controlled lightning. Have you ever heard of ball lightning? That was the best that I could do with it." He was laughing at himself, then continued when he regained his composure, "it took me about three or four shots at it to hit that van, I damn near knocked a telephone pole down on the other side of the road. That's one invention that still needs some work, but that's the second time that they lost a van out there." That struck me as odd, why would they park a van in nearly the same place.

"Maybe it is a different bunch of guys," I commented thinking about the circumstances.

"You know you might be right," he didn't even look up when he spoke, "but I wondered what happened to them after the lightning hit their van. I know that it melted their electronics and didn't you say something about a guy pounding on the door. I wonder what happened to him." He suddenly got quiet and was staring intently into his computer. "Oh my God, there are three guys out there with guns drawn and one of them has got an automatic rifle." Sidney pulled his phone and called the police. "The Tulsa Police are friends they will be here in a moment." Sidney eased back in his seat and continued to peer into his computer screen.

"I hope these guys don't have the explosives like the guys at Eureka had." I said and Sidney cast me a worried look.

"I see the guys, they look like they are waiting for something," Sidney was searching his computer screen. Boom, came the sound of a big explosion. I leaned over to see what was happening. We could feel the shock waves of the blast but I knew that it wasn't anywhere near the garage. "Those bastards just tried to blow a hole in my house. I hope the police get here soon, we need to get the hell out of here." Sidney sounded really concerned and a little helpless.

Then we heard the sound of the sirens coming down the road and I started feeling better. Boom, boom, someone started pounding on the garage door. Sidney motioned for me to stay quiet and I reached into my fanny pack and touched the handle of the Glock. Then I heard, boom, boom, boom like someone was shooting at the garage door. Sidney motioned to me to stay calm and he returned his attention to his computer. I heard someone milling around outside and messing with the lock on the door. I thought that I could hear shooting around the front of the house. I knew that the police had arrived.

"Okay, get ready," Sidney whispered, "we will be leaving in a few minutes." I nodded in agreement but I didn't know what he was talking about but I knew that he was watching from several angles on his computer. I could hear whoever was outside start firing in the opposite direction. I could hear firing going on outside and around the house but all the police that I had ever been around would want whoever was involved to fill out a mile of paperwork, especially if there was a shooting involved. He hit some keys on his computer and the garage door started opening. "Let's go." Sidney buckled his seat belt and I watched as the sunshine of the afternoon sky filled the garage and I hit the accelerator and moved slowly out of the garage. There was a police car sitting in the middle of the driveway and I could see that there were several holes in the windshield. "Stop up here at the supervisor's car," Sidney motioned where he wanted me to stop and he rolled his window down.

"Can you believe what these bastards did to my house?" Sidney asked the supervisor as he approached the truck.

"Sidney, I don't know who you pissed off," he began, I couldn't really see him all that well but I knew that he had a helmet on with the sun shades pulled down. "I got your report and all the pictures. You write one hell of a report. These bastards will be behind bars for a long time." Sidney just stuck his hand out the window and shook his hand.

"We have got to get going," Sidney responded and turned to me to move on. As I turned onto the road outside of the house I could see the damage done to the house. The explosion looked to have taken place in the entry enclave of the house and it didn't look like the damage was significant enough to allow anyone to get into the house. I drove on the past the burned out van and there was another Suburban sitting about fifty yards behind the van. Both had several bullet holes in them. "The van had all their tracking equipment;" he said flatly, "the Suburban had their enforcers." I wondered if Sidney knew more than he was telling or if he had seen something on his surveillance equipment.

I didn't know why Sidney felt safer at the house in Eureka than he did in Tulsa. It seemed to me that he was up to his old tricks of being paranoid and super cautious again. But when we pulled into the drive at the Eureka Springs house I could see where the gate had been blown and the left side of it hung helplessly open and it looked like a Sheriff cruiser was still there.

"Hey, Sheriff," Sidney shouted in a real friendly manner as he climbed out of the Suburban. I wanted him to open the garage door and let me get in. I thought it was strange the way that the man reacted. He didn't get out of his car or answer back.

"Sidney, something is wrong, open the door." I shouted as the hairs on the back of my neck were standing up. Sidney closed the door and started working the keys on the laptop and the door started opening. It was about open when someone stepped in front of the truck with a handgun pointed at us. I stepped on the gas and just before I was going to hit him, he dove out of the way. He had a very surprised look on his face and the motor of the truck roared as he jumped out of the way to the right. My heart was racing, the Sheriff was supposed to cleared all of the people that were after us out of the area. But I guessed they didn't.

"Close the door," I shouted and rolled out of the car and began firing my pistol into the opening wildly because I didn't see anything. The door finally closed and I felt instantly better.

"Can you believe that?" Sidney asked, "I wonder what the hell went on around here." He paused as he was watching me reload the gun and snap the first round into the chamber. "You're pretty handy with that thing. I was hoping that we wouldn't need it, but I'm glad you had it tonight." Sidney climbed out of the truck and placed his computer on the table. I could hear someone moving around outside. Sidney walked over to the safe door that led to the cave entrance and started working the combination. "Let's get the gear into the cave, we'll be safe there." I grabbed one of the bags with the computers from the back and carried it to the door.

Boom, Boom, someone was firing shots at the garage door. Sidney didn't act like he cared in the least and continued getting the computers out of the truck. The guy must have fired ten or twelve shots at the door and still Sidney was not concerned at all. I picked up one of the cases and started into the house. "Hey," Sidney shouted getting my attention, "let's put the computers in here." He was motioning to the door that let into the cave and he began working the combination to open it. "I have a workshop back here and I have all my connections to where I can communicate with the people that I need to communicate with." Sidney displayed his satisfaction by the smile on his face.

He opened the door and a stepped in. I didn't know if I liked the idea of staying in a cave, but when he turned on the light it looked like daylight in there. When I walked in a big conference room or something and it had florescent lights throughout the ceiling. On left side of the room there looked to be some rooms and one of them was a kitchen area and dining room. On the other side was Sidney's work bench and he took his bag of computer to his bench and started unloading them.

"This place is nice," I said as I was still looking over the place and taking the computer case that I had to his bench.

"You didn't think that I would work this hard to get back here if this place was a dump, do you?" He laughed and continued to hookup his computers. "I have got to find out what happened here. Things just don't seem right." He connected and turned on one of the computers and clicked the keys and a picture appeared on the screen. He moved it to fast forward until he saw something and then turned it back to where the action began.

He clicked some more keys and the screen divided into ten screens, then he started selecting specific screens. "Now take a look at this." He said as he picked up a remote control and clicked it. Suddenly a big digital flat screen elevated from a cabinet. The first camera looked like it was right over the yard of the house. I could see the people that blew the gate drive into the yard and suddenly gunfire broke out and they scrambled for a position of safety to return fire. I saw a couple of them go down. "This was at nine o'clock this morning and now watch what happens next." Sidney had a grim look on his face as he watched. I didn't know how he knew what was coming next but I took a seat and settled in to watch. The two guys remaining from the Suburban just started shooting that anything that moved pretty much just standing in the yard firing at anything that moved, then they ran off into the woods.

"I wonder where those guys went," I asked Sidney point to the screen.

"I don't know where any of them went," Sidney laughed as he clicked the screen and we could see the Sheriff's truck pulling into the drive and suddenly both sides starting shooting at him. He fell just outside his truck. "God, I hope that they didn't kill him." Sidney uttered under his breath showing his concern. Then they went back to shooting at each other and then they all just disappeared into the woods leaving two people from the truck down and the Sheriff Deputy. I couldn't believe what I was seeing.

Shortly after that an ambulance showed up and gathered up the people. It looked like the Sheriff was wounded in the leg but he had sense enough to lay quiet and wait until the shooting stopped before moving. Evidently the remaining guys went back into hiding and were waiting for us to arrive. "I wonder how in the world those guys new that we were going to be here." I asked more or less trying to understand what was happening.

"Welcome to the wonderful world of GPS," Sidney began and I know that I was about to get one of his lectures on the terrific world of electronics. "It is a crazy thing, all you need to know is where someone was at in a place in time and you can track them to almost anywhere in the United States. You just follow them until you find where they are at in real time. The troubling thing to me and one of the reasons that I liked this place is that this place has never been on any GPS grid that I have ever seen." Sidney looked puzzled as he spoke and went back to his computer.

"I knew that you liked it for some reason," I joked and continued, "but I didn't know all this was back here."

"Oh, you haven't seen anything yet." Sidney lit up as he spoke, "let me set some of these cameras and we'll go get something to eat." I couldn't imagine that Sidney would want to go somewhere to get something to eat but he acted like it was nothing.

"Let's go," Sidney stood up and motioned for me to join him. He was walking toward the rear of the big cave opening and he opened a door and I felt a cold rush of air coming from the bowels of the cave. "Believe it or not this cave has an opening in downtown Eureka Springs and we can get there before the kitchen closes if we hurry." I followed Sidney through the cave and for the most part it was wide enough for the path but in a couple of places it was pretty tight. I was glad that he handed me a flashlight before we started down path all in all it was fairly easy going but I wouldn't have wanted to through there without a light.

When we reached the end he stopped and turned to me, "Now when I throw this door open you are going to be looking at about a fifty foot drop," Sidney was smiling at me as he spoke, "you're not afraid of heights are you?" He laughed and swung open a door and the city of Eureka Springs suddenly appeared. It was lit up for the night and I could hear music being played from several places and the huge hotel loomed just to the left of us. "Now there's a path that leads to the left that leads to the stairs behind the Basin Park Hotel, just follow me." He motioned for me to follow him and when I stepped out of the cave there was a little drop and it made me feel like I was falling down the cliff for a second and my foot hit solid ground. Sidney laughed at me, "Are you still with me Ricky?" Sidney asked as he closed the door to the cave. It was cool and I could see wisps of smoke coming from several of the buildings. Eureka had always been a very picturesque town that was built in the mountains by craftsmen from Sweden where they were accustomed to building buildings in such terrain. "Now, this is the Basin Park," Sidney said as we approached the walk bridge that led into the hotel, "it is the only hotel that is a five story hotel and each floor is a ground floor." He laughed as he stepped onto the bridge, "I think that we are on the third floor." I followed him as he opened the door that led into the hotel and down to the second floor restaurant. It was small but had a big bar on the back wall. I noticed that the majority of the seating was outside on the balcony of the hotel I stepped out there and being above the town I could see all around the town including the illuminated cross that was across the valley. It seemed like a peaceful little community. It was strange that I thought I could smell a faint odor of marijuana being smoked somewhere in town.

"It's really pretty out there," I said taking my chair at the table that Sidney where was seated. There were only eight or ten tables in the whole place and only two or three of them were occupied and the people looked like they were locals.

"This is a pretty little town," he began while taking a sip of his beer. "but during the week is the only time to visit. On the weekends the tourists come in and take over. This time of night on the weekend this place is packed." Sidney looked up at the waiter and placed an order for both of us and was careful to wait until the waiter walked away to began again. "I told you that this was going to get hairy," He smiled at me as he was leaning into me and now talking with a little whisper. "I was proud of you for the way that you handled yourself at the house. Do you think that you shot anyone back there?" He had a smile on his face as he asked his question.

"I don't think so," I began sipping my beer, "but I think that I think I might have scared a few of them. I just didn't want them slipping into the garage before the door got all the way down." Sidney chuckled in response.

"This is not going the way that I had planned that it would go," Sidney was visibly distressed as he spoke, nearly to the point of tears. "I never thought that they would kill anyone, with a gun anyway, but it looks like there are several people that have ended up dead over this." Sidney was waiting on a response from me and I didn't know what to say. I had always felt that the motor needed to get into the hands of the people.

"I think that we have to keep going," Sidney looked surprised to hear me say that, "the people that are against us are very committed to stopping us. We have to get this motor on the market." Sidney chuckled a little and I didn't know what I said that he thought was funny.

"I was ready to quit and to slip out of here and disappear into the woodwork." He was laughing a little in between his words and then calmed before continued, "I have tried to hire an advertising firm to advertise the motor. I hired a public relations firm to promote the motor and get us news coverage and most importantly none of that has gotten us anywhere. They have completely closed down all our access to the media. They are going to keep us in the dark and crush us like a bug, just like they did Stanley Myers." I could tell that Sidney was frustrated, but if he was even half way scared of these people.

"You are the one with the plan," I began between bites of my steak, "don't we have orders for a thousand motors. Can't we just deliver them and lay low for a while?" I was grasping at straws and really didn't know what to say. Then a strange thought hit me, "You know I had this guy come up to me at Des Moines, Randy Morgan I think he said his name was, anyway he was very persistent about wanting in on this deal. Then he showed up again when we were in Vegas. He didn't say much then, but he is definitely interested in helping out in some way, do you know him?" Sidney was gathering in all the information that I was giving him and then suddenly, he leans back in his chair and slaps himself in the head.

"Oh, my God," Sidney suddenly became jittery and picked up the pace of his eating, "hurry up we have to go." Soon he was tapping his empty fingers on the table encouraging me to hurry. Finally I just gave up and stood up and took the last swallow of my beer.

"Come on, come on," he flipped the waiter a couple of twenty's and started pushing me down the hall. "I think that they have a GPS tracker implanted in your tennis shoes." He led me down the stairs and out of the door onto Spring Street. "Let me see your tennis shoes." He was very demanding and I sat down on the ledge outside of one of the stores and took my shoes off. Sidney began looking them over intently. "There it is," he exclaimed, then produced the steak knife that he had used in the restaurant and started digging at it. "You see it, right there it is, just under the surface of the rubber of the sole." He was pointing to it but I couldn't really say that I saw it. Soon he had cut a chunk out of the sole of my left shoe. He checked over my right shoe and handed them both back to me. "We have got to get this on something that is moving. Come on we have to walk up to the highway." I put my shoes back on and followed him to the highway.

"I'm walking a little funny now." I said joking with him.

"I know that damn Randy," Sidney said as we walked down the road to get to the highway. "he always cheats, when we were racing against him he was sanctioned by the track officials more than anyone. He got to be a big joke, whenever we would see the track officials come out to pit road it was because Randy had either done something or told on someone for doing something." As we walked toward the highway I noticed most of the stores were closed but a couple of local bars were open that catered to the local people. One looked to have a biker theme and had a few motorcycles parked out front.

Sidney began huffing and puffing as we started up the grade just before the highway. There was a stoplight up there that looked like its red and green lights were illuminating the road instead of the moon. "I would like to find a truck or something that was traveling through the area so maybe these people will give us a break." We reached the intersection and walked a few feet from it and leaned on the retaining wall of a huge hotel and waited.

"How in the hell did they get that thing in my shoe?" I asked sounding like I couldn't believe that I had let that happen. "I don't even remember anyone being around my shoes."

"It only takes a second," Sidney had regained his breath and was relaxing leaning on the retaining wall. "They have a gun that shoots them in, air powered. Most of the time they use them to track dogs and cats. If Randy is behind this, I think that we can cope with him, but I think he is a pawn in a much bigger game." Sidney watched as a couple of cars stopped going east along the highway and was shaking his head as both had Arkansas plates.

"I didn't think Randy would have done all this." I started remembering all the things that happened to me on the way to Vegas. There were several tracking bugs on the car but I didn't think about one being on me. "Wait a minute," I began as realization hit me, "that was how they always knew where I was and when you blocked them they couldn't find us. He has known exactly where I or we have been all the way." I was amazed at the technology and I started hearing a truck revving its way through town. Sidney handed me the bug still enclosed in the rubber of my shoe and told me where to put it on the truck in between the bars of the door locks.

"Maybe the bastards will leave us alone for a while," Sidney said as we both watched as the truck disappeared into the night. We were walking back to the hotel when a dark Suburban charged past us and their headlights caught both Sidney and I full in the face. "Oh, my God," Sidney yelled as the truck skidded to a stop about a hundred feet past us. "We have to get off this road," he pointed to a motel up ahead, "we have to get up there." I took off running and made it around the corner of the motel when I saw the lights pass slowly by the hotel. But Sidney wasn't anywhere around.

"Ricky, where are you?" Sidney asked as he rounded the corner out of breath.

"Me, where were you?" I asked not really expecting an answer.

"We have to get out of here because it won't take too long for them to figure out that we are not where they thought we were." Sidney laughed and motioned for me to follow him and to continue our walk back to town. It was getting very late, after eleven and the night was still and cold. I had an oversized sweatshirt on to help cover up the fanny pack that Sidney insisted that I wear and I wasn't all that cold, but Sidney just had a button down shirt on and was making sounds like he was freezing as we walked.

"Sidney, don't you think that we had better get out of the country or something." I asked showing my concern about all the people after us.

"I don't believe in going down without a fight," Sidney began between his gasps for air as this was probably the most exercise that he had in a while. "and if I'm going to fight I want to be in a place where I have the advantage. And in this mountain, I have a big advantage."

Chapter Nine

"Boys I think that we have good news," Herbert began as the others were taking their seats. "I've heard that we spotted them in a little country town in Arkansas," he paused as he watched the others settle into their chairs. "My man says that he's in a house out in the country and that there have been some shooting going on out there and a County Sheriff got shot in the leg. We've told him that we were shooting a movie out there and that he was going to be in the middle of it." Herbert laughed at the absurdity of the cover story. "I think that we are going to have blow the damn house up to get him and the records." Herbert settled back in his chair with a huge smile on his face of self satisfaction.

"I know that he has shipped some of the motors," Price interjected, "but to who and how the money was transacted I don't have any idea yet." He shrugged his shoulders and held his palms up.

"I'll guess we'll have to pay him a visit to find out what we need to know." Herbert broke in nearly laughing at his own suggestion.

"Knowing you and your friends when you and your friends blow up the house it will probably kill everyone and we won't get a thing." Hugh sounded like he was sour on the whole proposition. "Look if we let this motor out to the public the oil exporters will have to lower the price of oil and we all will benefit." Hugh was hesitant in his speech and was looking for any sign of acceptance of his idea.

"Hugh," Price addressed him sounding a little disgusted, "if we don't stop this guy, everything that we have and our families have worked for all these years will disappear. Herbert is right if anybody is going to introduce this motor it has to be us." Price was reasoning with him but Hugh was shaking his head that he didn't like the idea.

"Let me get this straight," Sammy broke in, "you guys think that we have to blow the guys house up in order to kidnap him and make him tell us where he shipped the motors and how he got paid on them." Sammy was supporting Hugh and sounded reluctant to the heavy handed plan that Herbert had put forward.

"I would be interested to hear what Joe has to say on the matter," Price was searching for backing to his and Herbert's plan and he knew that if Joe sided with Hugh and Sammy then Herbert and his attempt to handle the threat the way that they thought best would be out voted and then who knew what would happen.

"I think that Herbert has always tried to do right by all of us and I'm inclined to go with him," Joe began, "but I think that if we end up killing him that the FBI or someone will track it back to us." A couple of the others tried to interject something but Joe raised his hand to calm them before continuing, "you know that no one has ever been caught and tried for the Randy Myers death, then there was the Karen Silkwood and one after another we are leaving a string of dead bodies all over the country." The others greeted Joe's words with solemn resolve.

"I think that we can come to reason with his man once we let him know how serious that we are," Price was slow and cautious in his speech and was choosing his words carefully. "I think that if we can't reason with him he could always come down with a stroke or some other medical condition that would render him useless." The others listened intently to him but questions started appearing on their faces.

"And how do you propose we do this, if and when we catch him?" Sammy questioned his proposal.

"I would be interested in hearing about that myself," Hugh interjected and several of the others indicated their desire to hear the answer to that question.

"There is any number of ways that we can." Price suddenly became quiet in mid sentence as Herbert responded to a knock on the door. All watched as Herbert rose slowly and answered the door. There was mumbling at the door but it was indistinguishable. Everyone watched as Herbert marched back to his chair carrying a folded piece of paper. He sat down slowly and unfolded the piece of paper.

"According to this report we have them holed up in a little town in Northwest Arkansas." Herbert began as he from the paper, "this says that after the shoot-out up there that the foreigners seemed to have moved out. I tried to tell them that we had everything under control and that our cover story has been accepted by the people up there and they even want to know if we need any extras. " Everybody laughed when he read that part of the letter, and then he continued. "I think this is good news, I think our guards that we have up there have everything in hand and they are waiting on us to give them the final go ahead to make their final assault on the place." Herbert was nearly giddy when he read the letter.

"I thought that you were going out there and talk to this man," Sammy interjected.

"There may not be any reason to go out there now." Joe blurted out like he wasn't interested in going nowhere. "I would think that everything is well in hand now and there is no need to go out there now." Some of the others laughed at Joe's assertion.

"Joe, all you are worried about is not missing dinner at the country club tonight," Sammy chuckled as he spoke and the others continued to laugh.

"I don't think that traipsing out into some God forsaken place is going to change anything," Joe defended himself but turned beet red in the face as he spoke.

"I don't think that I will go either," Sammy interjected, "I think that I will let Herbert and Price do what needs to be done. I will give you my proxy." He saluted Herbert as he spoke and then settled back in his chair.

"I think that I am going to stay on the sidelines as well," Hugh began as he saluted Herbert and Price, then adding, "I hope that you men know what you are doing, this could turn out very bad for all of us." Hugh was shaking his head in a sort of disbelief of what he was hearing and what was happening.

"You never did say how you were going to accomplish rendering him harmless," Joe asked of Price who had gathered his things up and filling his brief case.

"Well," Price began settling in his seat and turning to address the group, "as I was saying there are two ways to induce a stroke in a person. One is by electrical means and the other is chemical, either one can cause permanent damage in the brain and render the person to such a condition that they will have to be taken care of for the rest of their lives. Actually they are quite peaceful; it is like they have Alzheimer's or something." Price was pleased with himself and it showed in his words that proposed the plan.

"Well it is better than killing them," Sammy interjected, "but not by much." Sammy as was shaking his head in disbelief.

"I just want this whole thing to be over with," Hugh said flatly as he slapped the table.

"Not anymore than the rest of us want it over with," Herbert agreed, "but we have to get his plans, we have to take possession of any and all motors that he has ready and we have to go and get the motors that he has already shipped. I tell you in just a couple of days this thing could get traction in the media and we won't hear the last of it." Herbert had always been greedy and to him the ultimate in greed was the power to control technology and this technology was the ultimate power.

"I think that it leaves me and you Herbert to handle things out there in Arkansas," Price concluded, "all we have to decide on now, are whose jet we are taking to Arkansas." Price settled back in his chair and waited for a response.

"I've got to find out a few things first," Herbert began," we think that we have got them holed up in the house, but one of the guys said that he was rolling through town and thought he spotted him on the road. Then the GPS tracker that we had in the kids shoe took off on us and was discovered attached to a truck that rolled through town. Then I want to make sure that the area is safe, there has been a lot of shooting up there and before I get there I want our guys to be in solid control." Herbert had a big smile on his face as he spoke and the others laughed when he finished.

"Well you call it," Price concluded, "give me a call when you get ready." Price saluted him as they all stood to leave. "Herbert do you think I should I plan on bringing my stuff to give them a stroke or not?" He asked as he stood and gathered his things and prepared to leave.

"I think that it would probably be best," Herbert began as he watched the others stand to leave, "since Sammy, Hugh and Joe won't give us the okay to deal the problem in a more permanent way." They all broke out in laughter as they walked out of the room.

"Ricky," Sidney shouted knocking on the door of my room. For some reason he thought that we would be safe staying the main house and I slowly returned to consciousness as he was beating on the door. "We've got movement out here, let's get out of here," he shouted. He didn't act like he was in much of a hurry. But I knew that I had to move quickly.

"Okay, I'm going to hit the shower and I will be downstairs," I hoped that I had time to do all that but I knew that he would tell me if I didn't.

"You've got ten minutes," Sidney shouted sounding like it was urgent for me to get down there and he was a little aggravated that I didn't share his urgency, "I'll have the door open to the cave, I'll see you there." When he said that I started thinking that he wasn't all that worried about our company.

When I entered the cave, Sidney rushed to the door and closed it, locking it down. "I can't believe these guys," Sidney uttered beneath his breath, "I have to get this information out before they start messing with us. Lock the door, will you." Sidney was working intently on his computers and went to the kitchen to get something to eat. "You better get something to eat now; there is no telling when you will get the next opportunity." I wondered what Sidney meant by that. He, I was sure, would be checking all the surveillance equipment that he had rigged around the house. “It looks like they are out there waiting on something,” Sidney was talking to himself and then started closing the lids on his computers.

“What are they doing out there?” I asked finishing my breakfast. I was thinking that Sidney was acting strange.

“I’ve got to crash these computers,” he acted like he was still talking to himself. “Okay,” he said turning to me. I have a lot of things I have got to tell you. If anyone lives over this thing I want it to be you.” Sidney was nervous and it showed in his voice, “I want you to take this and put it in a safe place outside of the cave.” Sidney was clearly thinking as he spoke and was being very deliberate in his choice of instructions. “This little card has all my business affairs on it; it has my bank account numbers, my drawings for all my inventions, deeds on everything I own and in the event of my death, my will leaving it all to you. We have to keep this safe.” I was floored at what he was saying but he had said similar things like that in the past. “I have cleared all my computers and about to crash all of them except the one that I’m watching them on, but I never had any of this stuff on this computer. If they find this one I won’t make any difference.” I started to say something but didn’t really know what to say.

“Do you have any idea of what you want me to do with it or how I could hide it?” I asked not really having any idea of where I could hide it. I was thinking that I could take it to the post office and mail it somewhere, but I didn’t know. “What about mailing it somewhere?”

“Oh, that’s good, but we can’t mail it, but what a good diversion?” Sidney hurried to his desk and addressed an envelope and handed it to me. “Drop this in the mailbox outside the post office.” He was smiling at me and I knew that he was really worried about what was going to happen in just a few short hours.

"So you want me to hide it under a rock or something," I was about halfway joking when I noticed his face light up.

"That sounds good but you have to get out of the cave before you hide it." Sidney sounded like he was a little scared but was more than willing to stay and face what might be an impending doom. "One more thing, I want you to get out of here and never come back. I will stall them as long as possible to give you as much time as possible. I want you to buy yourself a car or truck or something and get the hell out of here. You can come back in about a month or so and get the card and you will be able to get money or anything that you want." Sidney was down hearted and spoke like he expected an impending doom.

"Are you sure that you want to play it like this?" I asked as the full weight of what he was telling me sank in. He wasn't planning on making it.

"It has been a good ride son," He swallowed hard before continuing, "since my wife died this is all that I have had to live for and if I can't do it, I might as well go. Well you know." I couldn't believe what I was hearing. "Come here I want to show you some of the new tunnels that Al Capone's boys dug into the mountain to hide their booze from the revenuers." He opened the door that led out the back to the path that we had taken the night before. He handed me a flashlight and I followed him about hundred yards into the cave he stopped and pointed to a pathway. "This leads to an opening on the side of the mountain and it comes out at one of the springs that are in somebody's yard but they won't bother you. Just get that memory card out of your hands as soon as you can and then get out of here. I hope to God that you don't get killed." He grabbed me and gave me a hug and I could see his eyes tearing up. I knew that he really liked me but he had never been affectionate to me before. He released me slowly and held my arms, "Now go, don't you look back on this place." He pushed me gently towards the passage and I reluctantly took a step forward and stopped.

"Are you sure that you want to do it this way," I began in an attempt to reason with him, "We can both get out of here if we go now."

"They would just continue to hunt me down and they would kill us for sure," He began, "If we split up now, I will be the one that will have to deal with them. You are my only hope that my motor will live. Maybe in a few years you can fly to Australia and start producing a few of the motors. I don't think that the people chasing us have the same kind of power down there as they do up here. Don't worry about me; I've got a few surprises planned for them." I smiled at him thinking about the ball lightning machine that he had in Tulsa and suddenly I knew that Sidney would not be taken easily.

Boom, suddenly feel the whole mountain shake, "You get out of here, it sounds like I have some business to take care of." He smiled at me and I knew that he would surely have some surprises for them.

Herbert and Price jostled down the overgrown part of the drive that led to the house, "This is out in the woods," Price commented as the rolled down the window of the limousine that he and Herbert were riding in. "Who in the hell would want to live out here?" Herbert started laughing.

"No one will be able to live here after we get through with the place." Herbert was still chuckling as another blast rocked the house and the mountain.

"My God, what is that place made out of," Price asked rhetorically as he watched the dust clear from the explosion. He watched as his people were placing more charges around the garage door.

"Driver back us up some, I don't want any of the debris hitting the car." Herbert gave instructions to his driver, "no sense us getting blown up too." He said to Price finding it funny and laughing about it. "Driver, get me the supervisor of this squad, will you." Herbert was short and demanding with his driver.

"You must have ten or twelve men out here handling this," Price commented.

"I've got a team of twelve on this, the guy I talked to said that I could have a team of six or twelve, so I chose the twelve." Herbert sounded a little too jovial in his response as he rolled his window down to talk to a man approaching the limo.

"How's it going," Herbert asked but didn't give him any time to answer, "when can I see this man, I'm ready to get out of this God forsaken place. We have to catch the plane in about an hour." The man just shook his head.

"This man is probably the premiere security genius in the whole country," Robert said showing his confusion with the reaction and extending his hand to his boss, " By the way my name is Robert but everyone calls me Bob." Herbert took his hand and looked very uncomfortable.

"I'm Herbert and this is Price," Herbert said motioning to Price.

"We have tried to blast the door but it is made of tungsten steel and we barely made a dent in it. We are setting a new charge to try to take off the whole back section of the house. We are going to have a pretty big charge so you might want to stay in the car." Bob just innately knew that his bosses didn't have the stomach for taking care of the things that they wanted him to. Bob looked like he was somewhat ticked off that the boss wanted him and his team to hurry. He just rose to his full height, turned and walked away.

"How dare you walk away from me," Herbert yelled, "I'm not through with you." He turned to Price. "Can you believe the audacity of some people? I'm paying him." Herbert had turned red in the face as his anger boiled.

"Yeah, you're paying him but he probably won't live to be able to spend it." Price interjected to calm him down. It was pretty much standard practice to hire these mercenary teams and then when everything was over to put out contracts on each of them. No witnesses. No links back to them.

"What are you paying those guys?" Price asked rolling his window up and settling himself back into his chair.

Herbert raised his hand to his mouth to signal Price that the chauffeur was able to overhear everything that they were saying. "I think that we just have to sit back and wait," Herbert began pouring himself a drink. "Care for a little taste?" He asked Price.

"I think that I want to go up there and see what is going on," Price moved to climb out of the limo.

"Are you sure that is wise?" Herbert asked grabbing him by the shoulder.

"What can it hurt?" Price began, "if this man is such a security genius I would like to see some of his methods in put in practice, maybe I could improve the security of my own house." Price climbed out of the car and began walking toward the house.

"Hi, men," Price approached the men that were drilling into the rock and concrete wall on the corner of the house. The men looked like they were black operations agents or something. They were all dressed in black, black jump pants with big cargo pockets and black tight fitting sweaters and all wore the same black knit stocking caps that were rolled up onto their foreheads. "What are we trying to do here?" Price asked as he watched the men drilling the holes.

"We are going to have to place charges in these holes and hopefully we will be able to get into the garage," Bob responded while the others only nodded to acknowledge Price's presence.

"Why can't you just blow the door open or smash it open?" Price asked pointing to the door.

"I don't know what kind of door that guy has there, but you are not going to break it in and it does not respond to charges like every other door that I have ever seen." Bob acted as if he was really frustrated in having to explain his actions. Price overcame the urge to ask more questions and inquisitive about their actions and the reasoning behind it. "We are about ready to blow this corner of the house," Bob sounded short in his tone like he was trying to say turning to Price, "Will you get out of here and let us do our jobs?" Price sort of jogged away towards the limo.

Boom, the charge went off as Price was about a hundred feet away from the house but it still knocked him down to the ground. Herbert raced out of the limo to help the much younger Price to his feet. "Price, you crazy thing are you all right?" Herbert shouted as he approached where he was lying. Once Price returned to his feet, both watched the smoke clear to see if they had gained entry to the house. The roof of the garage was sagging a little but the door had blown wide open revealing the Escalade sitting in the garage. It didn't look like it tore the metal but merely moved it off the building and laid it out like it was meant to open that way.

"Let's get the hell out of here," Herbert began as he and Price started back to the limo, "I'm about ready to just tell our guys to kill these guys and get it over with." Herbert was showing his frustration and anger at the slow pace.

"They should be getting them any minute now, why don't we wait and see if they can get them pretty quick now." Price was trying to reason with him as they reentered the limo. "Let me go back up there and check with that Bob guy and see where we are at. Then you and I can make some decisions." Price reached for the door handle and Herbert caught his arm.

"You be careful this time," Herbert began, "let them take the risks. You stay safe." Price nodded and started walking away from the limo.

"Bob," Price yelled as he saw him going into the garage, "where are we at? How much longer before we can get to Mr. Cain?" Bob laughed at him in response.

"This guy does not want to see you and he is making it very hard." Bob motioned for Price to come into the garage. "We have checked the house and we think that he is in there," he said pointing to the big safe door that was in the entry of the cave.

"Yeah, I'm in here," Sidney said over the intercom, "you bastards having a little fun, are you." He was laughing at them then turned his tone to become more serious. "Who is that in the sports coat out there, what's your name?" Price reacted by ducking his head and moving out of the garage. "I've got your picture, you son of a bitch. How much is he paying you guys, I'll pay you double." Sidney was shouting over the intercom before Bob spotted the speaker and took out his pistol and shot it into silence.

"Herbert, we have got to get the hell out of here, that bastard knows what I look like and he probably knows what you look like to." Price slammed the door of the limo showing his disgust and anger. Herbert looked shocked at the news and became quiet as he stroked his chin in deep thought.

"I think that we have to up the ante a little," Herbert was rolling down the window to where the driver could hear him. "Driver, I need you to take this note to the guy named Bob up there at the house." He had taken pen and paper out of the compartment in the limo and jotted a number and the following message. "Call us at this number when you have him, we are now offering you a million apiece to take care of this problem for us." He ripped it off the tablet folded it carefully and handed it to the driver.

Herbert and Price watched as the driver headed toward the house, "I think that we ought to fly back to New York and let these guys handle this problem." Herbert sounded like he was ready to wash his hands of this problem and move on. Price look shocked.

"We can't do that," he protested, "what if they can't get him. He's got pictures of us now, we have to stay here and make sure that we prevent that video from getting out." Price was adamant in his reasoning.

"By God," Herbert exclaimed, "I'm going home, if you want to stay it will be on you." Herbert had always been the one that was in control and willing to see everything through to the end but this was strange behavior for him.

"Herbert, what is the matter?" Price asked like he couldn't believe what he was hearing. "You have been the one that wanted to talk to him and find out how the motor worked and everything about his invention. Now you just want to kill him and move on.

That doesn't make sense." Price was pleading with him and it didn't look like it was having any effect.

"I don't figure that this guy is going to give up very easily," Herbert began sounding very disgusted, "I think that we are drawing too much attention to ourselves by blowing up this house and shooting people out here in the yard. I don't like being in the scene. I want to be behind the scene." Herbert sounded very solemn as he spoke and twisted in his seat to show his resolve in the matter. "Let's drive back to the plane and let Bob and his guys handle this, they'll call us when they get him." Both watched at the driver returned to the car. "Driver, let's go. Did he have anything to say to me?" He asked the driver as he watched him prepare the car to go.

"He said that it might be awhile before he gets through the safe door," the driver reported, "he said that they are out of C4 and they have to get some more."

"Oh my God," Herbert blurted out, "this crap is just taking too long." Price motioned for him to shut up while he rolled the window up so the driver couldn't hear them. "I'm going home."

"Now let's think about this a little," Price interjected showing his anger on the waffling of Herbert, "we can get back here in a couple of hours. Once they get him, we can jump on the plane and get back here in a short period of time." Price expressed his anger through his words.

"I'm just about through with this fool," Herbert bellowed in his anger, "what makes him think that he is going to be able to introduce a motor that would put us out of business."

The constant beep, beep of his phone, Herbert pulled it out of his pocket with a smile on his face, "Maybe they have got him all ready," Herbert said to Price and pushed the button to answer the phone.

"What's the matter, you sorry bastard." Sidney shouted through the phone, "You don't have the stomach to watch your men blow my house apart." Herbert acted as if cold chills ran up and down his spine. He started to answer but words wouldn't come out of his mouth.

"Maybe I can help you," Price said calmly.

"You must be the one that was wearing the sport coat," Sidney concluded, "I assume that you want me dead, but I don't like that idea." Price and Herbert laughed at Sidney.

"Mr. Cain you are a brilliant man," Price began, "but you surely don't expect us to allow you to put your motor out without a little resistance do you. We had Pritkin offer you a billion dollars and you turned him down. You had to expect that there would be another level of reprisal didn't you." Price was over his emotions and surprise that Sidney had found his phone number and was trying to offer some kind of reasoning to resolve the matter.

"You are not that big of a fool," Sidney responded angrily, "once you got all my notes and motors, I wouldn't live six months anyway." Sidney acted like he had won some sort of battle, when a huge explosion came over the phone. Herbert and Price acted like they were relieved and might have secretly hoped that Sidney might have been injured or eliminated.

"Are you bastards still there?" Sidney asked not sounding like he was at all concerned with the blast. Herbert grabbed the phone and switched it off.

"We don't need to talk to him," Herbert blurted out angry that Sidney had that audacity to call him. "How did he get this number anyway?" Herbert asked.

"Don't you remember that you wrote your number down on that paper that you gave your guy?" Herbert acted as if he was about ready to throw the phone out of the window as Price spoke. "Here let me have your phone, I'll talk to Mr. Cain should he call back." Price smiled a little sinister smile and acted like he had other motives in taking the phone from Herbert.

"Your dad was always calm like you are," Herbert said as he settled back into his set in the limo. "He was always rational and deliberate in everything that he did. He would have been proud of you." Price received the information positively.

"Well think you, Herbert," Price began, "my dad was truly a special man." Somehow Price seemed to feel uncomfortable with the conversation.

Ring, ring, the phone went off and Price noticed that there was a different number on the screen and handed Herbert the phone. "Hello," Herbert responded into the phone and listened as the person on the other end communicated with him. "Okay, well give me a call if you need anything and let me give you to my associate, he will be taking over this operation and he will help you with anything that you need." Herbert handed the phone to Price.

"Hello," Price said into the phone, "Hello, we are running into quite a few problems up here, we just tried a gasoline bomb and it basically did nothing but get a little fire started. I've got two men going after more C4 but it is going to be awhile before they get back with it." Price accepted the information with great concern.

"Do you still think that you can get into the cave where he is?" Price asked questioning the abilities of the men that Herbert had hired to do the job.

"We will get there," Bob responded, "but we may kill him in the process." He sounded concerned about what might happen.

"Don't worry about that," Price said calmly, "if it happens it happens. Just call me the minute that you get into the cave." Price punched the phone off and settled into his seat for the ride back to New York.

I had made my way through the cave and emerged out the spring just like Sidney had said, but he didn't mention how close it was in places. I came out on the north side of town and once I got my bearings I decided that I needed to walk down the main street through where all the shops were. It was mid-morning on a bright November day and it was a good day for a walk, but I had to find a car to buy somewhere.

About halfway down the street I found a leather shop that had some boots and a jacket that fit me. The only thing that I didn't like about the boots was that they might be hard to run in, but since they were not cowboy boots, I thought they would be all right. I dropped my old gym shoes in the trash outside of the leather shop. I liked the jacket I picked out was a soft black leather and long enough to cover up the fanny pack that Sidney had insisted that I wear. I knew that I had to get out of town. While I was in the leather shop I saw a couple of dark colored Suburbans pass by, and it made me nervous. I walked to the bottom of the main street past where we were when we ate at the Basin Park Hotel, and I tried to search the mountain behind the hotel to see if I could see where the opening to the cave was. I couldn't.

I stopped into a little bar and café that was on the outskirts of town and grabbed a sale paper from the rack outside to look for a car that I could find somewhere around here.

"You don't know where I could buy a car, do you?" I asked the waitress who looked like she was young but was more of a hippie from the old days when my parents were young. She had long dark hair and looked like she had a tattoo on the corner of her eye.

"Oh, my boyfriend has a car for sale," she said and grabbed her cell phone to call him. I was thinking that I probably would not be interested in anything that this couple had for sale but at present I didn't have much of a choice.

"Just tell him to bring it on down and let me look at it." I responded while she was trying to explain to her boyfriend that I was interested in buying a car. From the second that she hung up she became so chatty that I could barely stand it. I ordered a burger and fries just to shut her up for a while.

In a few minutes a shabbily dressed young man came in the restaurant, he had long hair and he looked like he hadn't bathed in a while and he was wearing bell bottom jeans and he spoke like he had smoked a little too much marijuana. I followed him out to the parking lot to where he parked the car. He was giving me a long sob story about how everything closed up in town for the winter and his girlfriend wouldn't be able to work and they had to sell the car. I about half expected that they would have some clunker or something, but when he motioned to a fairly nice older model MGB sports car. It was a yellow convertible and it looked fairly nice to my surprise. He flipped me the keys and as I climbed in I noticed the sign that he had in the rear window that read that he wanted twenty five hundred for it. As I claimed in I was greeted with the over powering odor of marijuana. The car started and seemed to run all right. I pretended to check the car over and raised the hood and raced the motor and surprisingly it didn't smoke for such an older model. He kept saying something about how fast it was. I thought to myself, it was a four cylinder, how fast could it be.

"Okay, I'll take it," I began as we walked back to the restaurant, "she said that you wanted two thousand for it, it that right?" I pretended I didn't notice the sign in the back window that read twenty five hundred.

"Yeah," he began, "the restaurant is closing for the season soon and we are getting a little tight on money." I excused myself and went to the bathroom and counted out twenty five hundred dollar bills and stuck them in my pocket before I returned to the table.

He had the title on the table when I returned. "Let's get this paperwork over with," I began picking up the title and looking it over. "I will need a bill of sale and authorization to use your license tag for a while." When I said that he looked at his girlfriend and I was wondering what might be wrong.

"We don't know anything about a bill of sale," the waitress interjected and I motioned for her to give me a paper and pen. I quickly wrote out a little bill of sale and authorization to use their license tag in lieu of a paper tag. I didn't know if all of that was legal or not but I thought that it was worth a shot. I paid the pair the full twenty five hundred and took the keys and walked out. Knowing that I would soon be out of town, but I forgot to hide the computer chip and I became painfully aware of it when I pulled the money out of my pocket, it nearly fell out on the floor of the bathroom.

I noticed a public restroom located on the side of a big block building that was some kind of theater or something. I thought that if I could hide it somewhere in there it would be safe from the elements and open all year long unlike he restaurant which was about to close for the winter season.

I eased into the stall and closed the door. I was looking around for a place to hide the disk where it wouldn't be discovered by the cleaning crew or someone nosing around in the bathroom. I looked overhead and decided that I would hide the disk in the above the ceiling tile. I stood on the seat and as soon as everyone was out of the restroom I lifted the tile up and placed the chip on the board behind it.

I started the car and the first thing that I noticed was that it was out of gas. I drove out to a gas station that was a little out of town and was standing outside pumping gas into the car, when I noticed a big black limousine pass by. I started thinking that they might have something to do with Sidney and the explosions that I was hearing while I was buying the car. I knew that Sidney was not going to allow a few explosives get to him. He was in a fortress and by the way that he wanted to get back to that house in Eureka, I was sure that he had a few surprises for them. I fought the urge to drive by the house and check on him, but I did think that I could send him a text. "Ok on the move. Limo at the house?" I hit send on the phone and paid for the gas and decided that I would follow the limo.

I liked the way that the car handled. It drove more like a race car than even the Corvette did and the motor could really wind up. I had to drive with the windows down to air out the marijuana smell and I wondered how such a small town could possibly have so much marijuana use.

The limo had about a ten minute head start on me but the road was so hilly and curvy that it couldn't make very much time and the MGB that I was driving was very quick on the curves and I could race my way down the straight-aways to make up time.

Beep, my phone signaled me that I had a text message, I grabbed it and pushed the button, "Doing well, I think they burnt part of my house but I'm ok, I'm about to bring out the big guns. Text me tonight." It felt good to know that Sidney was safe in spite of all the explosions that I heard.

I was pushing eighty when I caught a glimpse of the limo about three miles ahead of me as it was going around a curve and then disappeared from sight. I pushed the car a little harder. I didn't know why I was following them but if they were involved with the assault on Sidney, they might be the ring leaders.

I kept thinking about Sidney. He wanted me to run and get to a place of safety while he was staying there to give me some time to get away. It didn't seem right considering all that he had done for me and all that he wanted to do. I felt like going back and fighting those guys myself, but I knew that I couldn't do any good by myself. I began thinking of how I could get to get people to help Sidney get out of the cave and end the siege.

I caught up to the limo to where I was about a half a mile behind them and they were going fairly slow and I wondered if I was being conspicuous hanging behind them. I pulled down my cap that I had bought at the gas station and tucked on the shades to where I would not be as easily recognized and pushed the car closer to them. I had noticed that they had pulled to the shoulder to let other cars pass and I thought I might get close enough to get the tag number. Then I started thinking that it might be a rental and it would be more important to get the tail number off their airplane, for that matter I might as well get them both. Maybe Sidney could at least figure out who was after us.

As I was following the limousine I was starting to get mad, Sidney did not have to die for trying to better the world. I just didn't know what I could do and getting both of us killed would useless. There had to be something that I could do besides run. I didn't know anything except that there was a motor and that I had driven it, which probably meant to them that I was highly expendable in their eyes. Running meant that I had to run somewhere and I would constantly have to be looking over my shoulder for the rest of my life. That was not my idea of a life no matter how much money Sidney was willing to give me. Most importantly he was willing to give me time to make my run as successful as possible. I just couldn't do it; I had to find a way to help Sidney. I knew that

Sidney was depressed and he sounded very fatalistic. The thought crossed my mind that he might wanting to die and doing it this way was his way of fighting for what he believed in.

I caught up with the limo and watched as it pulled into the airport and they drove across the tarmac to what looked to be a small jet that was something like a Learjet. Two men got out of the limo and hurriedly walked up the ladder steps to board the aircraft. From the parking lot of the airport I could see the tail number on the aircraft, N7501E, and I watched as the door closed and the ground crew motioned for the pilot to taxi onto the taxiway.

The only thing that I could think of was to go by the security company and see if I could get some of the guys there to go back with me and help Sidney get out of his predicament. I knew that they were my last hope and if they didn't want to take the risk, I would have to accept their decision.

"I have always hated getting involved in these little problems," Herbert sounded dejected as he settled into his seat on the plane and felt the surge of it taking off from the airport. "Did you get the name of that limo driver? Herbert asked as he pulled a pad of paper from his pocket, "he will have to go to." Price understood what he meant and shook his head.

"We are going to leave a string of dead bodies all over the country if we are not careful." Price sounded disgusted as he spoke.

"We are not responsible for this," Herbert began sounding irritated, "it is his fault that this stuff is happening. He is making us do all of this." Price was astounded by how Herbert twisted the facts with his logic.

Ring, ring, Herbert's phone began ringing, "I hope that this is not that crazy man in the cave," he said to Price with a twinkle in his eye then pressed button to answer. "Hello," Herbert said into the phone, "Yes Bob," Herbert responded by signaling his ease with the conversation, he made several little guttural sounds to indicate that he understood or was accepting of the things that he was saying. "Well if the only way that you can get to him is to blow the mountain up, then blow the mountain up. When do you think that you will have it done?" He then made a couple of other sounds to indicate that he concurred with what Bob was saying. "I'll tell you what, wait until morning and we will get back here so that we will have an opportunity to talk to him. You might want to replace your three men. Okay, wait until we get here in the morning before you blow it." Herbert hung up.

"Well," Herbert began settling himself in his chair and putting his cell phone back in his pocket. "Bob said that they were going to blow the mountain in the morning so I guess that we can fly back in the morning. He said that somehow that damn man killed three of his men with some sort of lightning but they disabled his antenna, but that his men were getting anxious because they don't know what else he could do. I told him to just get some more men." Herbert was laughing when he finished.

"My God," Price reacted with disbelief, "don't you think that people will notice if you blow a mountain up."

"Screw them," Herbert spat back at him angrily, "this is not our fault. If people would just buy our gas and keep their mouths shut everything would be all right. Remember we are shooting a movie down there and we have a security force in place to keep nosy people out of the way." Herbert started a little chuckle to himself sounding satisfied with himself.

"I can't believe that you would go to such extremes to get these guys," Price was astonished at Herbert's attitude in dealing with this problem.

Beep, beep, Herbert's phone went off and he looked at it smiled and clicked it on speaker to let Price hear. "Hello," Herbert said, "don't you ever get enough, Mr. Cain."

"It's not me I think your hired boys have deserted you," Sidney was gloating a little, "but I'm sending you the bill for my house, Mr. N7501E," Herbert cut a look a Price when he heard the tail number of their airplane. "Before long I will be able to knock your plane out of the sky and you won't even know what hit you, maybe you're the one that is not safe."

"Why Mr. Cain you could be safe if you would just listen to reason," Herbert twisted a smile on his face and winked at Price. "Goodnight Mr. Cain," Herbert pressed the button ending the call.

"How did he get our tail number?" Price asked showing concern, "I wonder where the kid is. Could he have followed us to the airport?" Price twisted in his seat to look Herbert square in the eye.

"I don't care if he did, we will find him and take care of him, he knows too much," Herbert was very deliberate in his speech then added, "he is just going to be one more loose end that we have to take care of, Just like the people that are out there, all of them will have to be taken care of."

"This man must be a genius," Price commented, "People have been trying to reproduce lightning for a long time. The military had wanted to use it for a weapon for a long time." Price seemed anxious and twitched a little in his seat. "We have to get our hands on his papers, it could really be something that we could give our research and development people."

"You're welcome to everything that is left," Herbert smiled and stretched out in the plane. "My wife is having people over for dinner tonight and I can hardly stand it, maybe if you and your wife come it won't be so bad." Herbert poured himself a glass of wine and eased back in his chair. "Did you see that house; can you believe that people live in something like that?"

"Some people would have loved to have a house like that," Price nearly whispered in response, "but I think that he choose it for its defensive potential." Price sounded as if he didn't think that Herbert's men were going to have such an easy time of getting to Mr. Cain.

I was trying to figure out what I needed to do. If I did what Sidney wanted me to do I would run and I would never look back. I just couldn't get him out of my mind. I decided that I would go by the casino where Sidney stayed. I thought I would text Sidney and see what he thought of my plan.

I checked in at the hotel at the casino and went to my room. I started punching out a message to Sidney about how I should get some guys from the company and come rescue him.

Beep, my phone went off and I knew that I had a message from Sidney," No, don't, run, run, run. I'm ok. I think that I have them on the run. I've seen nothing in a while now. I text you with where I will meet you later." Sidney sounded like he had weathered the storm and had made it through the worst of the assault. But I didn't think that they would quit until they had him or had the motors or the plans and manufacturing information on them. There was something wrong. Nothing was making sense. Why did the men fly off in the jet if they hadn't got what they wanted? Where did the men go that were outside the house and the cave? How much damage did they do to the mountain and cave entrance? There were just so many questions and there were not near enough answers. There had to be something that I could do.

I milled around the room for awhile and I even tried to take a nap but I was so worried about Sidney that I couldn't sleep. It was dark out now and I always felt good about traveling at night but I needed to go out and buy some things. The one thing that I had always enjoyed about Tulsa was that they had a magazine where you could buy used merchandise. I wanted to buy a truck, a gun, either an AK 47 or an AR 15 or something that would have a big clip capacity and some ammunition. In the old days I would read those papers and dream about all the stuff that I could buy if I had the money and now I had the money. One thing for sure I was going back to get Sidney out of the cave whether I could get any help from the Security company or not.

It was after six in the night when I walked out of the casino and drove across the street to find the bargain paper. I found a couple of pickups in the paper; I wanted a four wheel drive and preferably one that had an extended cab. I called a couple of numbers and found one that sounded promising, I called them both and had them agree to meet me at the casino at nine o'clock. I then dove into finding a gun, I had the Glock that Sidney had given me but I would have felt better having more ammunition for it and I wanted to get a rifle. I found one listing and I called the guy and he sounded like he was motivated to sell the gun and he agreed to meet me at the convenience store in about thirty minutes. The rifle that he had was an AR 15 and he said that he had about two hundred rounds of ammunition that went with it. I bought them both.

I debated as to whether I should text Sidney back and let him know that I would be coming after him and finally decided that

I needed to wait in case that they had some way of monitoring Sidney's communications.

"Hello Bob," Herbert said into his phone, "is everything ready?" Herbert and Price were in the plane and flying back to the airport that was closest to Eureka. "We should be there in about an hour or so. Wait on us before you do anything." Herbert was nearly giddy for some reason. "This is going to be interesting," Herbert turned to Price, "he called me last night and said that he had almost a hundred pounds of explosives and they had drilled holes into the mountain for most of yesterday and that they were going to pack the holes this morning."

"What are they going to do, blow the mountain up?" Price asked sounding surprised.

"I think they'll do whatever Mr. Cain makes them do," Herbert jested and twisted in his seat. "We are about to land in a few minutes. We will see what happens in about an hour." Price reacted by shaking his head and snapping his seat belt.

"This is getting out of hand," Price began, "blowing up a mountain is just a little excessive, don't you think."

"When a bug is bothering you," Herbert laughed, "you have to squash it."

I got to the security company long before the six o'clock shift started, about the only people that I actually knew were my former crew leader and a couple of other people that I had met when Sidney took us all to lunch. I had to find Joe. I had a company badge somewhere out at Sidney's house. I walked to the guard shack that led to the entrance.

"Hi," I said to the guard, "I work here but I forgot my badge." He was looking at me with great curiosity. He was an older man, that had thinning gray hair and wore horn-rimmed glasses, I had remembered him from the few times that I had been through the there on my way to work. He looked was balding and had a paunch around his middle. He motioned for me to stand aside while he watched the employees that had their security badges file past him and scan their badges. There was slack in the line and I fell in back of the last person in line.

"Look," I pleaded with the guard, "I'm Sidney's race car driver, Sidney is in trouble. I need to get a hold of Joe, he was my crew leader." The guard looked like I had slapped him.

"Sidney is in trouble," The guard was letting the information sink in. I was getting really upset because I knew that every second counted. "I haven't seen Joe, yet, ah, ah." And he started fumbling with his directory and punching the keys on his computer.

"Come on, Sidney is holed up in a cave over in Arkansas and there are a team of men over there trying to blow up the mountain to get to him." I was trying to explain the urgency of the situation, but I knew that I would have to be explaining this problem several times. I just happened to notice one of the companies newsletters posted on the wall and my picture was there standing outside of the car. "Here, look here, this is my picture with Sidney's car." The guard grabbed the newsletter out of my hand and looked at me and the picture.

"Okay," he said becoming very frantic, "you stay here and make sure that everybody that passes has a badge. I'm going to go get some people that will help you." He nodded at me and took off into the main building.

I stood there and watched as other employees marched through the line and passed their identification badges under the card reader and I noticed when they did a picture of them would flash on the computer screen that only the guard could see.

I noticed Joe walking into the guard station even before he got there and I was glad to see him. "Hey Ricky, long time no see," he blurted out entering the door with several other men in front of him.

"Joe, I am so glad to see you, Sidney is in trouble," I pulled him to the side and several other of the people that were coming in to the facility suddenly stopped to hear more. I looked into the eyes of Joe and instantly his face turned to concern. I was uneasy about continuing but I felt that I had to, "he's holed up in a mountain cave over in Arkansas and I'm afraid that they are going to blow the mountain up to get to him." The news impacted them all and they turned to silence.

"I will get the guys," Joe acted like he was mad and was willing to take on whoever it was that was holding Sidney by himself. Joe pushed his way through the building through the other employees and through the door into the facility.

I watched as Joe exited that guard shack and was met by the guard who was returning with several people wearing ties. It sort of shook me a little. He met with them and Joe went on into the facility. The guard motioned for me to follow him and I pushed my way through the crowd that was now jammed into the guard shack.

"Ricky, follow us," one of the men wearing a tie said and they pushed the crowd away as we marched into the building.

"This is our situation room," one of them said, "sit down, now where did you say Sidney was?" The room was laid out with a conference table in the middle of it and to the back of it was a group of people that worked on computers and on the other side was a huge screen that had the All Tech Security symbol in the middle of it.

"He's in a cave at a house just outside of Eureka Springs," I began and I could hear the key of computers clicking behind me. "There are a group of men that are trying to get to him and I'm afraid that they are going to blow the mountain up."

"Come on people let's get it up on the screen." The leader shouted. In a few seconds a picture of the house in Eureka Springs popped on the screen. I could see that they had blown the garage almost off the house and the safe door was still prominent. I could see the men around there crawling over the mountain and one was rappelling down the front of the building. I watched as the limo that I had followed yesterday pulled onto the property. "That's the limo that I followed to the airport over there yesterday, the tail number was N7501E." I heard more clicking of the computer keys and a picture of Price Culver flashed on the screen.

"It looks like Sidney has ticked off some mighty big people," the leader quipped.

"Look something is happening, they are running away from mountain," the leader shouted. Then the whole screen erupted in a huge explosion and smoke and debris was everywhere. "Get the team ready we are leaving in thirty minutes." With that demand everyone scattered out of the room, except for the computer people who were suddenly busy working on their computers.

I didn't know where everybody was going and suddenly someone from the computers came down to me and began fitting me for a headset. He slipped something in my back pocket fitted something in my ear and motioned to another person.

"Testing, testing, one, two, three, got it," I heard someone say in my ear phone and I motioned that I had heard him.

I was kind of astonished because no one had asked me if they wanted me to show them where the house was or told me what they wanted me to do. I continued to watch the video on the big screen and as the dust cleared I could see that the big door that led into the cave was down and they were men preparing to go in.

"Ricky, what did Sidney tell you to do?" someone said into my head set.

"He said for me to run and I can't leave him there to die," I said to the person that I was talking to.

"Then I think that you had better do what he said," he responded.

"I'm going back, there are two passageways into the cave from the town side of the mountain, and I know where both of them are. I'm going back there." I demanded as forcefully as I could.

"Be at the helicopter pad in ten minutes." The voice ordered and I felt a little better that I was at least valued.

"They are clearing the debris out of the way and they will be going in to get him in a few minutes." Bob said into his phone to Herbert.

"Okay, let us know as soon as you get him," Herbert replied turning to Price, "things are going a whole lot better today. We should have this thing wrapped up shortly." Herbert was very satisfied with himself as he spoke.

"I think that Mr. Cain is full of surprises and if we get out of here with our skin I will be happy." Price concluded attempting to douse the flames of joy that exuded from Herbert.

"Nonsense," Herbert blurted out sounding like he had taken offense by Price's reluctance. "Let's go up there and see what is going on." Herbert was getting out of the limo as he spoke.

"Are you sure that is a good idea," Price shouted to ensure that he was heard. "He might be able to do something. Bob said that he killed three men with some kind of electronic gizmo. He could be dangerous." Price continued his reluctance and slowly approached what was left of the house as Herbert raced ahead of him.

"Bob, Bob," Herbert shouted as he neared the entrance of the cave, "Where is he at? Do we have him?" Herbert gingerly made his way through the debris into the cave and finally into the room that Sidney had made in the cave. Bob had raced out of the back out of the passages in the back of the room.

"We've got him," Bob shouted to Herbert "We will have him back here in a few minutes." Price had zeroed in on the computer and was attempting to discover all that he could from it.

"Herbert he has been watching us all this time," Price shouted as two men forced Sidney to walk back into the room.

"So nice to meet you, Mr. Cain," Herbert jeered at him in a victorious tone. "I believe that you have some information that we require." Herbert began as the two men wrestled with Sidney to get him into a chair.

"Here," Bob shouted pitching one of the men a roll of duck tape, "wrap him up with that." As one of them reached to catch the tape Sidney broke a hand free and grabbed for the gun of the one that caught the tape. The other one hit Sidney across the head with his gun knocking him out. The two men pulled him to the chair and began taping him up. "It looks like Mr. Cain is a little hard headed and he is going to have a knot on his head for a while." He laughed a little and turned to Herbert, "I guess that he is safe now if you want to talk to him for awhile." Herbert walked to the sink and drew a glass of water and threw it in the face of Sidney.

“Wake up you sorry bastard,” Herbert grabbed a fistful of Sidney’s thinning hair and held his head back as he slowly returned to consciousness.

“Well, you shitheads finally have me,” Sidney blurted out the obvious and was met with a slap in the face from Herbert.

“Anybody getting cussed around here, it’s going to be you,” Herbert justified his actions and swelled with his new found authority. “If you have any hopes of living through this thing we will required certain information.” He turned to Price who was working over the one remaining computer on the desk.

“Mr. Cain,” Price began approaching him, “we want to congratulate you on your diligence and discovery of your motor, we would like to see one of them and we have looked through the things that you have around her and we can’t find one.” Sidney responded with a cold stare into the depth of his eyes, he jumped up and walked behind him to continue his questioning. “We know that one of them was blown up down in the Keys and we heard that you had a thousand of them shipped from somewhere and that would mean that you had to have them made somewhere. We would like that kind of information.” Sidney just sat there and acted like he was going to sleep or something.

“I don’t know what you are talking about,” Sidney laughed and struggled against the tape that had him stuck in the chair. “Motor, what motor?” Herbert reared back like he was going to hit Sidney again and Price motioned for him to hold up.

“Now Mr. Cain we know that you have invented an electromagnetic motor and it sounds like it is a great motor,” Price was patient and deliberate as he motioned for one of the men that were still clearing the debris out of the way to come to him. “I have a bag in the limo; will you get it for me?” Price was smiling as he talked, almost like he was about to enjoy what was about to happen.

"How long is this going to take," Herbert was impatient as he spoke and took a seat in Sidney's recliner and stretched it back. "Hey this is comfortable. I think I'll buy me one." Price laughed as they both watched the man that he had sent out to the limo was returning with the case that Price had brought to provide the chemical persuasion that he thought was necessary.

"Now Mr. Cain," Price began pulling the table closer to where Sidney was sitting, "we intend to get some information from you whether you are willing to give it or not." He smiled as he readied an injection.

"You might want to hurry it up," Bob stuck his head into the room, "I think that we've got company." He hurried out as quickly as he came but this time he had his rifle at the ready.

I had told the men in the helicopter about the entrances to the cave and how I thought that Sidney had one of them booby trapped but that the other was clear. They had agreed to let Joe and I down on the cable so that we could approach from the back side while they went and made their assault from the front.

I didn't like the idea of being lowered on the cable out of the helicopter but I didn't have a choice. Joe had been the only one of those men that I had ever seen before and they looked like they were from the military or something and they were very professional. They acted like they welcomed a chance to use their skills.

I looked at Joe, "are you ready for this?" I asked over the roar of the helicopter.

"It's like riding an elevator," He joked and then added over the noise of the door that was now open. "All you have to do is put your foot in there and hold on." He smiled at me and stepped into the harness and motioned for me to do the same. When I swung out of the helicopter I almost lost my breakfast, if I would have had any breakfast. It was like we were on a big swing for awhile and finally it calmed down and I felt better as we went straight down. I was never so glad to hit the ground and get out of the harness and on solid ground. The locals were coming out of their houses and watching us and I fought the urge to wave and them. I grabbed Joe and we ran into the spring that served as the cave entrance.

I searched in the darkness for the light that I had left the day before and finally found it. Joe was being very quiet as we started into the cave. "Are you okay?" I asked as he followed slowly and I was trying to go as fast as I could. There were a couple of places that were really tight and without a flashlight Joe was having a hard time catching up. From time to time I would see him ignite his lighter. I had told him that we needed to be quiet because the echo in the cave could be heard easily from the room where I figured that they would have Sidney. I made it up to the main hall in the cave and I shined the light to where Joe could see better and he quickly closed the distance between us. I motioned for him to be quiet and we started into the cave toward the big room. I leveled my rifle and chambered a round into the rifle and watched as Joe prepared his rifle as well. I could hear someone talking in the room and I knew that Sidney was probably in there. I switched my gun off safety as we approached the door.

For some reason the door was ajar and the light from the room filled the passageway. I grabbed Joe by the shirt and motioned to him where I wanted him to go when we broke into the room. He nodded that he understood. I eased the door open a little bit more and slipped into the shadows of the room. The room was now lighted from the sun. The majority of the rock and stone that had encased the room were completely blown off the front of the mountain.

As I eased into the room I could see a man sitting in Sidney's recliner but couldn't see a gun on him. I had instructed Joe to go around to the right side of the cave were the rooms were and he had made a few steps in that direction. Suddenly gunfire erupted in the room. Joe went down. I couldn't see anyone doing the shooting so I trained my rifle on the man in Sidney's recliner. Boom, boom, I fired and he got up and ran out of the cave where I heard sporadic gunfire coming from outside.

"Why Mr. Bristow it is so nice of you to join us," Price said calmly holding a pistol on me. "drop your gun and come in here and join us." Price motioned at me with the gun and I got up and followed him into the bedroom that he pointed towards.

"Sidney," I shouted when I saw him ducked taped to the chair. He looked like they had really worked him over and his face was swollen and bloody and he looked like he had suffered a pretty good beating as well. I guessed that they were trying to get some information out of him and I knew that he was not telling them anything. I rushed to him while Price held the gun on me. The bedroom was the only one that had the lights on for some reason. "What have you done to him?" I shouted my question to Price.

"Mr. Cain has been a little tight lipped," Price smiled as he took Sidney by the head and pushed it back. The lifeless unconscious Sidney didn't even respond. "What do you know of his business affairs?" He asked laying the gun on the bed and picking up a syringe from his case.

"What are you doing?" I asked shouting and lunging towards him he quickly retrieved the gun from the bed and pointed it to my nose. I eased back a little and he laid the gun back on the table.

"Mr. Cain is about to have a stroke," he smiled at me when he spoke and continued to draw the chemical into the syringe. I knew that I had to do something and I hoped that he would need both hands and his full attention to give Sidney the injection. When he did I knew that I had to be ready.

"What are you giving him?" I yelled and wanted to lunge at him again but he was looking straight at me and I knew that I wouldn't have a chance. "For that matter what have you given him?" Price slapped Sidney across the face. "He's just taking a little nap right know. Sodium pentothal, he's had maybe a little too much and he will definitely be out for a while. But this is the really good stuff this will really blow his mind. He will never be the same. The poor bastard will be lucky if he can even talk." Price had giddiness in his voice as he spoke. He drew the chemical out of the injection bottle with the syringe and flicked it with his finger. "Well Mr. Cain are you ready to take your trip." He grabbed Sidney's arm and found a vein and turned his head for a second to insert the needle.

I quickly and as easily as I could I opened the secret compartment that held the Glock and quickly pulled it. "Stop it right now." I shouted and Price looked at me and then continued to push the liquid into Sidney's arm. Boom, boom, I shot hoping to kill him instantly. Price fell to the floor and I thought that one of the bullets had caught him in the head because blood splashed over the back wall. I rushed to Sidney's side and pulled the syringe out of his arm. About half of it was left in the syringe. I rush of dread swooped over me. That Sidney might have a stroke because I wasn't able to act fast enough to save him.

Chapter Ten

Six Months Later

"How are you feeling today," I asked Sidney as he relaxed by pool as he watched the people frolicking in the pool and around it.

"I had a pretty bad headache this morning but I'm doing better now," he saluted me with his drink as he spoke.

"I've got some business questions that the people in Tulsa want an answer on, are you up to it?" I asked pulling the brief case of paper work from under my chair.

"Maybe later," he responded slowly, "I am still seeing double a little." He motioned to a bikini clad young woman about to dive in the pool. "I would like to see her double." He laughed at the thought.

"You have been through a lot," I responded putting the brief case back under the chair, "I wished I would have shot that guy quicker, maybe he wouldn't have given you so much of that stuff.

But the three months that you spent in the hospital might have had something to do with your headaches." I was trying to get him to talking because the doctors said that the more he talked the better he would get. They were reluctant to let him out but he was getting so restless that he was no longer making any progress and I convinced him and them that he needed to come back to Key West for a while. We had been here for about a week and he was doing better but he sort of did things as he felt like doing them and if he didn't feel like it he just didn't. I made sure that he took his medicine and his doctors and all the business of the company came through me and I got back to him when I could.

He just nodded at me and eased back in his lounge chair and dosed off into a nap. We had heard nothing from anyone that was chasing us. One of the reasons was that I imagined that they might have thought that Sidney was dead. Sidney's men loaded up the dead men including Herbert and Price and flew their jet out to sea and Sidney put his identification on one of the shooters that had met with an unfortunate end. We thought it was the only way that they would leave us alone, if they thought Sidney was dead. They had the company pilot fly the plane into the water and he jumped out just before it crashed into the ocean. We figured if they thought we were dead they would leave us alone. That meant that I inherited everything Sidney owned. The men that really ran the company would send papers that needed signed occasionally but for the most part we had very little contact with the company. We decided that we would rehab in Key West and just let the world pass us by. Of course we had put the motors in Sidney's Hummer, a Corvette, a boat, and even an airplane.

"Man I feel good," Sidney said stretching his arms as he woke up. "let's go get the women." He sat up and started getting up. For an older man there was something about the mini-stroke that Sidney had disrupted something in his mind that reversed his amorous prowess, instead of getting worse with age he was chasing women like a teenager.

As well as I knew Sidney, I knew that one day that he would take a crack at reassembling the motors and marketing them. He was a hard driving man and taking a few months off to get his thoughts together was not out of the question. But I wondered who else was out there. Who would want to kill us and take the motors locking them away in some warehouse forever? For now at least, we had some time to relax.